ANGEL'S CREED

REV CARVER SERIES BOOK 2

PAUL SATING

Cover Design: A massive Rev Specialty for Natalie at https://www.original-bookcoverdesigns.com for this amazing Rev cover. Thank you for bringing him to life!

ISBN-13: 979-8-9857203-8-9

THREE FREE NOVELLAS

To Maddog. With you, all is possible.

WANT YOUR WINGS?

Be a good mortal. If you enjoyed the book, leave a review on Amazon, Goodreads, and/or Bookbub. Remember, the head cheese is watching your good deeds!

1

RUN, RUN, JUST AS FAST AS YOU CAN

What do you do when your latest target doesn't want to die?

You chase them, of course.

The problem is? I'm too old to find joy in running. If I'm moving swiftly, there better be a damn good reason. A Hellhound chasing me. Something burning on the stove. A sale on wine at the local package store. Running is low on the list of my priorities. Chasing after a drug dealer whose name was on the scroll tucked away in my jacket was even lower on the long list of things I had to accomplish this week.

But, here I was, running through an empty home improvement store parking lot in Olympia, Washington on a bitter January night. Puffs of clouds billowed before my face as I panted. The blacktop flickered in the yellow light where ice patches waited to send me flailing to my ass. I swear, if I slipped, I would make Roger Baskin's last minutes alive a living hell.

"Stop running!" I shouted, shaking my head. "No one outruns the Reaper, you dumbass!"

What I didn't tell him was that I'm too old for this nonsense, and if he was determined enough, he just might.

"Leave him alone!" a voice screeched just as something slammed into me.

We tumbled to the frosty blacktop. Had it not been for a lazy customer and even lazier employees leaving the abandoned shopping cart in the middle of a parking spot, I would have met the icy surface with my shoulder. Guess I should thank them for their lack of initiative. As it was, the welded metal cart took most of the impact. My only injury came as one of its hard plastic tires poked into my hip when it tipped and I landed on top of it. At least my leather duster prevented the bolt from ripping open skin.

I rolled as a flurry of fists slammed into my chest. Even though my attacker threw them in fury, they were nothing more than an annoyance.

"What the hell is wrong with you?" I said as I deflected the fiery but meek blows.

Usually, I wouldn't complain if a woman straddled me. Not that I'd remember what the experience was like. I've been divorced for decades and remember little about the sensations of intimate contact with a woman. What I do remember didn't include fists. Alisha, my ex, wasn't into that sort of thing. Not that I was, to be clear. Not that I'm judging. I'm a Reaper. An assassin. Heaven's clean-up hitter and Mr. Fix It. I'm not an arbiter.

And this woman throwing fists didn't seem interested in any of that. Apparently, she had one thing on her mind; beautiful, glorious violence. By the twentieth punch, her square glasses flew off, rattling across a patch of ice. She squinted, still swinging. By the way she pinched her eyes, I think she was aiming for any blur that could possibly resemble the human form.

As another punch flew, I snagged her thin wrist.

I don't like being touched. At all. I'm not big on being hit either, no matter how light the punches.

I held her arm in place. She tried to jerk it free, but couldn't break my grip.

This woman had the look of a librarian and not the dirty kind. What the hell was she doing in this store's parking lot at one in the morning, and why was she attacking me? I hadn't pissed off a woman who wasn't my familiar or a member of the Order of Thirteen in a long, long time.

Unless good ole Roger was her supplier and my appearance had ruined an exchange, dampening her night?

This twenty-something didn't have that look about her. Instead, she was the type that hung out in coffee shops until the battery on her tablet died. The type that didn't know if her town had a home improvement store or not, and if it did, she wouldn't know what to do there. Not the type to throw fists with a Reaper.

"Get off him!" another feminine shout pierced the night.

I smiled. The voice belonged to an ally, my partner.

Billee came up behind the librarian-looking woman, grabbed her black, pinned-up hair, and pulled.

My attacker stopped swinging and tried to grab Billee's arms. A pointless use of energy. My mortal familiar is a badass. The spunky librarian was no match.

Billee pulled the woman off, and they toppled to the blacktop.

I scrambled to my feet, seeing the dark of night beyond the parking lot lights absorb Roger's form.

"You going to be okay?" I asked Billee.

She had the librarian in a chokehold—I told you she's a badass. "Go get him. I've got her."

Billee wasn't even breathing hard. Damn showoff.

"Be careful, Sparky," I said, casting a wary glance at the librarian before dashing off to chase down a drug dealer.

Past the protective shell of the parking lot lights, the night grew still. Sporadic cars and trucks raced north and south alongside the I-5 interstate, but they were the only signs of life in this small city, in the middle of winter, in the dead of night. Either Roger had gotten away or he hunkered down somewhere to avoid detection. The problem was, he wasn't fast enough for the former. So, I began my search.

"Where are you, Roger?" I called into the darkness over the din of traffic. "This ends with you and me heading off to the great beyond. It's cold, and I just want to get this over."

I did. I had more important tasks to complete besides escorting a drug dealer to the Veil Gate. Insignificant things like finding and fighting a behemoth. A giant beast. You know, the type spoken of in the Good Book? Yeah, that kind. And I wanted to get to it while this newest version was still in diapers. With that beast loose on the world for the first time in over ten thousand years, I wasn't interested in dragging out this pursuit. Roger Baskin was hiding, and that pissed me off. This task, to act as a Reaper to escort a mortal to their afterlife, was one more mundane thing to get done when time was already at a premium. That doubly pissed me off.

I crept toward the row of bushes lining the road and stopped. Streetlights provided enough illumination that I would have seen the drug dealer if he'd tried escaping along the road. That meant he was still in cover. I'd need to cross the street to explore the multitude of hiding places. That sucked. I'd be out in the open. Vulnerable.

I mean, I don't want to sound obtuse or anything, but a drug dealer not packing some kind of weapon was as likely as not seeing a single Confederate flag at a NASCAR race.

This was the Overworld, the one place where angels can die. I was not taking chances stepping out into the street and being cut down by a lucky shot.

Reaching inside my duster, I slipped my hand into the specially made pocket where I kept my .327 Ruger. I named it Maggie. The revolver was small, just the way I liked it. I don't need the weapon to use my Angelfire Ability, but it sure is a lot cooler when you blast a jackass with a ray from a temporal weapon instead of using your hand. Plus, my aim is better with Maggie, and I don't look like a dork who'd just fallen out of a van carrying him and his buddies to some LARPing event when I tap into my angelic magic. Just the sight of Maggie often induced compliance. This drug dealer seemed more like a butter knife than a steak knife, if you catch my meaning. I had a feeling he'd need more convincing than me just swinging the Ruger around.

Roger had proven he wasn't going down without a fight. He crossed the line when I first appeared to escort him to the Veil Gate, explaining what I was there for and that he was about to step into traffic and be struck down and killed. I was trying to play the considerate, nice guy. Billee had even tried to help with the explanation.

But Roger wasn't having any of it. He pushed Billee into the road, putting her in danger, and took off. After pulling her from the semi barreling down, I had a new level of determination to separate Roger from his crime-bound life. No remorse, no regrets. Plus, he was already a scumbag.

Staying low, I moved along the road. To the south, civilization gave way to the green of uncultured land as Olympia faded away and pockets of homes and farms sprang up. People like him didn't do well in the country. Not enough vulnerable people to take advantage of. They needed city life. They needed suburbia and kids with mommy and daddy's money to explore the mind-altering relief people like Roger provided. So I made my way north.

A loud clang drew my attention to the building ahead. The Great Wall of Dumpsters gave it away as a Costco.

At this time of night, the store had already been closed for hours, so either someone was rooting around and looking for an evening meal, seeking shelter, or they were hiding.

Using the sporadic spread of trees and blanket of black of the night as my cover, I moved toward the sound. The lid of a dumpster, one of those thick plastic ones, was closing so slowly it was comical. Roger might as well have called out to taunt me that I'd never find him in a million years.

Moving to stay hidden behind the closest tree, I shouted across the forty feet divide. "Come on out, Roger. I'm not going anywhere and, trust me, I can wait forever."

"Fuck you," came the reply, muffled by the container.

I shook my head. This guy had been sitting in a Corvette when I came to get him. A Corvette. Savvy enough to afford a car like that, yet no smarter than the steel surrounding him.

"You're coming out, buddy," I yelled back. "Now. In ten minutes. An hour. Tomorrow morning. It doesn't matter. This ends here. Don't make me come in after you. I already have to take my duster in for cleaning, but that doesn't mean I want to root around in trash. Especially to deal with trash like you."

The dumpster lid cracked open. The dark interior prevented me from seeing anything inside. "Fuck you!"

"Goddammit," I said, stepping out from behind the tree with Maggie in a two-handed grip, barrel pointed at the frost-covered grass. It crunched under my feet. The ever-present puffs of clouds formed around my face every time I exhaled. I was going to have to soak for an hour after this just to feel my toes again.

One foot into the open and the dirt near my booted feet split open just before I heard the pop coming from the dumpster. I jumped back behind the tree.

So Roger was armed, after all. A drug dealer with a gun. Shocker.

I leveled Maggie. Keeping the tree between me and the dumpster, I took aim.

The tree was wide enough to block most of me, but this was still a risk. Roger could be a crack shot, or he could be one lucky bastard and hit an exposed shoulder or my gut, and take out a vital organ. Imagine, the Upperworld's most senior Reaper, taken out by a dirtbag hiding in a dumpster? Good thing I didn't have children to shame with my potential demise. One more reason to be thankful to my ex. So level-headed, that woman.

"I gave you a chance."

Another pop. Bark flew from the tree.

I snarled and pulled the trigger.

Angelfire split the dark night. A beam of pure white, wholesome goodness—okay, I admit, the 'wholesome' part isn't necessarily true, but it makes me feel better about the duties I've been carrying out for eight thousand years. When the beam struck the metal dumpster, it didn't explode. The green metal simply became an ichorous mess, liquifying and plopping to the ground in molten globs. The metal container had no ridges, no sharp edges where I'd blasted the hole through it. Imagine a knife poking through a piece of paper held tautly. Clean, efficient.

I fired again, and again. Small beams; barely a workout. Each knocked another hole into the dumpster. With each, I reduced the room for the concealed dirtbag. By now, less than half the dumpster remained intact. With my next shot, I blew the last portion supporting the lid off. The black plastic clanged down into the dumpster.

Underneath my focus, someone howled. It could have been the drug dealer. It might not have been. One thing I knew for sure was that I wasn't losing focus and letting this bastard get a lucky shot. I knew what sort of mortal he was, and I knew the world would be better without him.

Pop.

More bark.

Pop.

The bullet punched the dirt five feet away.

I trained on the far corner of the dumpster.

A howl rose in the air, closer this time. Behind me.

"Rev!" Billee, somewhere in the distance.

I fired.

The last corner of the dumpster evaporated. All that remained was the crumpled plastic lid, resting atop the bags of trash my focused shots hadn't melted into goo.

No one would find Roger Baskin's body, not after tasting my Angelfire. But I doubted many people who didn't waste their lives smoking or snorting something would be worried about him. Beside the dumpster, looking down at a black trash bag sheared open by my beam of magic, was the energy residue in the shape of the former drug dealer.

An ethereal replication of his mortal form, he stood, looking at the spot where he thought he was safe, as if confused. Mortals usually are at this point.

He was no longer a danger in his bodiless form. His spectral body would linger next to the dumpster, waiting an eternity for nothing in particular, and terrorizing unaware employees on trash runs unless I finished my job. Sighing at the thought of his energy residue being added back to the All, I tucked Maggie into my duster's hidden pocket and stepped out from behind the tree. Halfway across the open lot, I heard footsteps.

I spun and stepped to the side, flinging my arm out and catching the back of my pursuer. Pushing, I propelled her forward, flinging her face-first into the remains of the trash.

Billee raced out of the darkness.

"Are you okay?" I asked.

She nodded. "You?"

"Yep." I tipped my head at Roger's energy residue. "He got off a few lucky shots, but nothing serious."

As a familiar to a Reaper, Billee could see the energy residue that had been Roger Baskin. When her eyes slid in his direction, she nodded. A normal reaction for a Reaper's familiar, even a relatively new one like her.

The most aggressive librarian impersonator in the world pulled herself out of the trash. Though she squinted—and probably would until she bought new glasses—she faced Roger's ethereal form.

That wasn't supposed to happen. Unless...

"You've got to be kidding me?"

"What?" Billee asked.

"She's a Guardian," I said, flicking a finger at the librarian.

2

AIN'T NO JOKE

"A GUARDIAN ANGEL?" BILLEE STRESSED THE SECOND WORD AS if doing so would further clarify the meaning that was already abundantly clear.

This woman, who had directly interfered with the grim-mother-freakin'-Reaper executing his duties, was a Guardian Angel. The order sworn to protect mortals from all unintended harm; she had broken a major golden rule tonight.

The scroll for Roger Baskin had been delivered earlier in the day. Usually, when I get a notification that a mortal had been entered into the Book of Planes, the eternal list of all who have ever existed but whose time had now come, I check them out. I lean on my own analysis to see if there was anything they might need to wrap up. I also check to see if they're with family or at a special event, like a concert or sporting event. For one, tickets are stupidly expensive in today's world. Second, if I get the impression they're contributing to the world in a good way, I don't mind giving them as much time before their deadline as I can. I'd done that recently with Delores Garcia. Good people deserve all I can give them. Someone like Roger Baskin didn't deserve the time it took for me to take a dump. I'd even rearranged my evening to round him up.

The rules bar Guardian Angels from interfering when their mortal's name is entered in the Book of Planes. Most Guardians don't even make an appearance. They have a unique ability to disguise their presence in the Overworld, from mortals and immortals, called masking. Basically, they only show up if they want to. Most don't. None interfere with a Reaper. That is as big a no-no as not sleeping with close relatives—well, except in certain areas of West Virginia.

As the Reaper Minister, I don't need anyone putting the Reapers I'm responsible for in danger if a Guardian Angel suddenly got the impression they could interfere with the execution of our duties.

"What the fuck is wrong with you?"

Her head snapped at me. Every muscle in her face twitched. "Why? Why did you do this?"

"You know why."

"It's too soon," she said. More twitching of her face. Her eyes glimmered. "Too soon. Why?"

I drew in a sharp breath.

"What's wrong?" Billee asked.

I jerked my chin at the Guardian. "She's in love with him."

"Wh—what?"

"Yep."

"Can that happen?"

"Apparently." I shrugged, still watching the Guardian twitch and try to hold herself together. "I mean, I've seen it before. Not the first time. Won't be the last."

"It's got to be taboo, though. Right? Against the rules?"

"Oh yeah. Big time. Just like interfering with a Reaper by physically assaulting him." I said that last part with extra gusto.

The Guardian got to her feet, not bothering to brush off the repulsive bits of... whatever it is this store threw out and stomped toward me. I backed up, pulling Billee. This was the Overworld. I was still vulnerable to injury and death here. Billee, being mortal, didn't need to be put at risk unnecessarily. As my familiar, she was already at higher risk than the average mortal. I'd be damned if she was going to face that because of some distraught Guardian Angel with terrible judgment.

The Guardian flipped her arms in the air. "You could have left him alone. You could have given him time. Before deciding, you could have talked to me.

I ignored her screeching voice that clawed at my eardrums. "No. No. And you didn't show until he forced me into a chase. Is that a sufficient response? Now, I've got to get him to the Veil Gate. You should head back to the Upperworld and check in with your boss. This stunt of yours won't sit well."

"Who do you think you are?" She lunged again.

I caught her wrist and held it in mid-air. This Guardian was out of her mind, but if my intuition was correct and she was in love, then she was also grieving. Throw in a good dose of shock, and I had one unstable opponent on my hands. Without taking my eyes off her, I said to Billee. "Hey, head home. I've got this."

"You sure?"

The Guardian's eyeballs bounced between me and my partner.

"Yes. Definitely. I don't trust her to not make another poor decision when I escort our drug-dealing friend to the Veil Gate. So, I don't want you anywhere around when I leave."

A quiet moment passed. The Guardian sniffed as tears threatened to pour over.

"Okay, Rev. If you're sure." Billee let the statement dangle, making it sound more like a question. She was concerned for me. That was cool. It was nice to be cared about by someone besides my crusty old mentor.

"Yeah, go on. After I drop him off, I'll swing by your place so you know I'm safe."

"Okay." A pensive tone. She was still unsure. Oh, ye of such little faith.

I waited, listening to the sounds of her footfalls crunching on the frozen grass and then disappearing into the night. As my familiar, Billee wasn't affected by the Interlude. Unlike the other seven billion mortals on this rock flying through space, time didn't stop for her while I dealt with Roger. The Interlude would mutate it, but it couldn't stop it completely for her. Otherwise, familiars wouldn't be of much use.

Because this Guardian was assigned to Roger, she wasn't affected either, unfortunately. She never flicked her eyes away from mine. Billee wasn't the target of her heartbroken rage. I was.

"Why?" the Guardian asked, now meekly.

"You know how this works. It was his time. No one outruns the Reaper, and no one gets out of life alive."

She snorted in what sounded like disgust. "No wonder everyone calls you the Grim Reaper."

We stood, staring each other down until I was sure Billee had enough time to get back to her car. I lowered her arm and slowly let go of her hand. "Are we done here?"

The Guardian's mouth twitched, but she stayed silent.

I stepped back and to the side, moving between her and Roger's energy residue. He watched us with passive interest. What remains of mortals after death is rarely the insightful, aware persona of their actual life. Most are so overwhelmed by what they've become, they barely cope. If they're a drug-dealing dirtbag, they probably weren't dazzling to begin with, so suddenly finding themselves in an ephemeral form kicks what little brain they have into shutdown mode. "Let's make a deal. You don't attack me as soon as I turn my back. You promise never to do something that stupid again. Agree, and I'll agree to not report you when I drop him off. Deal?"

The Guardian looked at Roger. Her face crumbled. Before she completely melted down, she blinked out of existence. The dark background of the trees obscuring the home improvement store parking lot replaced the spot where she'd stood a second ago.

Goddamn Guardians.

I turned to Roger. "Alright, my boy. Time to go."

Roger wore a plastic expression. "I don't understand."

"I know," I said, pointing at his neck. "Turn to the side."

He did, much more compliant in death than he was in life.

I nodded. Underneath the shoots of neck hair he hadn't bothered to shave when he was still alive was nothing but smooth, white skin. No mark of the beast. "Good. Let's go."

Snapping my fingers at the empty air a few feet in front of the dumpster, a Rift opened. A thick line of bright, sizzling light carved itself into the night sky ten feet above the black-top. It expanded horizontally for five feet and then oozed toward the ground. Once it struck the blacktop, it moved along the surface from both sides until it re-connected in the middle. Between the bright light, a rippling blackness silently waited. The air sizzled, sounding like hundreds of children's sparklers all condensed into this tiny space.

I stepped to and through the Rift. Roger's energy residue followed. It had no choice, and unlike my escort of Delores Garcia or any other commendable mortal, I wasn't interested in being accommodating.

We stepped out of the Rift and into the Veil Gate.

The utter silence was a smack in the face. Gunfights will give you that perspective. Above, underneath, and in every direction except directly in front of me, eternal blackness stretched away. For all I knew, I might have been able to hop, skip, and jump to the edge of eternity within a few bounces. Or, more likely, I might walk off in one of those directions and never be seen or heard from again. In all my visits to the Veil Gate, the realm separating this life from the eternal realm, I never found the guts to explore. The thought hadn't even crossed my mind. That endless blackness made my spine tingle, and not in a good way.

Plus, something told me the two massive Empyrean Knights guarding the Veil Gate itself wouldn't allow it.

Twelve feet tall and as broad as grizzlies, the pair donned gilded armor that somehow shined even in this realm. Their winged great helms, complete with narrow bands for their eyes, obscured their identities. I'm not sure I wanted to see what was under there, anyway.

The only light besides the Veil Gate itself came from a single lampstand to its side. The lamp, green metal formed by two thick vines wrapping around each other as they extended upward, cast a soft yellow light that somehow wasn't drowned out by the forty-five-foot tall gate's blazing border of white surrounding the rippling black of the All.

"Welcome, Rev," Harold said, its seven mouths moving as one.

"What's up, bud?" I asked, moving toward the Scroll Eater and pulling the scroll from the pocket of my duster.

Roger sidled up beside me, looking at the center of the Veil Gate with a mixture of consternation and fascination.

"What do you have for me this time?" Harold asked, seven pairs of lips spreading in a warm smile.

Harold, the name I'd given it long before mortals realized the world wasn't indeed flat, was the only Scroll Eater I'd ever dealt with when escorting. For all I knew, it—he?—she? was the only one in existence. I'd asked that question once, and Harold never answered. It has a way of talking around things it'd rather not explain. For the first hundred visits or so, the Scroll Eater helped me pronounce its actual name, but it seemed like nothing but a string of consonants. We both gave up, and 'Harold' stuck, the Scroll Eater never once complaining about being misgendered.

Five feet tall, the Veil Gate dwarfed both him and even the

two Empyrean Knights guarding it. That might be the only reason Harold seemed to blend into the background for most mortals. A creature with no eyes and seven mouths could unsettle mortals, but so many never seemed to notice its presence.

Roger didn't, and that was perfectly fine. The sooner I finished this job, the better.

"Something I wish I didn't have to contribute to the All," I answered after a glance at the energy residue at my side.

Seven mouths formed almost perfect concentric circles. "Oh, I see. One of those types."

"Afraid so, my friend. One day, your boss needs to design a dumping ground for types like this. The All would be better off."

I didn't know who Harold worked for and I doubted the jovial creature would tell me if I asked. "The All requires balance, my angelic friend. Both good and bad. The evil. The selfish. People who give. Those who create. Those who destroy. Without that amalgam, there is no balance, and without balance, nothing exists."

I squinted at the Scroll Eater. "You must be a hit at parties."

If Harold had a face, I'm sure it would have appeared conciliatory. Without one, I could only go off what I saw in its mouths and the way its seven arms moved. Which, right now, they weren't.

"I would quite like to attend a party one day," Harold said flatly. "From what I've heard, I believe I would find them to be fascinating."

"They're annoying, more than anything," I said. "Trust me. Fake conversations. Fake smiles. Bragging about things unaccomplished and sharing personal details of other people's lives in the interest of juicy drama. You're not missing much, my friend."

"Hmmm," Harold said, its seven lips pinching in unison, "possibly. Still, after so long at the Veil Gate, it might be nice to experience. These two," the Scroll Eater said, three arms pointing at the two guards, "don't talk about anything of interest."

I cocked my head at the silent guards standing on either side of the blazing border. "They talk?"

Harold sniffed. "All weapons and forging, battle tactics, and the greatest wars ever fought. If it weren't for the Reapers, I'd have trouble staying awake." In the hooded robe draping its lower body and back, only exposing its chest, it was difficult to tell what figure Harold had—I don't consider 'lump' to be descriptive or fair. So, I wasn't sure if it had a waist to bend. The Scroll Eater definitely leaned closer without moving. "Only when Reapers bring the residue, do they stop. It's an intimidation thing."

I watched the guards. "It works."

"They know," Harold said, straightening once more. "They'll go right back to it as soon as you leave."

"Speaking of," I said, pulling the scroll with Roger's name out of my duster and offering it to Harold, "I need to get back to the Overworld."

"Oh? A party?"

I chuckled. "Hardly. Had a bit of a problem with a Guardian and I want to check in on my familiar. Make sure she's okay." I looked at Roger, wondering what it was about him that had led his Guardian to attack me. That was bad, of course, but I would keep details of her actions secret as long as she followed through on her end. Worse, she'd allowed herself to develop feelings for the mortal. That was the taboo of taboos. Far be it for me to claim perfection. I've screwed up plenty. But falling for a mortal?

Harold took the scroll, holding it between two fingers, and opened a mouth on the side of its head. It slid the scroll in and wrapped thick lips around it, sucking it into its maw like a stiff, thick spaghetti noodle. Harold smacked his lips. "Accepted. Thank you for completing the delivery." Three arms extended in the direction of the Veil Gate. To the energy residue, the Scroll Eater said, "You may enter."

Roger's residue looked at Harold for the first time. He nodded, jerked to face toward his destiny, and stepped toward the Veil Gate.

The shimmering black, looking like the finest shiny, rippling silk you could imagine, wrapped itself around him. It was like watching someone floating face-down in a swimming pool before slowly sinking under the water. Exactly like that, but a lot creepier. The Veil Gate didn't make a sound as it enveloped the energy.

"Good riddance," I whispered.

"I hope the rest of your day goes well," Harold said. "Will I see you again soon? You don't come around as much as you used to. Compared to your peers, you rarely come by."

"My bosses have different duties for me now. I'm pretty important."

Seven mouths exposed seven sets of broad, flat teeth. Harold's dental plan must be top-notch. The mysterious creature laughed. "Well, I won't keep you, my friend. Though I will admit I hope to see you soon. Maybe you can share more about these parties next time?"

I turned. "You bet, Harold. I'll see you later."

"Travel well."

The Empyrean Knights said nothing. I wondered if they'd talk about me behind my back, then remembered I had bigger concerns.

Concerns as large as a behemoth.

3

AN UNSETTLED MEETING OF MINDS

STEAM FILLED MY BATHROOM, A HOVERING CLOUD OF MIST THAT filled the entire space. A shock I hadn't set off a fire alarm. The steaming water felt great on my back, every drop pressed like a tiny, heated masseuse's hand, loosening the aches and pains of being alive. I wasn't in a hurry to get out.

Chasing Roger Baskin through the frosty night was a miserable task, but at least it was over and everyone had moved on. The unnamed Guardian Angel was hopefully somewhere in the Upperworld, reflecting on every point in her journey where she'd erred. Billee was safe. She'd fallen asleep on her couch, watching a romance movie. I'd woken her, but she was grateful, telling me she'd be able to go to bed now that she knew I was okay. I was more than okay because I'd spent the last half hour letting steaming water caress my back.

Thank Yahweh for living in an apartment complex, so I could enjoy endless hot water. Thank Yahweh for my high pain tolerance, so I could enjoy the steaming water where it would have fried most people and angels. I almost thanked Yahweh for thirty stinking minutes of peace and quiet, but

I've been around. I'm a veteran. No peace is ever-lasting. Mine definitely wouldn't be.

At least no one interrupted me until the next morning.

I was making coffee when the scroll appeared. With a sigh, I broke the seal and unrolled it, pinning the top to my counter with my empty coffee mug.

A summons by the Order of Thirteen.

"What now?"

As soon as I finished making my coffee, I drank it as fast as I could and finished dressing. I drank while hopping into my pants, and throwing on my duster. I sipped in between tying my boots. And I even carried the mug into the adjoining apartment.

Years ago, I hired a contractor to tear out the wall between my apartment and the two adjoining apartments I also rented and kept empty of personal effects. I used one for training and exercise, and the other for Rifts and Gateways. Not that I needed two thousand square feet for opening portals—I'm actually quite an accurate caster—but because I didn't want to disrupt my personal living space by making room for them. I wanted the apartment I lived in to feel like a home, free of anything to do with the Upperworld. Maybe one day I'd come up with something else to do with the under-utilized space. They provided a pleasant view of downtown.

With regret, I set my mug on the floor. "I'm going to miss you," I said to it, knowing what kind of coffee the Order brewed in their meetings.

Snapping my fingers, I opened a Rift. A border of thick, white light, two-feet wide, extended horizontally and quickly formed a frame. A shimmering image of a long hallway came into view.

I stepped into the Eighth Level of the Upperworld.

"Rev!" a powerful voice boomed with a slight echo that carried down the hall behind me.

"What's up, big man?" I said, giving the mountain of an angel a smile.

Brock Illume was a guard for the Order of Thirteen. Long ago, he was one hell of a soldier. Now, he was too old for that type of fighting but still effective. He'd have to be to get this important duty. Outside Yahweh and His Council, this was the most important governing body in the realm. Protecting these angels meant more than just dumping a physical threat at their chamber doors. It meant having guards with the brains to know what to hear and what not to hear, and to watch for unspoken subtleties that might one day become threats. Someone who ate weights for breakfast, lunch, and dinner—and the other thirty meals these types seemed to eat every day—wouldn't provide the security the Upperworld's leaders and policymakers needed. Brock could. Brock did.

And I used that for my own purposes too. Not that I didn't trust the Order of Thirteen. For politicians, they're not —mostly—horrible angels. Still, a smart angel armed themselves with as much information as they could, especially when dealing with those who'd never earn my full trust even if there wasn't an end to the solar system, the universe, and everything in the All that lay beyond.

Brock was that source. When I stepped out of the Rift, I'd hoped to get insight into why I was being called to a meeting with the thirteen angels who determined my fate. Unfortunately, it didn't appear as if I was going to get the opportunity. Brock wasn't alone.

"More fun," he said with a warm smile. Angels his size shouldn't be able to make you feel comfortable with a smile, but he could.

"What's up with this?" I asked, tipping my head at the other guard, who was as muscular as Brock. "Didn't think you'd need backup. Pher causing you problems?"

My mentor wasn't a physical threat to Brock. Three Phers could fit inside the intimidating guard. Plus, Pher was the kindest, most-caring angel to walk Yahweh's realm. But the question served as a subtle way to test if this other guard was someone Brock thought I could trust.

Brock flicked his eyes across the hall toward his peer. The brown-skinned angel kept his cut short, just long enough that tiny curls spread across his scalp like moss on an Olympia lawn in the dead of winter. He stared straight ahead. Brock's yellow eyebrows drew down. "Pher isn't the problem, but it seems like someone has been sniffing around."

Interesting response. Giving without giving too much. If Brock needed to be careful, so did I. "Sniffing enough butts to make the Order jumpy?"

Brock's cheekbones creased. "Something like that." He tipped his head back toward the meeting room doors. "Too many jumpy Order members makes for interesting days. You be vigilant in there, Rev."

I moved closer, patting his shoulder. It was broader than my palm. "I will. Thanks. We'll catch up later."

"Let's do that," he replied and then snapped his head forward, staring down the hall again, a paler mirror image of the new guard standing across the set of doors.

I blew out a frustrated breath and pushed the thick door open.

The air always seemed different in the Order's meeting room. Staler. Stiffer. Polluted with something I couldn't quite put my finger on. The type of place I didn't enjoy visiting and couldn't wait to depart from as soon as possible. Impossibly, today it seemed even more lugubrious.

Order members spread around the room. Some hung by the tables set to the side, where they could refresh coffee or pile finger foods on empty plates. Influential angels took sporadic spots at the table, quietly writing notes or staring off toward the ceiling. Two hung in a corner of the room, their stiff heads brought together in conversation they wanted no one else to hear. That one of them was Jericho Judas, the eternal thorn in my side, made the other one less approachable. I had nothing against Uziel Verdant. She hadn't done anything I was aware of that made me decide to hold something against her or feel the need to hand over my heart. But you could never be too careful with Jericho and the circles he ran with.

He wasn't a fan of me either, and his snappy double-take in my direction confirmed my presence didn't thrill him. Recently blackmailing him might have had something to do with that.

One angel I didn't have to worry about being careful with was Christopher Montjoy. My mentor. I refused to use his full name and have called him only by his shortened moniker for nearly as long as I could remember. He stood behind his tall-back chair. At my entrance, his thick lips, pinched between a mustache and beard that were well groomed but still needed to lose a few pounds, spread in a smile.

"Rev," he said, coming my way, "glad to see you."

We hugged quickly. "What's this all about?"

"Everyone, let's sit," Puriel Bliss said from her station at the front of the long table before my mentor could answer. The President of the Order of Thirteen, she got the group of influencers moving like no one else. Despite being tall and thin, her presence dominated the room. "We have much to discuss."

Angels left the coffee station. Important influencers returned to the table with empty plates. Even Jericho pushed himself out of the corner and drifted to his seat.

Puriel remained standing, her hands gripping the headrest of her chair, the largest in the room that nearly reached her shoulders. Once everyone took their seats, she pulled her chair out. She sat like an iron rod propped her up in the most uncomfortable way possible, folding one hand atop the other. Her already small mouth shrunk as she considered those around her. Then, she met my eyes. "Mr. Carver, thank you for joining us. I know we do you no favors with these last-minute notices. That's something Camael and I are working to improve. Thank you for understanding."

"Of course," I said from the foot of the table, the spot reserved for guests, subject matter experts, and the Reaper Minister responsible for doing the Order's dirty work. What else could I say? The Order of Thirteen governed the Reapers and the Guardian Angels. They were busy and had the power to make my life even busier. Staying in their good graces was essential for survival. "How can I help? The note didn't say much."

Puriel's face scrunched. She turned to Camael. "You didn't mention what the meeting was about in the notice?"

Camael looked down at the table, nudging his black-rimmed glasses with a knuckle. His brown cheeks deepened with a flush. As the Secretary of the Order, he was responsible for sending out hundreds of missives a day while also over-seeing an entire office of angels who ran the escort assignments. "I did not. I thought it best he heard it directly from us here. Where it's safe."

If Camael's decision upset Puriel, it was difficult to tell. Her expression never changed. Ever.

"That's fine. Mr. Carver, you've been informed about the behemoth? You received the scroll?"

"I have."

Puriel nodded slowly. "Good. It's imperative your work begins immediately. Unfortunately, we lack details, but what we know, we'll share. Pher, would you mind?"

My mentor sat forward, his elbows on the table, as he turned to me. "We still haven't had eyes on the behemoth, so we can't give you an accurate description. All we have is information from the Council, and even that is…" He spread his hands as if he was giving up.

"Light," Jerah said from across the table.

"Unsatisfactory," Dumas agreed. His thick mustache, unkempt, twitched.

Pher bobbed his head. "We could do with more. That much is true. But we have what we have, and we'll share it."

"We need to move forward. Carver needs to get to work," Jericho said to Pher—because he didn't have the guts to look my way.

Jericho Judas and I disliked each other. We have from the very beginning of his service in the Order. Even before, going back to when his mother, who sat in the same position as he now enjoyed, took a dislike to me. Something that ran in the Judas family. You could say I had a predisposition to disliking him even before nepotism ensured the entitled jerk took such a prestigious seat without needing to work for it. Classism and privilege rock, even in the Upperworld, let me tell you. Yes, that's sarcasm.

"That's what we're doing," Pher said with the patience of, well, a patron saint. "That's why we called the meeting, is it not?"

Jericho sat back, still not looking my way.

"Carry on," Puriel said.

Pher cleared his throat. "As I was saying, we don't have much of a description. I wish we had something better. As soon as we get it, you'll hear from one of us. But we have a few tidbits. The impression we have is that the behemoth is as we would expect. Similar to what it was in the past iterations."

"So it's big?"

"Very," Raphina said, tapping a fingernail on her coffee mug. "The size varies, but we've heard anywhere between sixty and seventy-five feet."

"Nearly fifty feet long," Turial, the youngest member of the Order, said from the neighboring chair. Her shoulders pulled skyward together as if on marionette strings. "But we've also heard it might be up to a hundred feet."

"Sorry, Rev," Pher said. "I know this isn't helpful, but it's what we have and we wanted to share it as it comes in."

"I understand. Where are you sending me to track this thing down?"

"Fortunately, it seems to have manifested in your neck of the woods," Pher answered. "From what we understand, the Olympic National Forest."

"Good. No travel. But that's a big forest."

"It is. But that's all we have to go on at the moment."

"Not going to be easy."

"We need quick action," Puriel said stiffly. "Right now, we're being pulled in different directions by the Council. We don't like it any more than you. But with the pouring of the First Bowl, they're focused on mitigating the impact. They're calling on us for extra support. We, in turn, have to lean on those we can rely on to handle duties without our involvement."

"So, I'm on my own?"

"As soon as we can free up resources, you'll have them, Mr. Carver," the President said in a tone that said she had as much patience for an argument as I had tolerance for Jericho's face. "Until then, we trust you'll use the resources already at your disposal as you see fit."

"The Reapers are already over-taxed."

"Be creative," she said quickly, without a sparkle of life in her expression. Then she sighed, almost showing vulnerability. "There have been two million reported deaths from the virus kicked off by the First Bowl. Reported. We don't know the true impact of that travesty."

"We might not for quite some time," Uziel said, cocking her head and making her short hair bounce. "We might never."

"Sadly, that's true," Puriel said. "But that's a die that's already been cast. We have to work on what we can solve. Dumas, please brief us on what you know of the behemoth."

The older Order member, maybe the oldest ever, sat back, cupping his hands on his chest. His thick, white mustache twitched. "This is, by our records, the thirteen behemoth Yahweh has manifested in the Overworld."

"Thirteenth?" I interrupted. Didn't see that one coming. I knew about a handful of them, but nowhere near that number.

The fluffy white eyebrows of the eldest Order member drew down. "Please. Allow me to get through the information I have."

Jericho shook his head.

I held up my hands. Guilty as charged.

"As I was saying. We aren't sure which form this one takes since the previous twelve were distinct in appearance, but not nature, and the eyewitness reports we have vary greatly. Some claim to have seen a dinosaur-like creature. Others testify it looks like a ground-born sea creature. Like a whale, for example. Others have provided less-detailed accounts. We can safely assume, however, that it will be yet another monstrosity. Docile or not."

"It could be docile?" I asked.

"Others have been," Dumas said. His bottom lip pushed into his upper and his head tipped to the side slowly, as if an irresistible force were pulling it down. "The last two weren't calm, peaceful beasts, by any measure. The one before them was, but it didn't last. Savage mortals killed it in its sleep when it was barely a year old."

"Gross," Sidriel "Sid" Ruddy chimed in. Sid wasn't much of a talker, and I don't think anyone around the table expected much more from him than what he'd just contributed.

Dumas's admission of remembering the past three behemoths distracted me.

"Our records show they may have a good reason," he continued right through the brief interruption. "Not that the early hominids would have known that, of course. They lacked much in the way of communication, as we understand and appreciate it now. My research has been nearly completely dependent on angelic records of the ages."

"Did you find information from all seven ages? Something that'll help me understand what I'm looking for and what I could have to fight?"

"Not all seven," Dumas said with a shake of his head. Though his mustache and eyebrows were white, he'd spent considerable time and probably a decent portion of his income keeping his wispy hair an anachronistic dark brown. I don't know who he thought he was fooling, but hey, if it made him feel younger, more power to him. "Our earlier records do often suffer from neglect and mismanagement."

"Political editing too," Turiel said and Uziel, sitting on the other side of her, sniffed in agreement.

"That too," Dumas conceded. "So no, I don't have records throughout the ages that would be of use to you. But I've gathered enough of the pertinent details for you to read through." His hand hovered over a folder set out in front of him. The hand shook with the exertion of age. The hand lowered and Dumas tapped his thin fingers on the folder. "Read through it carefully. It was my intention to give you as much information about the past nature of the behemoths as possible. That will prepare you to devise an effective strategy to rid the Overworld of the beast."

The members along the table passed the folder along. I flipped it open. A scholarly overload, to be sure. Pieces of parchment and paper, even sticky notes plastered to the side, filled the folder. A snapshot of Dumas's thought process spilling out of his brain and into physical form. He'd even taken time to write notes in the margins of most of the pieces of paper, some of which were so puny, I had to squint to make out the letters.

"So you're not sure what I'm facing, but you are sure it's another behemoth? You can't provide any specifics about this one besides wide guesses of its size and possibly what it may or may not look like?"

"The research I've done into past behemoths will help."

"I'm sure it will. But I need to know what I'm walking into."

"I'm afraid we can't help in that," Puriel said before Dumas could answer. "No one reliable has seen this most recent manifestation."

"It could be very similar to a past behemoth," Dumas said, raising a shaking finger and pointing at the folder. "Which is why I provided as much as I could."

"And I appreciate it. But I need to know more. It's my ass on the line."

Dumas sniffed. Jericho muttered something that I was pretty sure wasn't a compliment.

"Obtaining specifics on this new behemoth is nearly impossible, Mr. Carver," Puriel said. "We need eyes on it. That's where you come in."

"Plus, it could take any form. Yahweh's will determines that," Dumas said, flipping his hand in the air as if I was being ridiculous. "Any form He wills. The same as before, or something completely new. We can't know."

"Not until you find it," Jericho said with a sneer I immediately wanted to wipe from his face.

"Great. So Yahweh just Godzilla'ed the world."

That got their attention. Even Jericho found the gumption to look my way.

I shook my head. "Movies. Giant radioactive dinosaur that keeps coming back in new movies but always looks different. An Overworld reference. Ignore me."

I think Jericho murmured, 'Gladly," but I didn't hear it clearly enough to care.

"We hate to put you in this position, lad," Pher said with something that passed as a sad smile. "You know we wouldn't if we didn't think you could get the job done."

"Oh, I know that very well," I said, raising a finger. "Here's the thing." I directed the question and finger at no one in particular. It was for all of them, or at least any of them willing to answer. "Do I have explicit permission to go after this thing? I mean, if it's one of Yahweh's creations, do we know His intent to the point that I won't piss Him off if I take down His new pet?"

"Have respect when you talk about Him," Jericho said, his dead eyes flicking in my direction, but only for a second. As soon as I looked at him, those crystal orbs of apathy dropped to the table.

Puriel said, "Mr. Carver, you've touched on an important aspect of this current issue. In fact, it's the reason we brought you in to discuss it here, instead of sending a missive." She paused. From my seat at the butt end of the table, it appeared she was drawing a slow breath. But the President of the Order was so prim and proper, so calculating in every movement and gesture, it was impossible to tell what Puriel was thinking or feeling. Guessing what thoughts swirled in her big brain was far beyond my capacity. So I waited her out. "There are concerns, among us and the Council, that the creation of the behemoth was an accident."

"An accident? What do you mean? Like, Yahweh didn't want to create it? He slipped?"

Puriel blinked slowly. "Something like that."

Pher cleared his throat, leaning forward, head turned to the head of the table. "Puriel, if I may?"

She nodded. A prudent gesture.

My mentor swiveled in my direction. "Rev, concerns circle the Council that Yahweh is somehow different. Acting outside His typical fashion and character. This manifestation of the behemoth is the latest example. Not the first. Hopefully, the last."

"We doubt that," Puriel said tersely. Which was strange. Not the terseness, but the interruption. She rarely interrupted unless she needed to wrangle the opinionated members of the Order.

Pher bobbed his head. "This is just one part of their concern. Granted, a major part, depending on the nature of the beast, but a concern."

"This ain't the old days," I said. "If this thing is stomping around the Pacific Northwest, it could hit major metropolitan areas."

"We should consider ourselves lucky if it's actually in the Olympic Forest," Uziel said.

Raphina pushed away from the table, coffee mug wrapped in tiny hands. "It might not stay there."

Without turning her head, Puriel watched the younger member refill her coffee. "Raphina is correct. Were the behemoth to wander out of this forest, we would have a major problem on our hands. Not only with the mortal population centers, but the Underworld as well."

"That's for the Council to deal with," Jericho said.

"It is." Puriel nodded. "But that doesn't mean we don't have a responsibility to find a solution."

"Isn't that why he's here?" Jericho looked at her while shooting an arm in my direction. "He's the solution. Let's stop talking and send him into this forest, and have him hunt the beast. If it's there, he tries to kill it. If it's not, he keeps looking until he does. Or until it kills him. Then we'll know what we're facing."

"Far be it for Jericho's concern to not touch me, but couldn't the Council simply approach Yahweh and ask what this thing is? Where it is? And, oh, I don't know, have Him undo this unfortunate action? For all we know, this could be part of His plan."

"They have," Puriel said stiffly.

"And?"

"He's not answering."

"What?" I looked at Pher for help. "What does that even mean?"

Pher shrugged.

Something had been discussed prior to my arrival. I saw it on his face. The Order had been given something, a drip of a large lake held back by a dam. Probably ready to burst. But that drip came at a price. Sealed lips was the payment demanded.

I sighed.

"Yahweh isn't Himself," Puriel said after a moment's silence. "How much unlike himself? We don't know that answer. Not yet. But when you partner the manifestation of the behemoth with the momentum of the Nephilim, along with the breach of the Safe and theft of the First Bowl... well, you don't need to be Dumas to understand something is wrong. Very wrong. What that is, though? That's for you to uncover. Starting with the behemoth. The Overworld is at risk. But so is the Upperworld. Should you survive this confrontation, we'll have further tasks. I wish I had better news, but honesty will serve us best. You'll need to act with haste. Get an answer and do what is necessary to remove it from the Overworld. We'll leave it up to you to figure out how."

I wanted to thank her for the massive vote of confidence that I'd survive this showdown with Yahweh's "chief," but Puriel pushed her chair away from the table and stood. The rest of the Order mimicked her. Meeting adjourned.

Most wished me luck as we departed—Jericho did not—and Pher walked me to the hallway.

Brock gave me a nod. "See you soon, Rev."

"I sure hope so," I said, snapping my fingers to open the Rift. Stopping before it, I turned to my mentor and best friend. "This is a mess."

"We know, lad," Pher said, gripping my wrist. "Just be careful. None of us know what you're walking into and things here are—" He turned, looking back at the closed oak doors shielding us from the other members. Brock and his new sidekick pretended to not be interested in our chat. "Getting interesting around here."

"Politics can be like that."

Pher shook his head. "No. Not the politics. That's never going to change, even when the faces do." One side of his face wrinkled as he smirked devilishly. "I think you have to look no further than Jericho to see proof of that. This," he said, pointing toward the ceiling and swirling his finger, "is something more."

"Like what?"

"No idea. Can't put my finger on it, no matter how much I think about it. But I'm going to keep an ear to the ground because I'm not a fan of what my gut is telling me."

"Oh? What's that?"

Pher reached up and stroked his beard. I didn't like that. My mentor only did that when he was thinking or stressed. And he admitted he'd already been thinking, so that left one possibility. "I'm probably wrong, but this is inside work." He tipped his head back toward the meeting room. "Some of them, too many of them, are convinced this is purely the Underworld's doing, but I'm not falling for that."

"Why?"

"Yahweh has been different for a while."

"Hanging with the big guy now, are you?"

Pher didn't even try to fake a smile. "Just the benefit of spending too much time in the Eighth instead of in my living room with my granddaughter." He moved closer. "Keep your head down and be careful. We need you." He glanced back at the meeting room door. "A few are fooling themselves about how serious this might be." He turned and tapped me on the forehead with a finger. "Use this as your primary weapon, Rev."

Uh oh. My mentor not using my full name to tease? This

was serious. Even more than worrying about some over-grown lizard.

"I will, boss."

Even before I stepped back into my apartment in Olympia, I wondered if I'd get a chance to fulfill my promise to the one angel I looked up to. More likely, I'd only serve as the prover-bial angelic shit for the behemoth to step in.

4

TITANS AND TOSTADAS

"This is nuts, Rev."

Billee wasn't looking at me. The marble countertop was her focus instead. She traced invisible lines in it with a drifting finger.

I moved closer, leaning over the counter and probably looking like some douche from a black-and-white film where men were men and women were the only ones in the scenes who understood how sexist those films were. With that dawning of awareness, I straightened and supported myself on the counter with just the flat of my hands. Less douchey. Trust me.

"It is," I said. "But it doesn't make it any less our responsibility. The sooner we get this over with, the sooner we can pretend like none of this happened."

"And then get another assignment to something equally crazy?"

"Maybe." I couldn't hide my smirk.

"Does it get crazier?"

Now, I allowed the smirk to spread. "Than a giant beast out of nightmares roaming the land? Oh, yes. And if you're lucky enough, I'll survive this behemoth and we'll have to take on the latest terror to fall out of the Upperworld. Who knows, maybe Satan will make an appearance too."

"That's not funny."

"Come on. Not even a little?"

"Not even a smidgen," Billee said, but I saw the corner of her mouth twitch. She shook her head. "This is how people end up in institutions. I swear. I've always been kind to my clients. It's part of the job all good counselors don't half-ass. But this is giving me a whole new appreciation for them. If I ever get to do my job again. This is a bad dream. One day, I'll wake up and that's all this will have been."

"So you dream about me?"

"No."

"Oh, then you consider me to be dreamy?"

Her head popped up. She snagged her wine glass and pushed it at me. "Make yourself useful and fill this up."

"Dinner isn't useful enough?" I asked, taking the glass and doing as ordered by my partner.

"Well," Billee said, taking a deep sniff. "You do have a talent for cooking."

"Of course I do. I'm basically an executive chef." I stretched to set her wine in front of her.

Billee took it and lifted it in a toast. "To the chef, and his swaggering self-image."

I found my glass and lifted it. "To me."

We sipped—the wine I buy is too expensive to enjoy in any other way—and I returned to the last of the dinner prep.

"Who knew executive chefs would lower themselves to make tostadas," Billee said.

"I like tostadas."

"As do I. Glad to see you can remain anchored to your humble roots."

I chuckled. Standing over the pan, I stirred my beer and vegetable concoction, adding a big pinch of salt and readying the stock concentrate for the final huzzah. "Listen, I know this interferes with your actual job, and I'm sorry. I wish I could do something, but the Order won't stop sending me taskers. I'm the Reaper Minister. You know, I'm kind of a big deal."

"You're insufferable is what you are."

"That too. And you're not the first familiar they've screwed over. They do that to almost all of them if I can be honest."

"When are you not? Sometimes brutally so."

"A consequence of the occupation," I said, stirring as a thousand memories flashed through my mind in an instant. "It doesn't matter how much time I have. With my duties, it's best to yank the Band-Aid off. The pain is more intense, but it's also over quickly."

"Wow, what an encouraging way to look at it. So, are you saying I'm going to experience pain from being your property?"

I smacked the spatula on the edge of the pan. "You're not pro—"

Billee laughed. "I'm messing with you."

"Oh."

"Some days I just get..." She stopped, pausing for so long that I stopped watching the contents of the pan to check on her. She gave her head a series of short shakes. "Don't mind me."

"What is it? Tell me." The beef and veggies sizzled. The combination of the aroma given off by pepper and onions made my mouth water. I could leave it unattended for a minute. Billee was worth eating drier beef if my proximity helped her through this struggle. So I moved to the bar, standing across from her, but giving her my full attention.

"It's hard," she said, her shoulders slumping. "I under-stand the importance of it. No matter how crazy it is to think that I've gone through life and noticed nothing strange enough to ping my radar. A world filled with immortals. Real people whose lives are turned upside down so they can serve as familiars. It's more than I was prepared to deal with."

"Well, to be fair, whenever a Reaper steps into the Over-world to escort, the Interlude stops life. So it's fair that you wouldn't have picked up on any clues when you weren't a familiar. No one does. But don't worry, those few who think they've seen evidence of the supernatural spend the next days and weeks of their lives talking to doctors and mental health pros like you."

She squinted. "You're not funny. And sometimes I feel like I'm losing my mind. I can't believe this is how I'm spending the best years of my life. I know we're helping people, but I could do so much more if I wasn't constantly being pulled away from my actual job."

"This is your job," I said, trying to not sound like an apathetic ass.

"I could do more good for people at the clinic."

"I know." I didn't enjoy hearing the tone in her voice. She was frustrated. I got it. I would be too if I were in her shoes.

Billee was still a new familiar. We'd been working together for a matter of months. Adjusting to a life as an immortal's sidekick took most familiars years to wrap their heads around. Longer, if they wanted to come to peace with their new reality. Well, if they didn't just give up, that is. Billee was adjusting nicely, whether or not she could see that.

"This will get easier," I said. "I know it's not perfect. I know it's not great. And I know you're probably just as ass-kicking a social worker as the world has ever seen, but this is a higher calling few can answer."

"And I'm the lucky one who picked up the phone," she said with a slight grimace. She shook her head and blinked rapidly, her disposition changing in an instant. "Well, I can't do anything about this. There's no get-out clause for me, and the pay is... honestly, sort of gross."

I couldn't not chuckle at that. She wasn't wrong. By a long shot. Billee wouldn't have to work again if I convinced the Order to let me go, or if I had the balls to step out into traffic and take the first step toward getting my morning star. "Yes, familiars tend to do well for themselves. Best part? It's all tax-free."

Billee sniffed.

"Just think of all the good you can do with it. The Order selected you as my familiar because, as Pher likes to say behind your back, you're salt of the earth."

"He calls me that?"

"All the time."

"So he's the one I should be mad at?"

"Yep." I had no problem throwing my boss in front of the Billee-shaped locomotive. It's the least he deserved for all the free dinners I made him.

We laughed as I returned to the stove. The simmering beef and vegetables filled the open floor plan of my apartment with its redolent scent. To me, there's nothing like the smell of onions in a pan. I know, I'm weird. The tortillas were done and Billee joined me at the counter to build the tostadas.

"Leave some for me," she said as I doused mine with a healthy dose of crema.

"I like mine spicy," I said as she took the bowl and began spooning the sour cream and hot sauce mixture onto her meal. "Be careful with th—"

Billee poured heaping spoonfuls of the crema.

"Remind me to sit on the other side of the table before that kicks in."

"It can't be that bad," she said, wrapping her finger around the lip of the bowl to wipe it clean. I blob of crema balanced on her fingertip and she promptly popped it into her mouth. Her finger came out with a pop and before I could finish topping off my tostadas with what remained of the sauce, Billee was fanning her face. "That's hot."

"I told you." I carried my plate to the table and returned to the kitchen, still chuckling at her discomfort and filling a glass of milk for her.

"Thank you," she said, taking the glass and drinking half of it.

I sat down across from her. "Nothing like getting free entertainment. I'm going to enjoy watching you polish those tostadas off."

"You're an ass."

Billee got through the first tostada like a champ. I expected nothing less. In her short time as my familiar, she'd shown herself to be tough as nails and as smart as an engineer—just with more personality. A dangerous combination. Which, of course, was why the Order had chosen her for this duty.

"Are you okay with all this, Billee? I need to know. Not like I can get the Order to change their minds, but maybe Pher can help. I could handle a lot of these jobs on my own if angels could do unsupervised work in the Overworld."

She fanned her mouth, which hung open throughout most of the meal. "I just had a weak moment. Trust me, I'm fine. And it's not like I'm not seeing my clients. I can't take on any new ones. I'm a big girl. I'll deal with this."

"Okay."

"But maybe you can talk to him about why it's always you."

"Always me?"

"Yes," she said, polishing off her second glass of water and standing.

I pushed back my chair.

"No, I'll get it," she said. "My punishment for not listening to you about the crema."

As she refilled her milk, I said, "Well, not like you gave me a chance. You were pretty gluttonous with it. Might need to be careful with that. I heard they frown on gluttony in the Upperworld."

She stopped filling the glass. "That's actually true."

Instead of answering, I scooped up the little that remained

of my dinner with my fork and waited for her to return to her seat. When I looked up, she was sitting, staring at me.

I almost spit out the last crumbles of beef and sliced pepper when I laughed. "No. It's not. Figured it was my turn to mess with you."

"Hilarious." She wagged a finger at me. "One of these days, I'm going to get you back. There has to be something about mortality or the world you don't know about, and I'm going to revel in holding onto that knowledge or toying with you."

"Billee, I've been a Reaper for longer than mortals have known how to write letters. Trust me, you won't pull the wool over my eyes."

"Challenge accepted." She pulled her chair in, shaking her head again. "Crazy. All of this."

"What?"

"Sitting at dinner with an angel who is older than the Sumerian language, for starters. Sitting at a table with the angel and helping him plan on how to find and fight the behemoth from out of the Bible."

"A behemoth. Remember, not the same one as in the Good Book."

"Still crazy. And when I asked why it's always you, I was asking why does it seem that you're the one who gets all these dangerous assignments? I mean, maybe there's more going on around the world that I don't know about. There might be a hundred Reapers out there chasing the baddies, but something tells me that's not the case."

"It's not. Guardian Angels pretty much mitigate the baddies."

"How so?"

I sat back, pulling my wine glass close. I couldn't ignore the feeling we were about to have a long chat that required nectar of cerebral revision. "Well, for starters, if anything the baddies are doing or about to do will harm the mortal, the

Guardian Angel can step in to influence the outcome. How they do that is usually up to them. Of course, it doesn't always work. Free will and all that. Plus, the Guardians have Rules of Engagement, but they're pretty gray. If the actions of whoever these baddies are that you've conceived over a wonderful tostadas dinner don't impact mortals, then it doesn't matter."

"And if the baddies kill mortals?"

I shrugged. "Then their names were already in the Book of Planes. The All needed their energy, and it was their time. Though, it is possible that the baddies... are we really going to keep calling them that?"

"Of course," Billee said with a smirk. "Makes it less unnerving than what I saw at the homeless camp."

I understood. Most of the jobs Billee was part of were nothing more than escorting deceased mortals, and petty tasks. That changed with the breach of the Safe and theft of Yahweh's First Bowl of Wrath. A Nephilim named Arakiel Hale had poured it on the world, kicking off a worldwide plague. The virus killed two million worldwide and was still spreading, though the mortals were doing everything in their power to slow it. Billee had been involved in my hunt for Arakiel and was there the night he showed his ugly face. Seeing a Nephilim in its true form can traumatize, even angels. I'd killed him, but stuff like that just didn't dissipate with death. I doubted Billee could ever put the event out of her mind.

"Well, if these baddies do something truly unexpected, it's possible a victim gets entered into the Book of Planes almost instantaneously."

"So, unplanned?"

"Yes, and no." I took a sip of wine and enjoyed its smooth texture. When you've dealt with crap like I have for eight thousand years, you learn little tricks to balance the bad with the good. The oh-so-very good. "Even angels don't understand the construction of the All. At some point in the development of the immortal lexicon, someone, somewhere named the consciousness of the All. They are called it One. Kind of like the brains to the machine, you could say. So if One changes their mind about calling time on a mortal's life, then it happens."

"Just like that?"

"Just like that."

Billee sat quietly for a moment. "So everything is tightly managed. Heaven doesn't need a bunch of Revs running around killing monsters. That's why it's always you who gets these weird assignments, and I'm the fortunate person assigned to the one angel who gets all the crappy jobs."

Still holding my wine, I extended my finger at her. "Bingo."

She snickered. "Lucky me."

"I consider you very lucky." I winked and waved at the two empty plates. "After all, how many people get invited to dine with an executive chef so often?"

Billee fanned her face, just not from the spicy crema. This time, she was being a smartass. "Oh, my, Mr. Carver. I am so fortunate."

"That's your southern accent?"

"I'm a social worker, not an actor." She raised her nearly empty glass, almost drinking but stopping at what looked like a sudden thought. "Though I took an acting class in college. An elective course."

"How did that go?"

"Terribly."

"You don't say."

She swatted the air. "Ass."

"To answer your question, I get these jobs because it's something my younger self agreed to. Something my older self would have smacked him in the head for doing if time travel were possible."

"Oh? Sounds like there's a story there."

"You could say that."

She waited.

I watched my wine swirl. With a sigh, I said, "You want to know, don't you?"

Billee smiled devilishly, lighting her face. Her smooth, brown skin radiated.

"You're a pain."

"So are you, Rev Carver, chef-extraordinaire. Now, out with it."

"You're going to think I'm a braggart if I tell you the truth."

"If it makes you feel any better, I already think of you like that."

So I began, giving her the quick and dirty of one of my first jobs escorting a tribe's leader who didn't feel like dying. He put up a good fight, and I hadn't received the best training from the Reaper's program. A few stab wounds and blood loss later, I was escorting the man's energy residue to the Veil Gate. "When I returned home, it shocked my supervisor that I hadn't died in the Overworld. They'd already started looking to fill my vacancy."

Billee's mouth fell open, which only made the re-telling funnier.

"Once they saw the ass-kickings I could take, I received tougher and tougher assignments. Since none killed me, I rose through the ranks quickly. My personality didn't hurt."

"Such a charmer, you," Billee said, then waved it away. "But seriously, you are a nice guy. I get why they'd see it in you. After how you treated Delores. That meant a lot."

"It's important."

"I know. But she could have been 'just another mortal,' yet you never treated her like that. As long as you've done this, as many as you've escorted, you could have just done the job as quickly as possible to move on to the next thing. But you didn't. You showed you cared by taking your time with her. I can see why your personality is attractive to your Order."

"My personality made me a great Reaper. My tolerance for pain and survival skills made me the perfect assassin. They said those very words to me." I grunted at a thought.

"What is it?"

"Just thinking about those times. Feels like a lifetime ago. Maize Judas said those words to me."

"There's something familiar about that name. Why do I know it?"

"You don't. But her son Jericho might ring a bell. I complain about him enough."

"Ah, yes. The guy you can't stand... his mother adored you?"

I nearly choked on my wine. Setting my glass down, I said, "Oh, no. Quite the opposite. But she saw something in me because she's the one who made the proposal to make me the first Reaper assassin. I was young, dumb, and full of myself. Back then, I believed in what the Reapers were doing. Believed in the Upperworld's processes and aims. I bought the Order's flirting, hook, line, and sinker and swore to the creed as if it was the greatest honor they could have ever given me. To protect the Upperworld from any threat, foreign or domestic, if you will." My thoughts turned dark and my voice drifted away at how screwed I was, knowing there was no end to my job. A slave to eternity. "And they've been using me ever since. Didn't hurt that I stopped an assassination attempt on Yahweh."

If I thought Billee's mouth had fallen open before, she took it to a whole new level. I swear, it looked like her jaw came unhinged. "You what?"

"Stopped an assassination attempt."

"On God?"

"Yep."

She pursed her lips, shaking her head. "Wait. Wait. Wait. God can be killed?"

"Yep."

"I need more wine."

"Let me," I said, getting up and finding a cabernet that would complement the meal we'd just finished. I grabbed two fresh glasses and brought everything back to the table without a word, giving Billee time to process the opening of the aperture I'd just provided. "Crazy shit, right?"

Her wide eyes confirmed she thought it was.

"And ever since then, I'm seen as untouchable. Even to the bigwigs. Even to those who don't like me."

"Like Jericho?"

I nodded.

"So you don't have a get-out clause either? You're going to be a Reaper until?"

"Until I'm lucky enough to get an assignment for someone with better aim than that dirtbag last night."

"I don't like when you talk like that."

"Like what?"

Billee slid her wine to the side and leaned closer. Her dark eyes were warm and welcoming. "Rev, I appreciate that I'll never understand what it's like for you." The corner of her mouth quivered. "I mean, this is nuts. For me. You under-stand? To comprehend everything about reality that's changed for me just in the past few months? It's like I don't know what's real and what's not. Not anymore. But I can try to understand your position. I get that you have a job you hate. A job you've performed well in for thousands of years. I appreciate you feel it's time for someone else to take up the mantle. My heart hurts to know you feel you've done your part and are now only asking for those above you to recog-nize that and make some concessions, knowing they won't. But I still don't like hearing you talk about death like that. You've done it before. You mentioned it to Pher when we were all together. This morning star of yours. Please," she said, stretching across the table to take my hand in her smaller, warmer one, "please, I'm asking you to hear me. I am not chastising you and meaning to imply that you're being selfish. I don't think you are. But there is so much in you. So much good. The world is better with you a part of it." Her dark eyes swung in the direction of the balcony doors behind me. "And life is so beautiful. Every moment. So precious. I want you to feel that. I'm sure you have before. Maybe a long time ago. All anyone has to do is watch you cook. When you're in front of your stove or at the counter preparing the ingredients, I see it. That's when you're alive. I want that for you. To embrace living life."

"I do, Billee," I said, kindly but firmly. "I do, and I have. But sometimes those moments aren't enough." I adjusted on my chair, trying not to send signals that her caring put me off. I didn't. There were too few who truly cared, not about me, but just about each other. I appreciate those, like Billee, who did and had the guts to show they cared by having real, sometimes difficult, conversations like this one. "Long before the world you know existed, I was doing this. At the rate I'm going, I'll still be doing this long after everything is gone. Normally, when an immortal is in the Overworld, doesn't matter if it's ten minutes or ten years, they begin to decay, and—"

"Decay?"

"Die," I said, maybe too bluntly, if the way her face flickered was any sign. "This isn't our realm. Though we can travel here, this is the mortal realm. One, the All, whichever. I don't know, and I don't care. It, they, devised that mechanism so immortals didn't overstay our welcome here. Doesn't matter who. Angel. Demon. Yahweh. Lucifer. When we come to the Overworld, our bodies begin to break down." I sat back, stretching. Raising a flat hand, I gestured along my body, from my face to my waist. "Yet, look at me. You won't see me on the cover of a smutty romance book, but that's mostly because I enjoy eating red meat that prevents having a six-pack stomach."

She giggled, sounding years younger. "You'd also have to comb your hair once in a while."

I allowed myself a laugh. "All the things I've been through. All the monsters I've chased, the crap out of children's stories you wouldn't think were real. I'm still rocking this bod."

"Oh, god."

"I've had ladies say that before."

Billee's hand shot to her mouth as she cough-laughed. "You're terrible."

"My point is, I'm not going anywhere. Literally. The Order won't release me from the Reapers, and every single time I kill an immortal being, I absorb their energy, prolonging my own life. You saw that in Seattle with Naaman, even though he was a demon. You saw that at the homeless camp with Arakiel. Imagine the amount of energy something like a behemoth holds. If that thing doesn't squash me and I kill it, I might outlive Yahweh." I tipped my head from side to side, smiling. "Actually, having it squash me doesn't sound like half a bad idea."

This time, when her hand moved towards mine, it wasn't to embrace them but to smack them. "Stop. It."

We'd had a lovely evening over the best tostadas anyone in Olympia would be eating. Today or tomorrow. Or this month.

I put my hands up. "I'm stopping."

"Promise?"

"Promise. Plus, we have to figure out our behemoth plan."

"You know," she said, pursing her lips, "you've just made me think of something."

"Miracles never cease!"

That deserved and received another hand swat.

"What I was about to say," she said as a smile illuminated her flawless features, "is that it's a good thing you're such a kind guy."

"Oh? Why's that?"

"Because look at what you just said." She held her wine in one hand while the free one made a rolling motion. "You're Heaven's assassin. You get all the dirty jobs that require the killing of immortal creatures committing harmful actions. That alone is scary because, in the wrong hands, someone might abuse that authority and power. But that's not the worst part. Not for me."

"I think you're complimenting me, but I'm not convinced."

She sighed playfully. "Besides the incessant need for ego stroking I seem to be reinforcing, I'm talking about something serious. You have ethics. You're morally faithful to your duty, to God's will, and to the people you serve. But hear me out. What about a Reaper who is less ethical than you? Someone who would abuse the power you have. Think about it, Rev." She swatted my hand with rapid, light strikes as her thought machine swirled. "Not only could they transform humanity with each action. But there's the immortal aspect to consider. If someone other than you was Heaven's assassin, absorbing the energy of immortals they killed, they could take advantage of that. A less ethical assassin could target and kill immortals and absorb their energy to live forever. They could become truly immortal. Have you thought about that?"

"Thanks. That's what I needed. One more thing to stress about."

"You're welcome."

"Just like mana stones, too. The combination of an unethical assassin possessing one of those stones would—"

"A what?"

"Mana stone. Powerful little devices that keep an angel alive far past their 'use by' date. Thanks a lot for the stressful thoughts, Billee."

She winked. "Just doing my job, boss."

I winked back. "Pain in my ass."

We stood and cleared the table.

As I reached for Billee's plate, she grabbed my wrist once more. Her grip was firm. Looking me in the eye, she said, "I mean it. Please don't go after your morning star too soon. You're needed. Maybe more than you know."

5

THROUGH PHER'S EYES

THE EIGHTH LEVEL OF THE UPPERWORLD IS WHERE THE ANGELIC movers and shakers do their business. Yahweh's residence—His throne room—His headquarters and the supporting staff's residences are located here. It's also where the Upperworld's head honchos govern. Definitely not a vacation spot. Especially for a long-hair, black leather duster-wearing assassin who enjoys life's casual settings over pomposity. Yet, here I was, walking the Eighth Level and having a chat with one of the movers and shakers.

Who could break me down so easily? My mentor, of course.

"Another beautiful day," Pher said as we walked past a park filled with children playing.

A mother squawked at a pair attempting to rough house. Before they tumbled to the ground, she was on her feet, pulling them up and snapping about 'getting their nice slacks filthy.'

"Why dress them up and then go to a park?" I mumbled.

"What?"

I shook my head. "Nothing. Just don't think anyone can consider this paradise when kids can't get a little dirty."

Pher glanced at the mother and children and then back at me. "Hmmm. Their pants probably cost a bit. No fault. I don't blame her."

"Then don't bring your kids to the park dressed like that. Plus, with their outfits and the fact we're in the Eighth, something tells me mom could buy new pants each time one of them gets a grass stain."

"True. Her family is well-to-do." Pher pulled up, watching me.

"What?"

His eyes narrowed. "You seem feisty."

"Someone has to stand up for a kid's right to just be a kid."

"Judge not, lest ye be judged yourself."

"Blah, blah, blah."

"Rev," Pher said, drawing out my name like he was my father and I was wandering into dangerous territory.

I rubbed my face, pushing my hair back. "Ignore me. Just been doing some thinking. I blame Billee."

"How is Sunrose?"

I started walking again. I needed to be away from the overlord mother in the park. Pher drifted with me. "Though she's fine, she would be better off being allowed to return to a normal life as a counselor. I don't imagine you're up for working miracles?"

"Sorry, lad. Billee is perfect for you. And you're not exactly slow on the uptake. You understand the importance of your task."

"I do. But I don't have to like it. I'd rather be chasing demons, and I don't want to do that either."

Pher grabbed my hand, laughing. "Speaking of, have you heard about Cassie?"

Now it was my turn to draw a name out. "Cassie?"

"Haniel," Pher said as if I should have known exactly who he was talking about.

Another sigh later, I said, "Oh good. What? Did another

entitled brat get another big break? An opportunity no one else gets because of who she's related to? Better yet, did she get a release from her contract? Did someone ignore the creed she agreed to uphold?"

"You really are feisty today," Pher said, dropping my hand. "Actually, it's an interesting story. And if you gave her a chance, you might find it interesting yourself."

"I don't know her, so I don't need to give her a chance."

"Well, it speaks to interesting events."

"In the Overworld?"

He nodded. "In your own backyard."

"Oh?" Okay, so now he had my attention.

"Apparently, she was involved in an altercation in Olympia last night. How did you not hear about this?"

"I had Billee over for dinner to draw up a behemoth of a plan. Then she got me thinking about other problems. Thus my less-than-cheery disposition."

"Ah, well, while you were trying to charm Billee—"

"I wasn't. She's my familiar."

"Cassie was in the Overworld, involved in a skirmish. She used Angelfire to set a squad of demons and mortals on fire."

I stopped. I'd like to say I skidded to a halt, but there isn't any gravel in the Eighth Level. The sidewalks here, to risk sounding like a predictable stereotype, are paved in gold. In case you're wondering, skidding on gold surfaces isn't easy.

"Literally?"

"Seems there was a nasty fight and got involved in. To help."

"Well, that's cool, to put her neck out there like that for a human. Didn't know she'd picked up Guardian duties."

"She hasn't. Someone with her station wouldn't be assigned those kinds of tasks."

"Beneath her, are they?"

"Don't beat me up, lad. You know she's involved in other

things. Plus, it wasn't mortals she intervened on behalf of. It was a demon. A demon you might be familiar with."

His teasing tone and the fact that Cassie Haniel was in Olympia, protecting a demon I might know, led me to the only conclusion I could reasonably reach. "Let me guess. Ezekial Sunstone?"

"The one and only."

"What's she doing helping the supposed demon in line to become Lucifer?"

He gave me a run-down of her involvement, at least what he knew about it. Learning Cassie had used Angelfire, purportedly a heavy dose, in the Overworld, was beyond the pale.

"Wow. Risky."

He shrugged and said, "Young ones," as if it explained everything.

"Hormones blocking their thinking?" I said with a chuckle.

"Wouldn't be the first time. Not even between angels and demons."

"No, but I don't remember someone in the elite wooing the future ruler of the Underworld."

"We don't know if that's what he'll become. Once you're back on his case, it might become a moot point. Plus, don't call her one of the elite. She's a sweet girl. Woman actually. I've got to remember she's grown up."

"Yeah, well, that's where you and I differ," I said. "Was she disciplined for using Angelfire in the Overworld?"

"Not that I'm aware of," he answered carefully.

"There you go then."

"'There you go then,' what?"

"Were it anyone else, especially someone outside the top three ranks of angels, do you think they would have been allowed to attack mortals and demons in the Overworld without approval? Would anyone else do that and not suffer consequences? You know better, Pher. She'll get away with it because she's one of the elite."

"Don't use that word like a cudgel. It doesn't do you any favors."

"I don't like angels who are allowed exceptions someone from the lower ranks wouldn't be afforded. Disparity pisses me off."

Just then, a young girl, maybe twelve hundred years old, walked by astride a unicorn far too big for her. The beast was pure white, even its mane, except for its horn. The deep purple spike rose from the center of the bridge of its muzzle. The beast was less threatening than the young girl, who looked down her nose at an angel assassin and a member of the Order of Thirteen as if we'd disturbed precious playtime. I had the sudden urge to steal the damn unicorn, sell it, and use the proceeds to help needy angels in my Level.

"Like that, right there," I said when she passed.

Pher turned to watch the girl. "What about her?"

"She's growing up in the Eighth, where life is calm and secure. Her biggest worry is probably dismounting and not stepping in a pile of unicorn shit. It wouldn't surprise me if she and the damn unicorn have handlers to remove even that worry."

"Lad, you don't know her or her family."

"But I'll bet I'm not far off. Just around the corner from my house in the Third, there's a family who enjoys children. They have six. The mother and father both work, and the older children make sure the younger kids are fed and finish their homework. Every damn night. The youngest kids are asleep by the time either parent makes it home, meaning they see their parents mostly on the weekends. The parents have to so the family has a roof over their heads. They'll miss their children's childhoods out of necessity. Out of the need to survive." I pointed at the little snob astride the unicorn. "Plop her into a situation like that, and she wouldn't last a week.

She's used to this." I waved my arm around, pointing out our surroundings. The park with its manicured grass and expensive playground equipment. Sidewalks of gold you could eat off. The subtle presence of patrols who made sure no one ever felt threatened—not in a police-state sort of way, but more like 'I'm the big brother and you won't bother my little sister,' level of protection. "So I feel justified in my stance. Look me in the eye and tell me you believe they'll hold Cassie Haniel accountable for picking fights in the Overworld."

Pher looked away from the girl and her unicorn, which dropped a load of shit on the sidewalk that would fill a shovel head, and turned to me. He didn't see the two sanitation workers move to the unicorn dung and clean it up before it caused any of the Eighth Level residents trauma by making them step around it on their evening stroll. Oh, the struggle.

"I can look you in the eyes and tell you that you're not wrong," Pher said. He started walking again. "The Council has said nothing to us, not even in passing. Not a surprise."

I snorted in disgust. I didn't know Cassie well enough to know if I liked her or not. I most definitely didn't like the fact that she could get away with something anyone outside the Seraphim, Ophanim, Cherubim, and Thrones would get strung up for doing.

"Rev, my boy, you have enough on your mind. Let this rest. Don't make me regret bringing it up. Focus on what you can affect. Like Jericho Judas. He's talking about you. Too much, if you ask me."

"Oh, is he now?"

"Yes, and I don't like it."

We continued down the sidewalk, passing a sidewalk café. Angels filled the tables, enjoying yet another perfect evening in the Eighth. The smell of lattes and light pastries filled the air.

The need to be protective against inquiring minds gave me a chance to think through my response. I still hadn't told

Pher about my risky tactic of blackmailing Jericho. I'd done so out of necessity, to uncover the truth behind the Nephilim Arakiel and how he obtained the First Bowl. All of which was a miscalculation on my part, one that came to nothing. Blackmailing a member of the Order of Thirteen is about the dumbest thing a Reaper could do. I might as well have asked Yahweh to throw down. At the time, I thought I had to so I could get answers and maybe save the Overworld and Upperworld.

Before I left Jericho trembling on the couch in his Eighth Level quarters, I promised him that the issue would stay between the two of us if he did the right thing. In the short days since the lack of uproar seemed to reinforce my notion that he'd play along nicely. But if Pher was worried about Jericho bringing my name up, I better be worried, too.

"What's he saying?"

Pher tipped his head. "Prying for updates on your activities. Encouraging us to pass a vote to have you supervised, among other things."

"Supervised? I'm the freaking Reaper Minister."

"His requests, if you can call them that, were dismissed. Trust me, he's making himself look a fool in front of the Order. But that doesn't mean he'll quit. If he keeps pushing, he might sway some of the more impressionable voting members." Pher stopped, turning to me. The glorious glow of the white hole—the flip-side of the black hole at the center of the Milky Way that hid us from mortal detection—all things are possible through One, don't forget—illuminated his globular cheeks. He kept his eyes closed as if he sought contentment. "While I appreciate the mutual disdain the pair of you have for each other, it helps neither of you. Jericho is young, and—"

"An entitled twat who benefited from nepotism."

Pher's lips twitched before he got his agreeing smile under control. "And he benefited from his mother's connections. Yes.

He is young, short-sighted, and if we're being honest, unequipped to be a voting member and in charge of security. But he's there, and that has to be dealt with. This matter between the two of you? Whatever it is? He won't listen to advice or guidance. Jericho is..."

"Jericho."

"Exactly. Which is why I'm coming to you about the effects of this toxic relationship between the two."

"My responsibility to fix?"

"Yes. I'm afraid so. He's not willing, and I doubt he's even capable."

"Great. One more task."

My mentor took my hand. "Rev, it's for the best. The Order needs solidarity now more than ever. Jericho will be a problem." He dropped my hand, and we started off again. "There is something else I wanted to discuss with you, but not out here in the open. Let's head back to my quarters and I'll cook you dinner."

I skidded to a halt, playing the role of smartass quite well. "You're cooking?"

Pher snickered, his nostrils fluttering. "Of course. Why not? I cook almost every evening."

"Every evening you're not mooching off me, you mean?"

"True. But your cooking is a level above most immortals. It's time I returned the favor."

"You sure?" I looked him up and down. "You look like you could use some 'Rev dinners'."

"Referring to yourself in third person is slightly concerning, my boy."

I flipped my hand in a faux flourish. "When one creates the epicurean experiences I do, one may refer to one's self in the third person. Plus, do you even own a pan?"

"By Yahweh," he chuckled, grabbing my wrist and hauling me along. "Let's go. I'm hungry."

WE SAT AT HIS TABLE IN HIS OSTENTATIOUS QUARTERS IN Yahweh's headquarters before Pher started the serious conversation. The lavish living space wasn't Pher's fault—all Order members were assigned these quarters while they served on that governing body. They needed to for those times they were called in for sessions that lasted for days.

However, the conversation was his fault, because he'd been thinking, and now he wanted to wrangle me in as well.

Damn him. If I didn't adore that man, I swear...

"You seriously, I mean, like no-shit genuinely, believe Hellion is behind this?" I asked as I sucked down a noodle. The spaghetti was hard. The sauce, bland. But I was a guest, and this was a free meal I didn't have to prepare, so I was going to try and enjoy it.

Pher poked at his spaghetti like he was angry with it. "I've gone over and over this, and it's the only thing that makes sense."

"And you rode my ass about making assumptions," I said, meaning it to be light.

Pher ignored the poke. "The Safe was breached. Sure, it's secure now, but for how long? We still don't know the how or why of it, and until we do, it's a massive problem. Everything is at risk. You talk about entitlement. Yes, the residents of the Eighth have it easy. The Upperworld does not differ from the Underworld or the Overworld. Those with resources have access and opportunity those without can only dream of. That's a fact of reality. But most of those angels you get agitated about because they snub their noses at supposedly lesser angels aren't a threat to everything. Hellion has been the Lamb of God for..." He flipped his hand in the air. "I don't even know at this point. As long as I can remember. She's one of the most ancient Nephilim and has been sitting in that seat for the better part of seven ages now." He shook his head. "She's involved. Somehow. Some way."

"You think she's the one who breached the Safe?"

"Arakiel couldn't have."

I didn't disagree. I'd fought the Nephilim. He was tough, but as Nephilim go, not that much of a struggle. Someone like him couldn't have penetrated the Safe, found the First Bowl, and navigated their way out without help.

"I can't get access to the safe," Pher said. "No one in the Order can. As much as you dislike the higher ranks of angels—"

"I don't dislike them. I dislike their privilege."

"Be that as it may," Pher said, swatting away my interruption with the hand that hadn't dropped yet. "None of the ranks have carte blanche. They're not able to access something like the Safe, no matter how much pull they have. As far as I know, no one on Yahweh's Council can either. Not individually. If one needs access, they all must attend in order to ensure transparency." Pher stabbed his spaghetti again, eating none of it. This was an angel who could barely afford not to eat. I didn't want to have to point that out. Not now. I would. Later. "It was her, Rev. I don't have any proof, but I know it in my heart."

"Well," I started, cautiously, "best be careful who you're exposing your heart to, boss."

"I have told no one but you."

I nodded once. "Keep it that way. I don't want to think about what she'd do if she found out you were implying she was involved in a criminal act of this magnitude."

Pher leaned forward, his fork dropping. The metal striking ceramic was a harsh sound over what was supposed to be a relaxed dinner between two lifelong friends. "She's taking advantage of something."

"What do you mean? Taking advantage of what?"

He shook his head as if he was trying to free cobwebs. "No

one is talking. No one in the Order knows anything." He wagged a finger at me. "But something is happening. The Council has been acting strange lately. They were before confirmation that someone stole the First Bowl. Add that to the behemoth manifesting, and my gut tells me whatever is going on has to do with Yahweh's situation."

"If the Lamb of God is manipulating Him, would anyone know?" I asked, the sudden dawning of dark subversion jumping to the forefront of my mind. Political intrigue can do that, you know, even to angels like me who couldn't give a rat's turd about politics.

"That's the thing," Pher said, his finger leveling and holding steady on me. "No one would if she could keep everyone an arm's length away." He sat back, crossing his arms. "I mean, that's the role of the Lamb of God, isn't it? To keep a checks and balances system on anyone serving as Yahweh. For all any of us know, especially if the Council is staying hush-hush on this, Yahweh might have overstepped and this is her reaction to His actions. The First Bowl, causing Him to manifest the behemoth, whatever might come next. All of it could be a reaction." He outstretched his arm, the dangerous finger extended again, and tapped the table with it. "But I'm telling you, I know this like I know my granddaughter's favorite ice cream. Something has changed, and she's involved."

I stared at my cooling spaghetti, unloved and becoming forgotten. Pher was convincing, I had to give him that. My mood turned sour. "This is bad, boss."

A moment of nothing passed, measured only by the ticking of the grandfather clock in the other room.

"And it might be worse than imagined."

I stifled my groan. "How so?"

Pher stroked his beard. "If I'm correct about Hellion playing this game, don't think for a second she isn't also using the Four Horsemen to move the pieces around the board."

6

OLD FRENEMIES

THE FOUR HORSEMEN OF THE APOCALYPSE. YEP, THAT'S WHO Pher was talking about. Imagine trying to get sleep after a conversation like that. Needless to say, mine wasn't restful.

I woke the next morning more tired than when I'd laid down. Though I may be immortal, in a few ways, I'm only human. Thinking Hellion broke into the Safe and stole the First Bowl, using the Four Horsemen to accomplish the feat, made sense. Too much sense. And if that was the case, who was going to say 'boo' about it if Yahweh remained silent? That's the crap that steals sleep.

But I chose to re-frame life into something productive, even when it stinks. Productivity equals contentment, if not happiness. If I'm getting something done, then I'm engaged with the world. Engaged with life. Inertia is the bane of existence. Live while you're living. So when I woke from a lousy night of tossing and turning on a mattress that cost as much as my last car, I was ready to get something done.

That's when I thought about Bear and Bolt.

A few text messages later, we were meeting at the abandoned brewery site on the west side of Olympia.

The two mortals came from my very recent past, thanks to

the First Bowl being poured on the world and the now-deceased Nephilim known as Arakiel. Both men, well, Bolt was really just a kid, had fallen under the influence of Arakiel. He had used them and their friends to cause chaos in the city, to distract authorities from his more devious actions —namely terrorizing mortals for their energy and wreaking havoc with the First Bowl.

Neither they nor those who ran in their circles were bad people. That was as clear as day when I discovered they weren't in control of themselves. With Arakiel's influence removed, they both had potential. More importantly, they had utility.

I'd done them favors when we crossed paths. It was within my power to change the course of their futures. I could have made decisions that led to both of them having their names entered into the Book of Planes, thus calling time on their lives. But I hadn't. They were alive because of me. Their friends were too. They had the promise of a future because of me. And now they were going to repay me.

I pulled into what used to be the abandoned brewery's employee parking lot which was now a carpet of blacktop nature that was slowly reclaiming. Because I'm a rebel, I parked across the white line. Edgy, I know.

The day was brisk. After all, it was January. Thick gray clouds should have shrouded the sky. Rain should have been pelting my face and soaking everything that was absorbent. Instead, an expanse of blue formed a dome, giving the sky plenty of sunshine even as it robbed us of the relative warmth cloud cover would have provided. I'd take it. There's never enough sun in this part of the Overworld.

The brewery site was quiet. It always was nowadays. When the beer stopped flowing here, so did life. A sad but clear example that, no matter what happens, life goes on. The form may change, but the nature of existence never does. Life will find a way to continue.

My car door closing echoed against the barren factory walls. I regretted clicking the clock and making the car's security system chirp. If I'd been smart, I would have punched the lock before getting out to prevent drawing attention. Too late. Any curious eyeballs would now see me near the abandoned site. Nosy people might call the cops. Cops might send a patrol. A patrol would not only ruin this meeting but might permanently rob me of a strategic place for future needs. After all, if shit was spinning up in the Upperworld, I'd need to expand my network to deal with it here in the Overworld. Bear and Bolt— what a great professional wrestling tag team name that'd make —were the start of my net casting. They just didn't know it yet.

Bolt, who got his nickname as an ode to his acts of vandalism with a bolt cutter while under Arakiel's influence, was already inside the brewery. I heard him before I saw him in the dusty and dark guts of the building.

Sitting on the wire mesh mezzanine, kicking his feet back and forth as they hung over the edge, he tipped his head at me in the way teens do when they think they looked cool or brash, or coolly brash. "'Sup?"

"Hey, B—" I said, stopping myself from calling him Bolt because his real name was Brad, and I can't think of a douchier name than Brad. Maybe Chad. Yeah, that's close too. "Doing alright?"

"Yeah," he said, gripping the railing and pulling himself up. "I'll be down in a sec."

I moved to the center of the vast room where employees had brewed a cheap beer that would have never survived in today's microbrew world even if the factory had. Most of the equipment was long gone, liquidated in the death throes of the business. The expansive concrete floor was empty, except for conveyor belts, discarded pallets, and a fermenter that was tall enough to hold skydiving lessons inside. The abandoned brewery was a perfect site for the types of discussions I routinely needed to have with mortals, which sometimes included having to use my Soul stone to manipulate them. A dirty place for a dirty job.

I did a quick search while I waited for Bolt to join me on the floor.

"No one's here," he said as he drifted my way.

A thin kid of eighteen, Bolt had long blond hair that could benefit from a visit with a bottle of shampoo. You'd think his cut would have died out with grunge music, but this was the Pacific Northwest, and we cling to that era of identity like Alabama holds to its ironic 'sweet home' national anthem. Bolt had to weigh a hundred and thirty pounds if he was lucky, and a tenth of that came from his nose. An ugly kid, it was easy to understand why he spent most of his time hanging around other angsty teen guys.

"Good."

"That's what you wanted, right?"

"Yeah."

He pushed his hair back with the flat of his hand. "Are we in trouble or something?"

"No. Should you be?" I don't enjoy playing hard-ass, but sometimes, like with the drug-dealing scumbag I'd escorted to the Veil Gate, you have to be. With Bolt, it was different. I was still feeling him out. He came across as one of those types who constantly walked the razor's edge. Most eighteen-year-old boys do. A failure of mortal society. Teaching boys that to be 'real men,' they had to be tough. They had to ignore 'weak' thoughts and feelings. To be 'tough,' they had to shun showing and giving affection unless it was something they could brag to their buddies about in the locker room. As bad as that truth was, trust me, it had been worse over the past few thousand years. Mortals are slow to learn anything, but believe it or not, this was progress. Bolt might tip to the dark side, but he could also fall on the right side of what it meant to be a man. If I had a small role in pushing him, I knew which way I'd shove.

"No, man. We're good."

"How is everyone? Your friends? They staying out of trouble?"

"Yeah," he said with a nervous laugh. "That was really fucked up." His eyes widened, flickering. "Oh, sorry. I mean, the other night. That stuff at the homeless camp. We're all still kind of freaked out."

"Oh?"

"Yeah." Now his hand rubbed her long locks. "We talked. Most of us kind of remember talking to you about something. Sort of. But we can't remember much. Then, wham! We're down at the homeless camp at night. Some guys were hurting. Like we'd just played football or something. Couple of guys have bruises they don't know how they got." He cocked his head to the side as if he didn't want to make eye contact. "We're kind of scared of you now. Guys think you had something to do with it. But none of us knows how or why. We told you we were sorry. Sorry about that shit at the storage units. We know that was wrong. We—"

I held up my hand. I didn't have the time nor inclination to explain the fact I'd temporarily brainwashed a bunch of kids to help me contain the homeless population at the camp so I could draw out and destroy the Nephilim. Outside, a car door thudded. Bear had arrived. "Tell your guys we're good. I thought I made that clear. Keep your noses clean. Take care of your brothers and sisters. Love your moms and dads. Keep your faces buried in books. Take your girlfriends and boyfriends out. Do that stuff and we won't have any more problems. That's not why I called you."

"Then why am I here?"

I gesture with a thumb over my shoulder, hearing Bear pop open the metal door. "You'll see in a moment." I turned. "Bear, thanks for coming."

Like most bald men in this region of the world, Bear wore a beanie. This one was a charcoal gray acrylic he'd pulled down as far as he could, even over his orange eyebrows. His nose and cheeks displayed an explosion of freckles and it was nearly impossible to see his mouth because of his unkempt mustache and beard combo. At least until he smiled in greeting.

There's something about big men smiling that is disarming. If you watch carefully, they give away their nature more than any other mortals. Big guys who are kind at heart are easy to tell by the way they smile. They're aware of their size and the intimidating effect it can have. Big guys who are dicks are also aware, and they carry that chip on their shoulders like the insecure twats they are. I'm not small, coming in at a nicely rounded-off six feet and two hundred pounds, but Bear made me feel like a prepubescent boy when he shook my hand, swallowed in his.

"Good to see you again," I said warmly.

"Thanks," he said, his gaze flicking to Bolt. "Hey."

"Hey."

Guys. Masters of communication.

"Is everything okay?" Bear asked, focusing on me.

Like Bolt, Bear lived through a run-in with me because of Arakiel. Bear's group of friends were beating up on a man who was well past being able to defend himself. Billee and I got the situation under control through the strategic deployment of beautiful violence. Some of Bear's friends fared far worse than Bolt's emotional bruises I'd left on fragile teen egos.

"Everyone good?"

Bear raised an eyebrow.

"Your friends I met the other day."

He smacked his hands. "Oh, them. Yeah. Everyone is recovering. The guy didn't press charges, so we got lucky.

Don't know why. I would have. Man, if someone did that to me..."

"You are lucky. Sorry about the broken bones, but it was necessary."

Bolt's mouth plopped open at that.

Bear chuckled, his broad chest bobbing underneath his thick brown jacket. "They'll recover. And we deserved it. Could have been worse. We all feel like crap about what we did. We've been taking turns running over to his house. Brian is his name. We walk and feed his dogs and help keep the place clean while he recovers. Pitching in to cook dinners every couple of nights, too."

"Not every night? A guy has to eat daily."

"We make enough to feed a church," Bear said, then chuckled again. "I'm pretty sure he has to throw most of it out. But at least it's there if he wants to snack."

"Well, glad you all are doing right by him," I said, patting his shoulder. "Keep it up. But I didn't call the two of you here just to check on everyone. I need a favor."

Bear raised an eyebrow again.

Bolt said, "From us?"

"Yep. This might sound crazy, but you've seen some crazy things recently."

"That's no lie," Bear said.

"Good news," I said, "is that the crazy doesn't end there. Bad news? It only gets crazier." Not wanting to leave them dangling, I continued before they could start asking questions or filling in the blanks themselves. "Have you guys heard any weird stuff coming out of the Olympics?"

Bear's face contorted. "They're not on this winter, are they?"

I laughed. "The mountains. Not the games."

"Oh, sorry. No, I haven't."

Bolt bounced his shoulders. "Me either. I don't go out there much."

Bear tugged his beanie down. It was chilly, even inside. "Why do you ask?"

"I need you both to check in with everyone you know, and," I said, putting extra gusto on the last word, "I need you to do so carefully. Don't go running around recklessly asking questions. Put a word out with those you trust and then keep your ears open."

"What are we listening for?" Bear asked.

"This is going to sound nuts, but it's as legit as what the both of you went through that brought me into your lives." I waited while they glanced at each other in instant under-standing and unspoken camaraderie. "So I'm going to shoot straight with you and expect you to keep this to yourselves while being smart about how you put feelers out."

"You're making me nervous," Bear said, stuffing his large hands into pockets that shouldn't be able to hold such meaty mittens.

"Good, because what I'm about to ask you makes me nervous, too. And if I'm nervous, both you and your friends would be smart to be nervous as well." I paused, drawing an unneeded deep breath that was more about influencing them to the seriousness of the situation than it was out of the need to calm myself. "There is a creature in the Olympics. An enor-mous bastard. Dangerous. One I don't want anyone going near. But the problem is, I don't know where it is in the forest or what it looks like. For all I know, it could be hiding out in a valley or chilling on the top of a mountain. I won't be able to find it on my own. Not soon. I need eyeballs. That's where you two come in. Between the pair of you, I know there's a few dozen people who've seen crazy shit in the past couple of weeks. Stuff you're all probably going to struggle to under-stand and come to terms with for a while. But you're aware you went through something strange, and that's a start. Ask around and see what your friends have to say. Those you trust, have them ask their friends. Keep details short. Leave the door open. Let them walk in with weird sightings. I need to know if anyone has seen anything in the Olympics that defies common sense and Mother-freaking-Nature herself."

Bear's lips fluttered as he loosed a breath he'd been holding. "That's a heavy load, man."

"I know. And I hate putting it on you, but we're talking about something that could hurt a lot of people if it ever comes out of the Olympics."

"You don't know what it looks like?" Bolt asked.

"Nope. Wish I did."

"How is anyone going to say if they've seen this thing if you can't tell us what you're looking for?"

"Trust me," I said slowly, making sure I had both of their attention. "When someone has seen it, they'll know. And you'll be able to see it in their eyes." They both still appeared unsure. To Bolt, I said, "You've got a lot of friends. You're at that age. They'll have lots of friends. I need as many eyes and ears on this situation as possible. I'm just hoping you're an active bunch and not lazy teens who sit around your basements playing video games."

Bear snorted.

"Some guys ski and hike and stuff," Bolt said.

"Do you?"

"Nah, not really."

"Then find more kids who do."

He nodded.

I turned to Bear. "Check with your military buddies if you still have anyone in the area."

"I do. Army. Bunch of us stayed around town after getting out. Know Navy folks up in Bremerton too. I can reach out to them."

"Do it. I have a feeling I'm going to need people with military experience before all is said and done."

"You got it," he said. Bear had two different sized eyes that looked offset. At that moment, they drew me in with his intensity. "Whatever we can do to make up for screwing with that guy, we'll do. I swear it."

"Thanks, guys. I know this sounds nuts, and I promise I won't be so cryptic when I get more information. But right now, I'm searching in the dark and need help."

"You got it," Bear said instantly.

Bolt simply nodded a few times.

We broke. They had their tasks, and I didn't want us hanging around longer than necessary. Try explaining to cops why two adult men and a teenager were passing time in an abandoned factory and see how far that gets you.

I cut through downtown on my way back to the apartment because I enjoy the drive around Capitol Lake.

Fate or fortune—I'll let you decide—the decision provided me an opportunity to realize Pher might be sniffing up the wrong dog's butt.

Up Legion Way, past Nicole's Bar, I was about to cross Capitol Boulevard when I saw something I didn't think I'd ever see. Something, someone I didn't want to see. An immortal who, in a flash of their appearance, made my day trickier and added another item to my To-Do list.

The broad form could have belonged to Brock, it was so large. Olympia isn't LA. We don't have beaches, and thus, we don't have a swarm of bodybuilders strutting around town to show off pecs, biceps, triceps, and every other strand of muscle. Seeing someone this large was an anomaly here, which was partially why he caught my eye. Except this wasn't Brock. This guy was black, not pasty white. He was bald instead of having Brock's military-esque haircut. He had blond sideburns where Brock was clean-shaven. Oh, and he was a demon and not an angel.

What the hell was Beelzebub doing in the Overworld?

7

TROUBLES AND SOLUTIONS

THE RIFT HAD BARELY WIDENED ENOUGH TO ALLOW MY FRAME when I squeezed through, stepping into the hallway of Yahweh's headquarters.

"Rev?" Brock said with a curious twitch—Brock is way too composed, and way too cool, to jerk in surprise. "What are you doing here? They didn't give me a heads-up you'd been called."

"Haven't been." I hitched my chin at the closed meeting room doors. "Are they in session?"

"Yeah," he said cautiously, his eyes swiveling across mine. "What's up? You look troubled."

"I am. Can you ask them to see me?"

Brock turned in a snap and stepped into the room. No knock. No verbalization of his request to enter. The big man just cranked down on the handle and stepped in like he owned the place. Of course, when you're Brock's size, who is going to stop you?

He was back before I could think of something to say to the new guard standing on the opposite side of the hall. "Come in."

I stepped into the Order's meeting room. Brock patted me

on the back and closed the door behind me, leaving me with the thirteen angels who kept me too busy to deal with anything effectively. Now it was my turn to give them something of a task.

"You wanted to see us, Mr. Carver?" Puriel said from the head of the table, her posture as stiff as a Congressional hearing on market manipulation.

"I did. Thank you for seeing me."

She nodded.

"What's the meaning of this? Shouldn't he be searching for the behemoth instead of bothering us?" Jericho said to the President of the Order as if I wasn't standing right there.

"Let's hear him out," the President said with the patience of a mother. To me, she gestured at the far end of the table. At this point, they might as well mount a placard on the chair with my name engraved on it. Though I imagine Cascade Cho, Minister of the Guardian Angels, might also have a claim. I was up for sharing it; I didn't enjoy being here more than necessary.

"I don't plan on bothering you," I said, reluctantly pulling the chair out and deliberately eyeing Jericho Judas as I sat.

"You look troubled, lad," Pher said. "What's going on?"

He knew damned well how bothered I was and had been. He and his theories of an Upperworld heading toward chaos were at the root of a lot of what had my mind reeling and my pulse racing. In a way, it was only fair I gave him something to think about. "I just came back from the Overworld."

"Did you find news of the behemoth?" Uziel said from her chair. She pushed her short, black hair away from her eyes and sat a little taller when my gaze slid to her.

"Nothing."

"Figures," Jericho scoffed.

"Yet. Though I'm setting up a network to help gather information."

"A network? You're involving others in a task we set

specifically for you?" Jericho asked, placidly staring at the wall. He fixed his sky-blue eyes there because, I knew, he didn't have the guts to look my way.

"More eyes, more of a chance to get information on where it's supposed to be."

"We already told you where to find it."

"Do you know how big the forest is?" I said, feeling my frustration with the whelp building. I was here for more important things than getting into a battle of the egos with someone who probably still needed his mommy's help tying his shoes in the morning.

"Still," Jericho said, sounding very much like someone speaking in order to get the last word in.

"I just left the Overworld where I have been working on the behemoth case. Came straight here because, as I was out and about doing the job I was assigned, I saw Beelzebub in Olympia." It felt good to cut off the notification there and watch the thirteen of them blink, faces scrunch, lips purse, and check with each other to see if they'd heard me correctly.

"The Prince of Demons?" Puriel kicked off the conversation. "What was he doing?"

I shrugged. "Wish I knew." After I explained the circumstances of the sighting, I said, "I figured it was best to report to you immediately so you can upchannel it to Yahweh's Council and verify that he's supposed to be bumbling around. It didn't look like he was actively causing trouble, but I don't imagine he would spin things up in broad daylight, anyway."

"Beelzebub in the Overworld is not a good thing," Pher said. "You did the right thing, bringing this news to our attention."

I gave him an appreciative nod.

"Camael?" Puriel said, her feminine but deep voice gaining a hint of huskiness as if my news bothered her on a deeper level.

"Yes, ma'am?"

"Send a note to the Council. They need to know."

The Order's Secretary stood and bowed to Puriel. I covered my discomfort at his formal and very public subservience.

"Dumas, what do you have to say?" Puriel asked the elder Order member.

His lips fluttered, which made his long-haired mustache flap, almost like a sprite's wings. "It's not unheard of for Council members to journey to the Overworld without noti-fying the Upperworld, of course. From my studies into our reports, they manage a few unapproved visits per month. Though we're in a periodic lull, I have seen concerning trends in my reading that activity has picked up."

"Without approved allowances?" Raphina asked.

"Of course," Dumas said. "They're demons. Hardly trust-worthy creatures. They've invaded the Overworld throughout their history. Were it not for our interventions, who knows what would have become of the Balance? I, for one, am not surprised at the news, though I wish Mr. Carver would have returned with more useful information."

"I'm already your Reaper Minister and hitman. I don't need to add spy or intelligence officer to the list of duties on my position description."

A smattering of chuckles welcomed that. Great, that they appreciated my humor, but I was serious. I wanted to set down a marker and ensure no one started entertaining thoughts of having me serve in that capacity. My cup was full, and I wasn't in the chugging mood to make space for more of their concoction.

"Be that as it may—"

"As it is," I said.

Dumas rolled his eyes. There's nothing more ridiculous than seeing someone with white hair—come on, everyone is far beyond being fooled by his shoddy dye job—rolling their eyes. "Still, this could be a sign of a larger problem. A troubling sign of things to come. Dependent on what the Council discovers, and if they share, if Beelzebub is in the Overworld without prior approval, fortune may have just smiled on us. This could give us a chance to become privy to the Underworld's maneuverings before they're able to leverage any advantage."

"If they're up to no good, they could wreak havoc. The Reapers and Guardians could be overwhelmed," Zephon Chary said. Usually as quiet as a mouse, when she spoke, angels listened. Zephon seemed aware of that. As soon as heads turned her way, she cupped her hands in her lap and stared down at them.

Around the table, now unseen to her, heads nodded.

I felt a headache coming. "Sorry for delivering bad news, but I figured it was best to pass it up the channels while it was hot off the presses."

"We appreciate it, lad," Pher said.

"You're welcome," I said, starting to stand. "I'll see myself out."

"Don't go just yet, Mr. Carver," Puriel said. "I want to speak with you after we adjourn."

I slowly lowered myself into my chair. Curious glances were cast at the President, but no one said a peep. Not until Jericho spoke up, of course. "Before you do, Puriel, I'd ask that we take advantage of Carver's interruption by addressing his recent actions. We were already in the middle of discussions, so we might as well finish it. His presence might be a convenient twist, but it should help us resolve the issue."

"What issue?" I asked.

Puriel answered Jericho as if she hadn't heard me. "Cascade isn't here. We won't find a resolution without her input. She is the Guardian Minister, after all. She must be present too."

That last part sounded like a chastisement of the younger Order member.

"Still," he said, his lips spreading in what I imagined he thought could pass as a smile but appeared to be more like a message that said 'I just spit in your soup.' "Should we not address his inappropriate behaviors?"

Puriel drew a slow breath.

"What inappropriate behaviors, Jericho? If you've got something to say, be an adult, look me in the face, and say it." I knew I was challenging his authority. He was an Order member. I was a Reaper. The Minister, but still just a Reaper. My place wasn't to chastise him. But he'd only fallen into his role as Chief of Security because his mommy held the same position. A position she'd had to give up, in part, because of me. But Jericho was cunning and devious, an angel with too much power for his undeveloped emotional intelligence. I didn't mind pushing that water bag and seeing if it might burst.

He sniffed, still not looking my way, as if responding to me directly were beneath him. "Puriel, we need to address it before he does it to someone else."

If I could have broken the thick meeting room table with my grip, I would have. I didn't realize I was squeezing the waxed wood until my thumbs throbbed.

"Let it go," Pher said, his voice cool, unfriendly. So un-Pher-like.

"I will not." Jericho's icy blues locked on my mentor.

"Will someone tell me what this twat is talking about?"

Jericho gasped. Dumas made a series of throat-clearing sounds that told me he desperately needed a check-up with his physician. Pher's lips quirked beneath his immaculate beard. My very accurate assessment of Jericho's personality hadn't humored only my mentor. Turial outright laughed.

Puriel's face was a mask, offering barely more life than Jericho's typical deadpan.

"Because if I've done something that needs to be addressed with the Order, I'd like to hear it. There's probably an excellent reason I did what I did." I allowed myself a slow grin as I watched Jericho struggle with wanting to confront me or deliberating what wood the conference table was constructed from. The table won. I knew he wouldn't meet my glare. "Once we get this matter out of the way, we can then talk about the actions of others that should concern the Order."

Jericho twitched at my hint of our little blackmail controversy. Good.

"Fine," Puriel said finally. "Not that we don't have other things to take care of. Not that we could simply rely on Mr. Carver and Ms. Cho to work this out. Instead, let's take precious time on this. But, I promise, we will move on. If the two Ministers cannot find a solution later, then we will. Agreed?"

The Order members responded with nods and "ayes," and Puriel looked at me.

"What's the problem?" I said flatly.

"It has come to our attention that you behaved inappropriately during a recent escort. Not only as a Reaper, but as the Minister. A certain..." Puriel paused, a single finger tapping on the table. "Oh, please. What was the name?"

"Sage," Jericho said, emphasizing the 'S' like he was mad at it. "Her name is Sage Eflin."

"Does that name ring a bell, Mr. Carver?" Puriel asked.

"No. Should it?"

"He's mocking us," Jericho said.

"I don't know what the hell we're talking about," I snapped. "Trust me, I've got too much to do to dance around drama. If I can answer something, I'll do it. But I don't have time for games."

"Nor do we," Puriel said, raising her voice, possibly from perceiving me as a threat to her authority. "It was brought to our attention that you had a physical altercation with a Guardian."

"When you escorted the drug dealer," Pher said softly.

"Ah, yes."

Jericho thrust a finger at me but still wouldn't turn his detestable face toward me. "See? He admits it. We need to do something about him. He's getting out of control."

"What do you want to do? He's the Minister," Pher said, his hands clasped in front of him, calm as you like. "We've tasked him with tracking the demon primed to become the next Lucifer. He's hunting the behemoth. Do you want us to sentence him? To lock him up? Are you going to assume his duties if we do?"

I appreciated my mentor giving Jericho grief. Quite enjoyable, actually. But this was the wrong starting point for the conversation. "Wait. Wait. Am I in trouble?"

"Should you be?" Puriel asked before anyone could say anything.

Ah, an opening. "No. I shouldn't be. If someone had asked for my experience with the drug dealer and his Guardian, they would have heard the other side of the story."

Another scoff from Jericho. "Oh? And what's this 'other side'?"

"Most likely? The truth." I spent the next few minutes briefing them about the Guardian's interference.

"She was romantically involved with her mortal?" Uziel said, her thick eyelashes nearly touching when she narrowed her eyes.

I shrugged. "I don't know about that, but she was quite taken with him. Listen, she was upset. Poor judgment on her part? Yes. But no one was harmed." The image of Roger Baskin ducking in a corner of a dumpster to avoid my Angelfire struck me as funny at that moment, but I didn't laugh. I'm a professional, after all. "Well, except for the scumbag. And I'm sure she learned from the experience. When I get a chance, I'll stop and chat with Cascade and we'll iron everything out."

"Fine," Puriel said.

"That's it? He's going to get away with assaulting a Guardian?" Jericho said, his voice squeaking. "We won't punish him?"

"You heard what he said, Jericho," Pher said. "Rev, do you have remorse about how you handled it?"

"Not really," I said honestly, even though I knew my mentor was trying to lead the conversation to a quick, peaceful resolution. But I wasn't about to cave. Not to Jericho. Not on the principle of it. "Listen, she put people in danger. She put my familiar in danger. Had that happened during the day when hundreds of people were around, who knows how it would have gone down? What if a newer Reaper had been assigned to the case, and she did that? They might not have set up the escort like I had and there could have been innocents in the way when she protected the man she loved. Talk about inappropriate. Talk about getting out of hand and causing serious headaches for everyone." I looked back at Jericho, holding the spoiled brat with my gaze. "Every single one of you should be grateful I handled it how I did, instead of thinking I had any fault or assuming I should feel any guilt about it. The only thing I'm regretting is that I didn't address this immediately and have her brought up on charges."

"You do not act with impunity," Jericho told the tabletop.

"Nor do you," I said icily.

"Enough!"

Heads snapped to the head of the table. A less-stiff angel would have slapped the table with the proclamation, but that wasn't Puriel's style. Her raised voice was effective enough.

"Both of you," Puriel said, her head swiveled to Jericho and then to me, back and forth, "will drop this contention. It is beneath an Order member and the Reaper Minister to act in such a fashion. Mr. Carver, you'll talk to Ms. Cho. As peers, I have full faith you'll find an amicable solution to this minor issue."

"Yes, ma'am."

"Jericho, we'll speak later."

He mumbled something I couldn't hear from my chair.

Impossibly, Puriel seemed to straighten even more. "Enough with your grudges. That's beneath angels of your stations. I'll encourage you, one time, to focus on your jobs. I won't say it again." An uncomfortable quiet settled over the table. "We're going to adjourn. Pher. Rev. Stay behind."

"Of course," my boss answered for both of us.

Turial and Zephon winked and when they passed. Jerah patted my shoulder and nodded. Uziel walked past as if she didn't see me. Dumas talked to himself even though he walked beside Jericho. The entitled brat didn't have the courage to even glance my way. I expected nothing less.

When the door slammed closed, Puriel stood and reached for the satchel she'd draped over the back of her chair. "Come down here, please."

Pher and I moved together.

"Nice view from this end," I said, looking back toward my usual seat.

Her lips curled. "You're going to give Jericho a migraine."

"Good."

"He's beneath you," my mentor said.

"I know."

"So stop letting him rile you up."

"I will. One day. Right now, it's too much fun," I said with a wink.

Puriel set her satchel on the table, resting her thin hands atop it. "Rev, you won't want to hear this, but I'm going to say it, anyway."

"Oh boy. Do I need to sit?"

"Maybe."

The creases around her mouth took form, as if she thought to smile, though I can't be sure. I'm not convinced Puriel's face can form those types of expressions.

"I'm going to ask something of you."

"Okay."

"I want you to agree to a creed."

"Another one, you mean?" I said, not hiding my exasperation. "Can't say I'm in the mood for that."

"Lad," Pher warned. "She's the President."

"I know," I said. "Puriel, I mean no disrespect. I'm just tired. Tired of a lot of things, and adding a new creed to the mix is one of the last things I want to do."

"What if I told you this one is easy?" she said with what I swear was a twinkle in her eyes.

"How easy?"

"This new creed I want you to swear to is nothing more than a promise."

"A promise to do what?"

"More like a promise to not do something," she said. "I want you to swear by and hold true to the creed that will guide you through this new future the Upperworld is facing. I want you to swear to hold strict confidence with Order members."

I could feel my face scrunch. Even Pher looked confused.

"Oh, come now," she said, looking between us. "I'm well aware the two of you share secrets like school girls. You don't fool me."

I shared a look with my mentor. Busted.

"As such," Puriel said. She rubbed the brown leather satchel as if it were a dear pet. "I share this with you. We face turbulent times, and I'm not sure who we can trust." Her eyes locked on me. "But I know you can be trusted, Rev. So, I ask you to swear to a new creed. A rider policy to what you've previously sworn to, if you will."

"Meaning?"

"What the members tell you in confidence stays in your confidence. Share only what you deem necessary with Pher and me. That is all. I already know you'll share everything with him, anyway."

Well, that wasn't true, but I silently agreed with the principle of it.

"I've never felt like you've withheld anything from me I needed to know," she continued. "I want that to continue. But I also want that perception to spread among the Order members. Not all of them are smitten with you like Pher is."

My mentor snickered but remained quiet.

"Some of them outright dislike you. That's no secret. Most keep you at arm's length, understanding your role and the power we bestow upon you." She fixed a troubled look on the satchel. "But that might not serve us well in the future. A future we can't yet define." She inhaled deeply and looked at me. "I am the President of the Order. Not its Queen. I can be replaced at any time, so I have to prepare for a future that doesn't include me. I have to entertain possibilities about how the Reapers and Guardians would operate were the Order to be presided over by another."

"And you think that if I build trust with the Order members by keeping their confidence, I'll be able to help when that future arrives?"

"If," Pher said.

"When," Puriel corrected, her eyes growing soft. She rolled her upper lip over her teeth and pinched her lips closed. "And this new level of confidence starts here."

"Okay." This time, the response came out with a dose of reservation.

"There is something wrong with Yahweh," the President of the Order of Thirteen said. "I've tried to ask. I've called on favors. Inquired. But the Council isn't saying much." She shook her head. "I can't remember the last time I felt such unease, but I feel it now. In fact, I have for months. A quick change, but a change nonetheless. Whatever is happening, we're deliberately being kept in the dark. The manifestation of the behemoth might not even be deliberate. The last time the mortal realm needed a reset, Yahweh was very open about why He was doing what He was doing. This current silence unsettles me."

"Last time, there was more than a single behemoth," Pher said, watching Puriel. Searching for something. He, like me, was disturbed, and that disturbed me even more.

"There was," Puriel agreed. "Between the behemoth and the First Bowl, this is nothing more than a scattergun approach to a reset. That's not His style. No. No." She dropped and shook her head. "Something is wrong. The Council is managing Yahweh, I'm sure of it. At the very least, they're managing the messages coming out of His throne room. So we, too, must manage ourselves. We start with the moves we make."

Puriel flipped the satchel open and reached inside with both hands. When she pulled them out, Pher gasped. I was too stunned to react.

She turned to me, handing me a quill and mana stone. "You will carry this now, Rev."

"Why?" I said in a voice that sounded wispy and foreign.

The mana stone was smaller than my palm and weighed as much as a small bowling ball. Okay, that's an exaggeration. It's light, but the weight of possessing one was as heavy as one of those balls of ugly shirt-and-shoes entertainment. When I looked at it, I lost my voice.

The mana stone displayed a name. My name. "Oh, no."

"As I've said," Puriel said, each word sounding measure, "troubling times lay ahead, and we must manage outcomes we cannot yet envision."

"That's a mana stone," Pher said, sounding as astounded as I felt, like he was trying to convince himself of what he was seeing.

Puriel laughed softly. "I'm well aware, my friend."

When I looked away from the stone to Puriel, I knew in that instant that the shit had just piled deep.

"You'll use it to keep yourself alive, Rev," she said as she regarded one of the ten stones in all creation. One of the most useful items in existence. Maybe the most powerful except for the Halo of Yahweh itself. "You will kill this behemoth, and the stone will ensure you do so that you can face our next greatest challenge." Puriel turned to Pher and said the words that made my throat constrict. "Because I don't think she's done causing trouble."

8

SECRET ARRANGEMENTS

HOLY FREAKING CRAP.

A mana stone.

In my possession.

Mine. Until, unless I bequeathed it to another, just as the President of the Order of Thirteen had done to me.

I wrapped my fingers around the stone, bobbing my hand.

One thing that became clear after Puriel's 'gift' of the mana stone, followed by my most recent training session with the new Reaper, was that I truly didn't have the time or inclination to play my Mr. Fix-It role any longer.

When I tried to attend to everything, I did a half-ass job. Sure, I made progress, but I'm not a fan of taking baby steps when I can sprint.

Now was the time to stretch, slap on the sneakers, and hit the pavement.

I stepped out of the Rift and into the Second Level transit station. I couldn't remember the last time I was in this Level, so I needed the mass transit location to ground myself. From there, I could get where I needed to be relatively quickly.

I wasn't here for a tour or to visit, but it was nice to take the solar train from the transit station to Anapheil's home. She lived in a small town, which was surprising. I expected her to live in a city's downtown high-rise. You know, to be around the movers and shakers, at the center of attention. Finger on the pulse-kind of stuff.

But the Reaper's own go-getter had chosen a different type of living. As the unicorn carriage pulled up outside her house, I had to give it an appreciative nod.

A white picket fence corralled a small yard with a carpet of grass so lush, so green, I was tempted to sprawl out on it and run my fingers through the shoots. Tactile comfort soothes the bestial mind, I've found... as long as I'm the one doing the touching. Finger fidget gadgets, guitars, working with wood. Having things in my hands helped me feel peace in the times I wasn't cooking and needed an outlet. Anapheil's lawn was a temptress.

A canopied bench swing occupied one corner of the green, angled to overlook the hillside that rolled away into a short valley before rising again to a sunlit pasture in the distance. Birds chirped in the single poplar tree in her backyard, standing high above the ranch home. Painted yellow, with white trim, including pairs of raised shutters bordering windows, the house was far more welcoming than her personality. Long boxes bordered the windows, neatly filled with various flowers of yellows and oranges. The homestead was an explosion of color.

A short gate with a black latch sat under a white arbor. The gate swung open smoothly, making me nervous about it slamming closed, so I escorted the bar way back into the latch. Hell, Anapheil's flagstone walkway was so immaculate I felt like I was supposed to take off my shoes.

I pressed the doorbell. A pleasant chime rang out in three slow notes. A moment passed. Inside, the shadow flicked across sunlight streaming from the back of the small home to the twelve-paned window running the entire height of the door. Footsteps thudded closer.

I set myself. Anapheil could be a handful, and I was visiting her home, uninvited, to talk business. Who knew what reaction I'd instigate?

There was a slight delay in the thudding feet once they neared the door, telling me I wasn't the only one with reservations. The lock clicked and Anapheil pulled the door open, confusion broadcast on her face like a Vegas nightlife billboard.

"Rev? What are you doing here?"

"Hi. I hate to do this, but I was wondering if I could come in and talk shop with you?"

"Now? Is everything okay?" she asked, pushing her glasses back with a finger, with just enough of a slight straightening of her posture to show me she was shifting from Anapheil Icogto, the angel, to Anapheil Icogto, one of the senior-most Reapers.

"Yes, it is. But I need a favor, and it's you I want to ask."

"Um, sure." She glanced back as if she was trying to remember if she'd left her dirty laundry lying around on the couch. "Come in."

"We can't really do this another time, even though I don't want to intrude. What we need to discuss is important."

She waved me in as she slid halfway behind the door. "Come in. You've traveled to the Second, so it must be something you've got to get off your mind. You're not interrupting." She closed the door behind me. Before I could take another step, she said, "Please take off your shoes."

"Sure thing," I said, not expecting anything less.

Against the wall, a spotless rectangular mat waited for me to deposit my footwear. Not a blade of grass, nor a single clump of dirt soiled the mat. I felt bad about defacing the mat with my heavy black boots.

The entry was modest and uncluttered. A smell of lemon hung in the air. I let Anapheil lead me into her living room. It, too, was respectfully modest. One overstuffed chair and couch set, white, formed an 'L' with a highly polished coffee table in the open space in the middle. The table was one of those that contained drawers, four to a side, split into two at each end. I was tempted to yank a drawer open just to see if there was anything in Anapheil's life that wasn't in its place.

She'd pulled her tight braids into a long ponytail. Even in her home, ostensibly not working, she wore tan slacks and a white blouse. Hardly a house-cleaning get-up.

"Would you like something to drink? I've steeped black tea."

"No, that's fine. Thank you. I really don't want to intrude." I flipped my hand in the air. "Nice place."

"Thank you," she said, sitting forward on the couch cushion and instantly making me feel guilty about sitting back in her chair.

I sat up. "What would you say about taking on greater responsibility with the Reapers?"

She cocked her head, asking with more than a hint of cautious skepticism, "How much more?"

"The Order has me involved in high-level stuff," I said, already having my plan of attack. If I was going to ask this of her, I needed to give her context. Anapheil was aggressive, but she was a professional, and that required treating her like one. "A behemoth has manifested in the Overworld, and they assigned me to rid the world of it as soon as possible."

If the news surprised her, she didn't show it. "I see."

"Between that, the escorting, and some distasteful tasks the Order has for me, I am stretched too thin to be good at any one thing. I need help. That's why I'm here. To ask you."

"For what sort of help?" She adjusted on the cushion, keeping her hands flat on her thighs. "I'm not an assassin, Rev. I can't do the things you do. I'll help the Reapers how I can, how you need me to, but that's a step too far." A smile flickered on her mouth, gone as soon as it appeared. "More of a hindrance than a help."

"No, no. You don't need to go hunting with me." I regretted the unrefined comment as soon as she flinched. I corrected myself. "Your talents serve the Reapers better in an administrative role."

"Supervisory?" She raised an eyebrow, pushing her glasses back again. "But I'm already working with the new Reapers."

"And I appreciate that," I said. Slow-dripping this conversation wasn't helping either of us. "But you're ready for something bigger. I know you are, and I'm asking you for that now. I want you to assume the role as the Interim Minister."

Her eyes went wide. "Of the Reapers."

I chuckled. This was about as disheveled as I'd ever seen Anapheil. "Yes. Of the Reapers. I need to focus on the behemoth before the Overworld gets out of hand and we all find ourselves in a far worse position. I can't do that when the Order is constantly pulling me in a hundred different directions. Plus, you're ready. You can do this. Of course, you'll have to hand off a lot of your assignments to Reapers you trust. I'll stay out of your way and let you figure out who that is."

"I'm honored, Rev. I really am. But, are you sure?" She rolled her lips. "What did the Order say?"

"I don't know."

She shot up straighter, even though I didn't think her back could be any more rigid. "You didn't ask them?"

I spread my hands. "They don't know I'm here."

A series of lip rolls later, Anapheil stood, clasping her hands and dropping them as she paced the side of the room. "I don't know about this. Without their prior approval, this doesn't feel right."

"They'll be a little perturbed, but that's okay. Politicians. They don't understand our business. I'm trusted to run the Reapers in accordance with their priorities, and I trust you. Shit rolls downhill. But so do opportunities."

"Rev, language, please. This is my home."

Rebuked, but needing to stay on topic, I said, "Sorry. I know you can execute the duties of the Minister without a hitch. The Reapers will be in excellent hands, and it's only an interim gig, so how upset could they be? Before I worry about the Order, I need to make sure you're okay with it."

"I am." With the flat of her hand, she smoothed the pocket of her slacks before reconnecting her hands. "I am."

Even from across the room, I could tell Anapheil was grinding her hands together, not content with just clasping them. Her dark skin was turning my shade as she pressed and pressed.

"Are you sure? If this is an imposition—"

She turned, facing me. Small dimples dotted her cheeks. "Not at all. I want this chance. I'm grateful for it. Thank you, Rev. I won't disappoint you."

"I know you won't. Remember, this isn't a long-term thing. So if you discover you hate every minute of waking as the Interim Minister, know that you don't have to do it for long. Well, unless the behemoth gets the better of me."

I chuckled. She didn't. She simply stared at me from across her living room, though she'd stopped wringing her hands.

"Am I allowed to change things?" she asked, taking a hard turn in the conversation.

"Like what?"

"Just small things in the daily tasks. Things I'd like to experiment with to see if we can run more smoothly."

I did say I trusted her. What choice did I have? "Sure. Just steer clear of long-term obligations. If I survive this show-down, I don't want to come back to a—" I almost said 'shit-load,' and then remembered where I was and who I was talking to "—a ton of work piled on my desk. The Order is sneaky like that. They'll try to get you to buy into their vision, but only tell you half the work it entails. Before you know it, you're drowning in tasks."

"I'll be careful, I swear it. Minor tasks on our daily work-flow. That's all. I promise."

"Sounds good," I said, spreading my hands. "So, do we have an agreement? You'll take the job."

She smiled, her bright, straight teeth glimmered against her dark skin and berry-colored lip gloss. "I agree. I'm really excited."

She only partially looked excited, but then again, partially excited was the extent I expected from my now second-in-charge.

"Good." I stood. "It's about time the Reapers had a woman in charge. It's been too long, and it's smelling like a locker room in the meetings."

"We haven't had one since I've been on the team."

"Almost fifteen thousand years now," I said. "Anapheil, this is great. It's the perfect opportunity for you to show everyone what you can do with more responsibility. It allows me to focus on the behemoth. The Reapers could benefit from hearing a fresh voice in charge, and the new ones will see that anything is possible if they work their ass—their butts—off. Everyone wins."

She nodded. "I like this side of you, Rev."

"Which side? The one that dumps his workload on other Reapers?"

She laughed. The sound was as pliable as concrete. "No. This pleasant side. Not so grim. Makes me think you fake that rough persona."

I winked at her. "Don't get too comfortable with that assessment. The job is yours now. Before you know it, you'll be a grim Reaper, just like me."

"Doubt that," she said with another tight laugh as she walked me to the door.

"Don't worry about the Order," I said. "I'll talk with them. If they've got a problem with this, they can take it out on me."

As I made my way down her immaculate flagstone walkway, careful to only step on the stone, I felt her eyes on me. The door hadn't clicked closed—assassins pay attention to things like that. She wasn't trying to be stealthy or fighting against calling me back to tell me she'd changed her mind. Honestly, I knew Anapheil was excited. Who knows, maybe after I was gone, she'd close her door and loosed a half-enthused 'yippee' to her tidy home. She might get crazy and crack open a bottle of carbonated seltzer to celebrate.

I loaded into the carriage, no longer needing to hide my smile. I was happy for Anapheil. She'd get a chance to prove herself. Leading the Reapers would also give her a dose of humility only angels who have taken leadership roles can appreciate. I was happy for the Reapers. They needed fresh blood. They deserved a Minister who yearns to do the job, someone who still believes in the mission. But most of all, I was happy for myself.

Anapheil didn't know this. Neither did the Reapers or the Order. Nor would they when they discovered my little switcheroo. With Anapheil accepting her new role, I'd just set up the first step in the future of the Reapers.

A future without me.

9

DIRTY DEEDS

"What's that?" Billee asked when she got into the car.

I lifted my hand, probably looking as anxious as a kid who had just discovered the truth about Santa Claus. "A mana stone."

She looked at me like I'd just told her I met a special woman and was running away to Bermuda. "Are you okay? You look like you just got bad news, or won the lottery."

Extending my arm, I said, "This basically gives me immortality."

"Aren't you essentially already immortal?"

My throat still felt tight. "No. Not really." I jiggled the mana stone. The smooth black stone popped into the air and dropped back into my palm, smacking against my skin. "But this is from the All. It holds a dribble of its power."

"Of its power? What does that even mean?"

"The All is everything in existence. All the energy of all matter, not just what we can measure. This little guy holds a fraction of a fraction of a fraction of that power. It allows its holder to tap into it."

Billee whistled. "What does that mean for you? When you

say you're immortal, does that mean you can't die now? At all? Ever?"

The mana stone sat coolly in my hand. An unblinking black eye taunting me with answers it wouldn't reveal.

"Less than a dozen of them exist. With good reason, too. As the possessor of this stone, I am more permanent than a god." I bobbed the stone again. It thunked meekly against my palm. "Put it this way. I could have a gang of demons pinning me down and beating me up, and the stone will continue to heal me faster than they do damage. They'd wear themselves out and then I'd get up and kick the shit out of them and still have enough energy to hit the gym afterward. The mana stone preserves the life of its holder. Even against their will."

"Wow."

"Wow is right," I said, tucking the item of great power away, not wanting to think about what Puriel had done. Sure, she'd ensured I had the best chance possible to survive the behemoth, but she had also condemned me to endless eternity with this calculated safety measure. As soon as was safe, I planned on unlocking the bequeathing and give it right back to the President of the Order of Thirteen.

"Start the car. I'm cold," Billee said, wrapping her jacket around herself.

"Buckle up." I cranked the heat as soon as the car turned over. "Are you ready for this?"

"No," she said in a tone so suddenly icy it could easily make a domestic partnership with the freezing condensation on my car windows.

"Billee, it's going to be okay. This might be the easiest escort we've ever had to do, and then we can snoop around local spots for word on the behemoth."

"I was hoping I'd never get one like this."

"Normally, you wouldn't."

She turned to me. She'd zipped her parka to her chin, pushing against her cheeks and rounding them into brown mounds. The look didn't suit the mood of the conversation. "Then why am I? Why did you get this assignment?"

"I gave it to myself."

"Why?"

"First, because I'm local. Easier than making someone come from the Upperworld. And, second, it's my job. I'm the Reaper Minister."

"You have to train all new Reapers? That's hardly an efficient way to run an organization."

I laughed. "Not for long. Trust me. There's nothing efficient about the way the Upperworld is run." I pulled out onto the main road and we started our journey to Elma, a tiny town due west of Olympia. It was going to be a decent drive, away from the city and through forested highways. Very scenic, very peaceful. "And, no, I don't train all Reapers. We have a training program for that. One I'm not responsible for running, thankfully. Those I trust do that dirty work. Since I'm local, this is easy, and you need the experience."

"What if I don't want the experience of watching someone kill themselves?" Her tone was passionate enough to melt the ice still clinging to the borders of the windows.

"Death with dignity," I said, cautious not to upset her.

"Semantics," she said, stuffing her hands in her pockets even though the car's heat had pushed the chill out of the small cab of the sports coupe. "Someone is still choosing to end their life."

I bit back all the things I wanted to say. For one, I respected Billee too much to fight her on deeply held principles and beliefs, no matter how ill-informed they were. I'd also learned throughout the centuries that some people and angels had moral values they wouldn't compromise on. Empathy and compassion were just as important to use with those opposed to the thought of someone ending their life as those who should be at the center of the discussion.

"The other familiar will need you," I said after we shed

ourselves off Highway 101, jumping onto Highway 8. "This is her first case, and she's going to be overwhelmed, just as you were."

"I'll do my job."

"I know you will."

"Not that I have much of a choice."

We stayed quiet for a few more miles. I'd never seen Billee pout. All those months of sucking up assignments for a job she didn't ask for, one that interfered with her personal and professional life, came cascading down the moment I put her in an objectionable situation. I understood. I'd had hundreds upon hundreds of those experiences myself.

"No," I said softly, "you don't. And it sucks. Just as it sucks that I'm making you help in a situation you're not okay with being part of. Don't think I don't understand that, Billee. Don't think for a second I enjoy asking you along."

"You aren't asking."

"Fair enough. I'm not. You need to do this because the other familiar needs you. Focus on that if it helps you deal. Before we get there, I want you to know I appreciate your position."

"But we're still heading to Elma."

I wanted to punch the accelerator into hyper-loop mode, but a speeding ticket would only amplify my irritation with this situation. "We are. And we're going to get there and do our job like the super tag team we are. You're going to help the familiar while I help the Reaper with the mortal. We're going to finish the escort, and then we'll go have dinner at a local dive and see what locals have to say about the behemoth."

"How can you say that? Someone is trying to kill themselves. How can you be so—so crass?"

Gripping the steering wheel, I said, "Because I don't know their pain. Who am I to judge them?"

Billee didn't speak the rest of the way to Elma. When we

pulled up to the red brick ranch house on a quiet street on the eastern edge of town, I watched something switch in her. Gone was the stubbornness, replaced by her warm persona.

She popped the car door open and got out into the chilly day without a word. Groaning, I shut the car off and followed.

Feeling for my soul stone, I wrapped it in my hand. I rang the doorbell. Seconds passed before a woman in her fifties opened the door. Her gray hair fell in loose ringlets. She'd been crying but greeted us with a smile.

"Can I help you?"

Hmmm. Interesting. She should have already expected us. Aria, the Reaper I was here to train, should have used her soul stone on any mortal in the house except the one we were here for.

"Possibly," I said. "Is your father Timothy?"

"Y—yes," she said with a look of skepticism. "Who are you?"

I pushed Ability into my soul stone, activating it as I pulled it out of my pocket.

The blinding light illuminated my hand, making it indistinguishable from the glow that consumed it. The woman squinted, backing away.

"It's okay," I said. "We're not here to hurt anyone. We're here to help your father. If you don't mind, we'd like to come in.

Her arms dropped to her side as she fell under the stone's influence. Dangerous tools in the wrong hands, soul stones are wonderfully convenient for Reapers. The stone's magic allows us to control the minds of mortals, which makes our jobs easier. I wouldn't want to return to the days before the Upperworld had these stones mass-manufactured, leaving Reapers to lurk around in the darkness to escort dying mortals to the Veil Gate. We were still trying to live down those old tales, passed through thousands of mortal generations, about the Reaper visiting. People feared us then, and that wasn't good for PR, even if it increased the power we had over the Overworld. Now, with a single slight push of magic, a Reaper could do their job and wipe the entire memory from anyone witnessing the event. I'm all for making this miserable job easier.

"Will you take good care of him?" she asked. "He's a good man."

"Of course."

"He'll be in expert hands," Billee said, moving to the woman's side and rubbing her arm.

The daughter's eyes fluttered with new tears. "H—he's in the back. His bedroom."

"Thank you. Would you like to say goodbye before I visit with him?" I asked.

"Y—yes. I would like that."

We walked with her down a narrow hall decorated with as many family pictures as could fit on the walls. Pictures stretching back to the time when black and white photos, huge cars, and men with greased hair were still a thing. From times before modern technology, when families actually spent time together, not letting it pass as they stared at small screens in their hands. From this brief journey down memory lane, it appeared Timothy had a good life, just as his report said.

The door at the end of the hall was open. His daughter stepped into his bedroom as we hung back. A moment later, Aria and her familiar Becs stepped out, closing the door.

"Hi, Mr. Carver," Aria said.

"Rev, please," I said, shaking her hand, before doing the same with Becs. The familiar's grip was firm.

Billee smiled and greeted them in a way that I knew was a situationally reserved and forced gesture.

From behind the bedroom door, the daughter quietly cried as she talked to her father.

"Let's move to the living room," I said, and we did. "Is he with a physician?"

Aria shook her head. "No, he's alone. That's how he wanted it. His daughter is the only family he has left. She's the only one here."

"Is that why you didn't use the stone on her?"

Aria's mouth drooped. She glanced up at Becs, who had a good five inches on her. "I wanted to give her as much time as possible before you got here. I was going to do it, but it felt wrong since we were waiting. Is that okay?"

"It's fine," I said. "Just wanted to make sure we're both clear on what the situation is. Actually, that's very kind of you. Make sure, if you do that in the future, that between the two of you, someone ensures it gets done." I glanced at the closed bedroom door. Soft shuffles drifted out before the daughter snorted and mentioned something about 'how silly you looked dressed like that.' My partner and the other crew watched the door. "None of these are ever the same, no matter how many you do. One day, you're going to walk into some-thing thinking you know exactly how it's going to play out and find yourself stunned. Mortals can be like that. Full of twists. So make sure, if you choose to not put them under the soul stone immediately, you have a safety mechanism in place to do it before you leave."

Aria nodded.

"Is it always like this?" Becs asked Billee in a deep voice.

"No," Billee said, stiffly at first. Her tone softened. "No, they're not. This is tough because of the circumstances, for me, personally. But I'll be honest. Even though they're not all the same, they're all tough. Just in their own, unique ways."

Becs clutched at her blouse. "How do you deal with it? How do you stay sane?"

"Lots of self-therapy," Billee said with a tight smile. She reached out for Becs's hand. "Let's go sit at the kitchen table and chat while they do their thing."

I didn't have to like how Billee said that last bit. I am a big boy, and I trusted her. She would guide the new familiar appropriately while I helped Aria through this experience.

"Are you ready?" I asked her after the pair of familiars moved into the other room.

Her chest puffed, and she drew a deep breath. She held it for a second longer and blew it out. "I guess so. I'm so nervous."

"Good."

Her forehead furrowed.

"That means you care about doing a good job." I led the way down the hall and knocked on the door.

"Yes?" A middle-aged woman, Timothy's daughter suddenly sounded like a frightened child from the other side of the barrier.

"May we come in?"

The door opened, but not by the woman who'd allowed us into the home. Instead, a Guardian stood there. She was short, lucky to hit five feet tall, but full of herself. The corners of her lips turned down when she saw me.

"I was hoping another Reaper was going to walk this one through the process," the Guardian said. "Not the Reaper Minister."

"Sorry. And you are?"

"Name's Heviena Yesker." She wagged a thick finger at me. "I've been a Guardian for a long time, so don't think you're going to bully me."

I put my hands up. "Not here to bully. Just to help a new Reaper through the escort. That's all."

Heviena backed away.

I started to enter the bedroom but stopped when I noticed Aria hanging back. "You coming? This is yours to deliver."

"She's—she's a—a—"

"Guardian Angel. Yes."

"But I thought—"

"They show up from time to time. Some like to make grand appearances." I looked at Heviena, who stood to the side of the bed, not hanging over Timothy and his daughter but remaining close enough to make it obvious she was there to protect. Even against the Reaper Minister. "They have a flair for dramatics. Theater kids, most of them."

"Oh. Okay." Aria looked like she took my words as literal.

"Come on in. Close the door. Let's get you through this. We'll talk afterward." I didn't need to clarify that I meant we'd reconvene when the Guardian was gone. Helviena's bratty sniff let me know my point had landed.

"Does Becs need to be here?" Aria asked.

"No. They're on site. Nothing in the Balance is changed by what we're doing, and that's the whole point of having them as familiars. That way, sensitive demons don't get their boxers in a bunch. Which is ridiculous when you think about it, since they never wanted these escort duties. They're too focused on themselves to give a rat's ass about this."

Aria swallowed noticeably, reaching into her pocket and pulling the scroll out. She had folded it.

I winced.

"What? Did I do something wrong?" Worry etched her voice.

I laughed. "No. You didn't. You'll see when we get to the Veil Gate, but the Scroll Eater isn't a big fan of folded scrolls. It's a little obsessive-compulsive like that."

Aria nodded rapidly. "Okay. Sorry. I'm ready."

The man in the bed was frail. Life had been ebbing away for a long time if first impressions were anything to go by. He wasn't my case, so I knew little about his situation, but I didn't need to. I'd been a part of enough of these types of cases, long before there were wise policies set in place by mortal governments. This man was tired. Tired of the pain. Of suffering. Tired of being tired. Mortals in these circumstances are almost always ready to go.

I changed my mind. "Billee? Can you and Becs come here, please?"

Heviena shifted.

"I thought they didn't need to be part of this?" Aria asked.

"They don't," I said, glancing back at Timothy and not feeling like explaining why I wanted my familiar to take the role of trainee now. "But I want them here."

Becs stepped in first, followed closely by Billee. She didn't look at me. Timothy had her full attention.

The bedroom was small and pungent, as is usual when someone has been restricted to such a tight space on the verge of the afterlife. We squeezed in together.

Billee lifted her chin. Not in defiance, but more a manifestation of her internal struggle.

"Just hang back and observe," I said to Aria, before going to Timothy's daughter and kneeling beside her. "Would you like to say goodbye now?"

She nodded as tears streaked down her cheeks.

I cut off the source to the soul stone, shutting down my influence over the woman.

Her head snapped in my direction, before swiveling around the room at the other two angels and two mortal strangers standing in her father's bedroom. Her mouth dropped open, about to cry out or scream.

I rested my hand on hers. "We're here for your father. We're angels."

In a flash, relief replaced fear. Her face crumbled.

"I knew it. Dad was a—a good man. Glory to God." She squeezed my hand. I squeezed back.

"But we have to take him now. He's being called," I said, always careful to not over-promise. This woman would understand the true nature of eternity in her own time. My third eye saw her fate clearly. She had another two decades of good living before her name would be entered into the Book of Planes. Long enough for her to celebrate her own mortality while holding out for hope that she'd see her father again.

"Yes. Yes." She cried for a few minutes, rubbing her father's arm. He was unresponsive, his breath coming slow and weak. Then she stood, ready to give her loved one over to us. She leaned over the bed, her quivering lips pressed to Timothy's forehead, and then stepped away.

I activated the soul stone.

Heviena grunted at the blinding flash. Becs yelped. I think I caught her by surprise. We really needed to work on our Reaper training program.

I stood next to Timothy's daughter. "You won't remember us. When we leave, you'll only remember your father and the last moments you had with him." My gaze went from the Guardian to Aria. I winked at both. "But you'll still believe in the goodness of angels."

I moved back to stand beside Aria. "Ready?"

She sniffed nervously. "I am. I think so. Yes."

"Are you taking him now?" Becs asked.

"Yes."

"Can we," she paused, looking to Billee for an answer, "can we go too?"

Billee shook her head.

"Trust me," I said, "you don't want to see the Veil Gate until it's your time." My third eye revealed when that would be for the pair of women, but I pushed the visualization out. Some things I just didn't care to know.

"Oh. Okay."

Looking toward the old man in the bed, I said, "Timothy, it's time to go."

A golden haze lifted from the body. Indistinct at first, as it rose, the ephemeral form contorted to take the shape of the man's mortal body. The energy residue got out of the bed, standing on the other side, next to the tube television that somehow still had rabbit ear antennas atop its veneered surface.

Like most energy residue, Timothy said nothing.

"It won't always be this easy," I said to Aria. "Some argue. Others feel remorse and regret. Those are the hard ones. Even tougher than those who put up a fight."

"They fight back?"

"Oh, yes. Not all, usually just the assholes. You'll see." I waved around the room. "Look at your surroundings whenever you go into a job. Imagine if he was stronger and had resisted. Imagine if he thought you were breaking into his house and had a firearm in here."

Aria looked around as if she suddenly didn't know where she was.

"Not much of an escape, is there?"

"N—no."

"Always have a plan before you call time on them. Do reconnaissance if you can. Figure out how, if you don't think you can. The more information you have before you go into a situation, the safer you'll be." I faced her. We locked eyes. "Never, ever forget that you are in the Overworld when you're acting as a Reaper. We can die here."

She swallowed.

"And on that cheery note," I said with such a quick pivot that Aria blinked as if she'd just woken from a bad dream, "let's get Timothy to the Veil Gate."

I led the way, squeezing past Billee and Becs, who filled most of the door. Timothy glided along behind us, his matter not interacting with the physical world. In the living room, I let Aria open the Rift to the Veil Gate, and we escorted Timothy across.

Aria's eyes went wide when she saw the Gate, the Empyrean Knights, and especially Harold. Admittedly, it's ugly enough to shock even the most jaded Reaper. Trust me, I have first-hand knowledge in that department.

I leaned closer. "Let me do the talking and maybe he won't push you through the Veil Gate for folding his scroll."

THE ESCORT WENT AS WELL AS COULD BE EXPECTED. NOTHING tragic or dramatic. Aria and I returned to the house, promised to get in touch again at the next staff meeting, and went our separate ways.

Becs impressed Billee, so that was encouraging. What was less encouraging was the dinner we had in town.

Elma is south of the Olympic National Forest. A good distance away by car, because the two-lane roads are often choked by logging trucks and passive drivers. Still, it's one of the few spots of civilization that are populated enough when you're on a broad monster hunt and looking to narrow your scope.

We were here for information, and getting none. Not a single conversation we eavesdropped on provided a single hint that someone had seen something untoward in the forest. When we finished dinner and headed to the dive bar outside of town, we came up just as empty-handed.

Billee had an ingenious idea when the bar proved to be a waste of our time. "Let's hit the truck stop and see if anything is going on there."

A spot filled with twenty exhausted truckers looking for a hot shower and meal at the end of a long day of driving sounded perfect, in theory. In practice, we came up as dry as a Steven Wright stand-up routine.

"Rev, I've got to get home," Billee said when the dining area whittled down to two remaining customers, neither of who spoke from their different tables. "I'm seeing a couple of clients in the morning, and no one is awake to creep on."

"We weren't creeping."

Her face scrunched. "We were."

I looked around the dining area. One of the remaining truckers now snored in his booth. "Yeah, we were. And we've got nothing to show for it."

"There's always tomorrow," my partner said as she slid out of the booth.

"Yes, there is," I grumbled as I joined her, patting the mana stone. "A million-million tomorrows."

10

TO HUNT

"It's creepy out here." Billee pulled her parka around her as we stomped through the underbrush and up the slope of the fern-covered hill.

I didn't agree or disagree. The Olympic National Forest is a wide expanse of 'creepy.' Deep forest, broken only by the mountains. It holds plenty of secrets, and probably twice as many bodies. Don't get me wrong, it's a beautiful, serene region of the world. A great place to escape the rat race of humanity and get back in touch with what the world used to be before mortals discovered the wonder of disease management, running water, and not throwing your piss and shit buckets out their windows. But the thick canopy of moss-covered trees can also be intimidating.

The population centers of Washington don't stretch this far. Mortals circle around the I-5 corridor, running north to south, from Vancouver, Canada, and down through Portland. The Cascade Mountains split the city-dwelling, tech-based population from the agricultural Washingtonians. Even though this forest is on the western edge of the state, it might as well be a world away from places like Seattle, Tacoma, or Olympia.

The thick vegetation makes it impossible to catch anything crawling toward you unless it's the size of a bear. With that much flora, sounds disappeared, too. Unless it was an eagle screech or the wind, the forest sucked all sound from the Overworld.

"How long are we going to be out here?" Billee asked after another quarter mile of hiking through thick flora and wet ground. I'm sure, if her thighs were burning like mine, that might have served as the inspiration behind her question.

"As long as we can stand," I answered as honestly as I could. "After I dropped you off, I hit some deep websites and dug up a thread.

"About the behemoth?"

I nodded. "The user didn't call it that, but he sounded convincing. From what I could decipher, we're in the general vicinity. The problem is, the forest is huge. There are six hundred thousand square acres of terrain to cover. Lots of mountains and more freaking plants," I said, tripping over an unseen root, "than I care to see for the rest of my life. No matter how long that is. Trust me, if either of us knew how to find this stupid beast, we wouldn't be doing this. I can think of better ways to spend a winter day."

As if on cue, a stiff wind cut across the slope, striking us square on and reminding me just how miserable of a task this was going to be.

"Too bad the rest of the gang couldn't make it."

"Damn school and work obligations. Bear felt bad and said he'd take the day off to help, but I talked him out of it."

"That was nice."

"I don't want to abuse them."

"I could say so many things about that," she teased and then shivered, looking up through the roof of trees. "At least it's not snowing."

We'd dressed for the elements. It wasn't like we journeyed out into the forest like unprepared city folk who usually ended up on the nightly news reports about missing people. I knew what I was doing, and we were here so Billee could learn as much as possible, as quickly as possible. Even so, this was miserable. After this job, I was determined to take Yahweh off my Christmas card list.

"And we're looking for tracks?"

"Tracks. Anything that looks like it might be a trail to a food or water source. A nest. Vegetation something has chomped on," I said, stopping and looking around at a forest that protected every one of its secrets. "Hell, I'll take bark rubbed off a tree at this point."

"Would the behemoth do that?"

"I don't know. That's the problem. Yahweh screwed us on this by putting the cart before the horse."

"How so?" She swung a long, thin branch as if it were a sickle and she was clearing a wheat field. The lady ferns were so large that even hefty swings wouldn't have budged them.

"No one has an idea what this iteration looks like."

She stopped. "It's not always the same? Like the one in the Bible?"

"Have you read the Bible?"

Billee was always unapologetic about the minor role formal religion played in her life. "All of it? No. Has anyone who doesn't want to make a career of religion? Parts of it? Sure, but was a kid then, and had a kid's imagination."

I chuckled. "You should go back and read it when you're bored. It's not what you remember." The far-off wind whirred through the Pacific Northwest on the other side of the rise, leaving us protected but aware of its threatening touch. "All the great beasts are different. Not only from each other, either. They can differ from themselves each time they manifest. This behemoth won't look like the ones in the past, because none were identical to their predecessors, either."

"What has it looked like before?"

"Ugly as the concept of original sin," I said. "Always big."

"Duh. Behemoth, remember?"

I almost stumbled over another root, deftly avoiding it at the very last second, and continued across the face of the slope. "Fair play. One I remembered was a wooly mammoth. Massive tusks. Had to be twenty feet long. Another looked like a triceratops, just with two horns and a mane like a lion. There was one, way before my time, that supposedly looked like a hairless sloth, just about fifteen times larger."

"Sounds gross."

"I don't expect much more from this one. Whatever it is, and whatever it looks like, don't let it shock you. Most likely, it'll be big, ugly, and stupid."

"Are they? Usually? Stupid, I mean?"

I rocked my head. "Seems like Yahweh likes to balance things out. Gives them plenty of physical presence while shorting them on mental dominance."

"So it shouldn't be too difficult for you to kill it then," Billee said, swatting a conifer leaf that was wider than she was. "No matter how big, even you should be able to outsmart it."

"That's the problem. If it is as mindless as those in the past have been, I'm pretty sure it won't be acting alone."

She stopped. The silent forest swallowed the sounds of her breath. "You mean it'll have a trainer or beastmaster?"

"Of sorts. Yes. The worst part? There's no telling who it will be. Could be anyone, from any rank of angels. If my suspicions are correct, that will be a problem. Especially if Hellion is behind this. She's got an army of Nephilim at her disposal. And worse things than them."

Billee groaned sound. "What could be worse than one of those things? The one you killed outside the homeless camp was an ugly bastard."

"And he was a rookie compared to a lot of the older ones. They're a lot like us Reapers, in that they get harder to defeat the older they get. That's bad news. But worse still is that she doesn't need to rely on the Nephilim. She can call on one of the Four Horsemen of the Apocalypse. All of them, if she wanted."

Billee pulled her chin toward her chest. "The. Four. Horsemen?"

"Yep. Like I said, bad news." I looked up the slope, rising another four hundred feet into the ashen sky. I wanted to make the summit during this trip to look around and get a lay of the land. Then we could head back to the car and the warmth it provided. Because of the access roads, I'd had to park far below us in one of the designated areas the park services had flattened and compacted. It felt a very long way away now. I tipped my chin toward the summit. "Let's keep hiking and talking through this. We need to be in the car before the sun even thinks about setting, which at this time of year, could happen before our lunch settles."

We picked up the pace, Billee exerting far less me, as we carved narrower switchbacks. The tighter turns ensured we got a decent thigh workout, but the extra effort would get us to the summit earlier. The journey was arduous.

Though I'd said we'd talk on the way up, Billee was the one doing most of the talking. I was clueless how someone who sat in a chair all day, listening to people talking about their problems, could be in such amazing shape. She was, and she didn't mind showing it off, either. When she was twenty yards ahead, I asked her to slow down. In part, because I didn't want too much distance between us. More selfishly, I didn't want to have to yell as we talked about behemoths, Four Horsemen, and other topics deemed strange by contemporary mortals. Loud voices drew attention. Loud voices discussing supernatural beasts and angels with so much power they could unweave the world typically ended with at least one participant on a couch, discussing their childhood with someone like Billee.

She put her hands on her hips, looking down—literally—

on me. "I was trying to get to the top, so I could check it out. Figured it'd be quicker than waiting for you."

"One. Not funny." I used the conversation as an opportunity to rest my hands on my hips. "Two. It's not safe. For all we know, the behemoth could be fast asleep on the other side of the ridge. This thing will be nasty, Billee. Just because I don't know what sort of nasty, doesn't mean we need to take risks. Don't go putting your neck out. I like it where it is."

She held her hands up. "Okay. Okay. Sorry. So, the Four Horsemen are a real thing?"

"They are," I said, sucking what felt like a half gallon of water out of my hydration pack. "And they make Arakiel look like a kindergarten brat. So, let's do this with caution. Every step of the way."

Somewhere deep within the shadows of trees and tall vegetation, a branch cracked with a thick pop! Billee jumped and even I reached for my holster. I hated being without my duster. I felt almost naked without it, even though I wore two layers of shirts and a heavy jacket designed for cold temperatures that threatened to dump icy pellets.

When nothing followed the sound, Billee and I shared a glance and nervous laugh.

"I imagine the behemoth will do more than crack a single branch," I said.

"Yeah." Billee stood where she was, waiting for me to join, with her hands stuffed under her arms and her hood now pulled up.

I pointed out hints of the forest's fauna as we continued up the slope. All insignificant life. Though it's hard to call deer and a mountain lion 'insignificant', they were nothing compared to a behemoth. The nibbles on leafy greens and the prints we came across belonged to more mundane animal life.

"Besides learning about tracking animals and spotting the behemoth, I also wanted to let you know about your bracelet."

"You mean my property band?" Billee said, lifting her arm and rocking her hand from side to side. Her gloves and parka hid the bracelet, but it was there because it would be until the end. Her end.

She smirked, but only because she knew the comment irritated me. Billee was wise to the uncouth Upperworld practice of forcing mortals to serve as familiars to Reapers. She had as much choice and power in the matter of her being a familiar and getting out of the gig as I did with my position as a Reaper. Still, that didn't stop her from giving me shit about it.

I ignored her comment. "The bracelet has magical properties. You'll be able to protect yourself and help others against minor injuries and wormwood."

"Wormwood?"

"The Upperworld's most popular poison."

Billee had stopped giving me the 'so-so' gesture with her hand, still holding her arm in mid-air. She now looked at the parka-covered place that hid her bracelet. "Magic? I have magic?"

"No. The bracelet does. Pull up your jacket. I'll show you."

She pushed her sleeve halfway up her forearm, exposing her brown wrist from which the thin bracelet dangled. Slightly wider than her wrist, it dipped an inch. I lifted the dangling chain with my palm and turned her arm over with my other hand. Hers was now pointed skyward. Rotating the bracelet, the gray day dulled the inset diamonds framed in fourteen-carat gold. I pinched the infinity loop between my finger and thumb, careful not to press it.

"You activate it by squeezing this with your fingers," I said. "Be careful. Though it's hard to set off by accident, it doesn't take much pressure. Totally effective against poison, which might come in handy one day. It won't heal serious injuries or stop bleeding. But it will keep you going longer than you'd be able to without it."

"I had no idea," she said, staring at the gold infinity loop as if it was her first time seeing it.

"Well, I hoped to never have you in a situation where you'd need it. This behemoth differs from anything you've ever faced, especially if it's not acting alone. I want you to be as ready as you can be." I let go of her hand and she slowly lowered it, glancing at the bracelet again before pushing her sleeve back down. "Whatever is going on, we've crossed the line into serious territory. Depending on whether I kill the behemoth or it kills me, I won't be making friends. If I end up walking away from this, you might become a target, too. Normally, we'd have more time. But things are changing and I'm leaning toward being ready for nasty surprises." I pointed at her bracelet, the Reaper trinket that kept her bound and loyal to me. "That will help you when you need it, to help yourself or someone else."

"This job gets more and more interesting," she said evenly.

"You can say that again."

We reached the summit a short while later. With the cloud cover, I only had a hint of the presence of the sun behind the thick blanket of gray. There was no accurate way to know how much time we had before the sun started its descent, so this had to be expedient. Three football fields away, the trees opened.

"Let's head over there. Maybe we'll see something."

When we reached the opening, we discovered the reason for the open view. A logging company had harvested the back of the hill. The slope below us was a wasteland of stumps and feller buncher tracks.

Beyond the decimated hillside, the Olympic National Forest stretched away. Mountains and the gray day blocked the most distant reaches. Cloud cover that seemed to settle over the world shrouded the closer heights.

"Not the best day to do this," Billee said.

"This is Washington. We won't see the sun until July. And we can't wait that long. Keep your eyes open."

Valleys and peaks taunted us from below and above, protecting the behemoth's secret. Intentionally setting low expectations, I didn't think we'd see the behemoth stroll by us on its way to find a snack. But I was hoping to find a clue to its presence. One trip to the forest wouldn't provide that. Ten probably wouldn't. Billee and I would be lucky to find something by our one-hundredth trip. And that's exactly why I'd done Anapheil the dishonor of asking her to take over as the Reaper Minister on an interim basis.

"This is why we need help," I declared to the gray day. It didn't answer.

Billee gave a frustrated sigh.

"Don't give up hope yet. This is our first attempt. We'll have a lot more ahead, I'm afraid."

"I know. That's the problem."

"How so?"

She walked toward the barren slope, casting a sad look down the hillside before swinging it out over the valley to the north. "This is going to take more from my job, Rev. It already is." She swung her arm out. "Look at that. It goes on forever. We could spend the rest of our lives searching this forest. Even if I was made for the outdoors, and I'm not, by the way, I don't have the time. My patients don't have the time. I've got a job to do, an actual job."

"I know, Billee. Trust me, if I could do this without involving anyone else, I would. This doesn't excite me, and I know what I'm asking of you."

"You're not asking."

"Like you, I don't have a choice."

"We're both slaves to the system, I guess."

"Happy, happy, joy-joy." I moved closer, feeling the distance between us impinging on the conversation. It definitely wasn't benefitting the search. Unless this latest iteration of the behemoth was shockingly super-behemoth-like, we wouldn't see hints of its presence from this part of the forest. "Careful, Sparky. You're sounding as grim as me, and I don't recall any urban legends about the Grim Familiar. Doesn't have the same ring to it." She didn't react. The wind blew across the open face of the slope, chilling in its embrace. "I can talk to Pher and get the Order to bump your pay if that'll help. They've got unlimited resources, you know?"

"It's not about money," she said, tucking her hands under her arms again and shivering. "It's about my patients. In the big picture, I get how this benefits people, even if I don't always agree with it." Her dark tone made it obvious she was talking about yesterday's escort job with Timothy. I left that alone for now. We'd have plenty more death with dignity cases if I lived to see the backside of the behemoth. "It's about time. I don't have enough of it to help the people I want to help. Unless the Order has a way of giving me more time." She sighed again. "I'm going to be frustrated. Plus, even if they could, they'd just fill it with more hunts for monsters and escorts. I still wouldn't be able to focus on my social work."

I almost rubbed her shoulder in apology when I saw her cheek bulge as she clamped down on her teeth. Wisely, I dropped my arm.

"I had to cancel with six people today so we could do this," she said, still facing the expanse of dark green Douglas fir tree tops. "Six people who need to work on their lives. Who rely on me to help."

"I hate to sound apathetic because what you do is important. I'm sure you kick ass, but if you help me find the behemoth, you'd be part of saving an untold number of lives. Depending on this beast's disposition and who might drive it on, imagine this thing loose in Olympia. Hell, plop it down in the middle of Seattle and think about the damage it would do. This is important work."

She was quiet for a moment longer before she turned and

headed back into the tree cover. "I know. And I'll do it. But that doesn't mean I won't be upset for the people I'm letting down."

She walked ahead, and I gave her space, keeping her within my sights. Sometimes, common sense was a priority over safety precautions. She wasn't an automaton, and I wouldn't treat her like one. Ever. Even if that was the way many in the Upperworld saw familiars.

We were halfway down the mountain when she slowed enough that I could shorten my strides. Soon, we were side by side again. Billee looked ready to talk.

"Tell me about the others," she said.

"What others?"

"Your familiars. What were they like?"

"I've had over three hundred. Want to narrow it down a little for me?"

"Give me the highlights and lowlights," she said, sounding thoughtful.

She was asking for more than a simple story time to fill in the return trip to the car.

"Okay," I intoned. "I've had plenty of good and bad times with familiars. Anything specific you want to hear about?"

"No, Rev. I just want you to talk about them. I want to understand their journey so I can put mine into context. Maybe then I'll come to terms with everything."

So I did. I spent the next two hours telling her about familiars from the distant and near past. The ones who walked with me from the time of hunter-gatherer clumpings of mortals to the familiar who she replaced. Billee interjected only sparsely, letting me do most of the talking.

When you've worked with so many familiars, there's a lot you can talk about. I kept the conversation focused on the light stuff, sensing Billee didn't want to journey into the stories I had about my mortal partners who'd been ripped apart by demons. Or the time two Nephilim pinned me down while their flock of giant horned rams cornered a familiar in front of a thousand-foot drop. Thankfully, I was too busy fighting to hear that partner hit the rocks far below.

Instead, I shared the times when familiars like Jessie Jenkins saved a little girl from drowning. When Ragnar Oleffsen put his own neck on the line to save my ass. He took an arrow through the shoulder, and even though his bracelet didn't stop the bleeding, it eased the pain until I could take him to the village's medicine woman. I made sure Billee heard about the familiars who jumped into freezing rivers to save pets. Those who spent their free time baking for the needy or sewing clothes for the needy masses. People like that. She needed to know what was possible.

By the time we reached the car, I think Billee was in a better head space. At least, that's what her expression told me. The deep lines of concern forming crescents underneath her eyes and at the corners of her mouth had smoothed away.

She waited at the passenger door for me to untie my filthy boots and replace them with clean ones. When I closed the trunk, she said, "Okay, now tell me about the costs of being a Reaper while you take me home."

"Costs? You mean besides the crappy pay and the unending life of pursuing demons, monsters, and baddies?"

"I'm being serious, Rev." She got in, rubbed her hands, and placed them in front of the vent as if my car could instantaneously blow hot air.

"Fair enough." I breathed slowly. "The job is tough on my psyche. I know you know that. It's not a lot of fun. It's depressing. Rough. Who in their right mind would want to spend thousands of years helping mortals deal with their mortality? Who would want to ensure the reluctant ones faced it?"

"Takes a special kind to do that."

"You can say that again."

"But what else? Besides that, what has this cost you? What have you had to give up?"

The answer was straightforward but private. But this was just me and Billee, sitting in a quiet car, far from satellite radio to distract us or cover awkward silence. Our conversation, accompanied only by the slow rolling of rubber over rock as I navigated the unimproved road, was our focus. She wouldn't let this go, and she was safe to share with.

"Love," I said, and felt the immediate release of pressure on my chest I didn't know was present until I eased with the admission.

From my periphery, I saw her head turn. When she spoke, she did so in that soft, empathetic way counselors do that makes you want to say more, even if you went into the conversation as closed up as a safe. "Love? What kind of love?"

"My wife," I said, feeling the release. I hadn't talked about Alisha in ages. Well, not technically. But it had been a long time. Years. The last one I shared my stories of her with was Abaddon. I couldn't even talk to Pher about her. He was too close to the problem.

"What's her name?"

"Alisha C—" I almost used the surname we once shared. Part of me wanted to forget that she had a maiden name—the Upperworld can be antiquated like that—she'd returned to after our divorce. "Rosi."

"Alisha Rosi. Pretty name."

I bobbed my head. "Pretty name. Gorgeous woman. Beautiful heart."

A silent moment passed. A memory of Alisha laughing at one of my terrible jokes filled my mind. No matter how much time and distance separated us, her spirit—if you will—was never far away.

"I take it the divorce was amicable?"

"Oh yeah. Alisha was a practical woman. Is practical. Well, at least I hope she still is."

"When was the last time you spoke to her?"

"Hmmm. Years. Four. Five. Eight. A decade? They all run together when you're immortal. Especially when the Order keeps me as busy as I've been."

"Is that the reason for the divorce? The job?"

"Yep." My mood darkened at what could have been, but that which I lost because of something beyond my control. The source of my happiness, sacrificed for a job. A job I'd done faithfully and well. A job I couldn't escape, even when it cost me the one thing I didn't want to give up.

I tried to laugh, but it came out as an angry bark.

"What's that about?" she asked.

"Just thinking about how Alisha is the whole reason I don't go home all that often. Instead, I spend almost all my time in the Overworld, even when I'm not working, in the one place where a car accident or a bullet to the head could take me out. The one place where each minute takes more and more of my life from me."

"You might be better at your job if you made peace with that part of your life," she said.

"How?" I asked as we exited the invisible line between civilization and hiking miles if your transport broke down. The radio blared a song rife with thick, distorted guitar chops. My kind of song, especially when I'm ramping myself up to fight demon spawn, wayward angels, or a behemoth. Not the most conducive music to having a conversation about the love of my life, though. I switched off the radio with a knuckle punch to the button.

"Go home," Billee answered with a heavy dose of tenderness. She waved out the window at the passing trees. "None of this is going anywhere. Go home. Talk to her." Billee smirked. "Assuming she wants to see you and you're not actually a creep in disguise."

I opened my big mouth to defend myself, but Billee's laugh and shoulder swat cut me off.

"Joking." Her voice softened. "Sounds like you could do with a real heart-to-heart?"

"You ain't kidding." The last conversation was the time Alisha told me she was leaving me, quitting on us. I couldn't swallow.

"Go home, Rev. Ask her out for a drink or something. Just talk. Check-in with each other. Celebrate each other. Make sure she is happy and safe. Healing starts with doing the simple things."

11

FRIENDS IN DIM PLACES

BILLEE IS AS SMART AS SHE LOOKS. TRUST ME. I BELIEVED THAT TO my core. Why else was I standing in my Third Level home?

A long return hike to the car, and a subsequent drive from the mountains to the city that took less time than the hike, was more than enough for me to see the wisdom in her words. Unfair, of course. She had me buying into her proposition before she even proposed it.

Like I said, Billee is smart.

So here I was, back in the Third Level. The second time within the past month when I used to count my visits by calendar year.

I inhaled deeply. The place smelled stale. Hiring a cleaning crew couldn't replace the aroma daily life brought into a place no matter how thorough the crew was. My Upperworld apartment was being neglected, and I was the culprit. The hardback autobiographies on the industrially inspired copper pipe shelves stood like sentries over the place, their bindings lined up perfectly. I meant to get to them. One of these days. My acoustic guitar sat in the corner on its stand. It smelled of lemon, like the cleaner had paid special attention to it when they wiped it down. I hoped they hadn't. Cleaning solvents on the wood and strings was going to have a permanent effect that would make me sound worse than my limited talents already did.

I looked at the rug, black with square gray tiles of fabric along the outer border. Not a spot of lint, dislodged hair, or oily pizza stain on the dark tract.

A waste. All of it. The mortgage on the place. Every unloved item filling this supposed home. The refrigerator that hadn't seen a carton of milk or an egg since 2G was considered fast cell service. Nothing but a waste, better enjoyed by someone else. Yahweh knew I sure as hell wasn't.

In that quiet moment, I realized how wrong I was. This wasn't really my home. This was a museum honoring my past. Like all things from an earlier time, I could only touch its spirit in my mind.

With a deep sigh, I headed out to see the "angel of the Abyss."

The bar was my favorite watering hole back in the day when I legitimately could call the Third Level my home. The angel in question was Abaddon Fulsome, owner of said establishment.

The day was bright and warm enough that most of the angels who dared come out limited their activities to leisurely strolls or sitting in the shade, chatting with neighbors, or quietly reading. There were a few new faces in the neighborhood, a marker of missing time.

Thing was, I didn't really miss it. Being here for even a few minutes wasn't fun. I felt my ex everywhere. Even on this sidewalk, walking the same street she and I used to stroll every night after dinner. Even when it rained. The sandwich shop with the outdoor iron tables we used to sit at and angel watch. The annoying second-hand clothing store she'd have to drag me into against my better judgment with promises she wouldn't buy someone else's discarded clothes. She broke that promise more often than I broke mine to never "Dutch oven" her again. Equally harmless, and painful to recall.

A zipping sound pulled me out of my dark thoughts, approaching fast and from the rear. I groaned but turned my frown into a smile. One, because I'm not an asshole. Two, the angel coming up hard behind me didn't deserve to share in my self-induced melancholy.

"Rev! You're back again," Jimmy Flitlight said as he buzzed past me at eye level, taking a hard banking turn and whipping around to float in front of my face.

I took a small step back. Jimmy is bad about recognizing personal space. "Hey, Jimmy. How are you? How's marriage treating you?"

I'd only seen the sprite a few days ago, but the way his tiny face brightened told me my question touched him.

"Estelle is wonderful," he said, turning in the air in a full oval but always keeping his solidly black eyes on me—I think. It's so hard to tell when the sclera is the same color as the iris and pupil. Something fell out of his pocket, too small for me to see, and the sprite dove, scooped it from the side-walk and stuffed his tiny hand in his pocket before I could tell what he'd dropped. "Marriage is wonderful. We spend so much time together and enjoy every single minute of it. The other night, we started cooking dinner early because we got off work at about the same time. Which is weird, because that rarely happens, and I was telling her about my thoughts on—"

If I didn't manage my favorite neighborhood sprite's chatter, he'd talk until I turned to dust. I liked Jimmy. He's a good guy. To be frank, he doesn't know when to shut up. I wanted to kill a few fairies with one stone, so I cut him off. "Hey bud, that's great. I'm headed to the Abyss to talk to Abaddon." His little face drooped. So I stifled my groan and said, "Want to join me for a drink and we can catch up?"

He brightened, and his long, thin ears twitched. "Oh, that would be great. I would really enjoy that! Thank you."

As I walked and Jimmy fluttered alongside, we shared the latest happenings in each other's lives. When I say 'we' caught up, I mean I spent the walk listening to Jimmy's update. The challenges of his job as a delivery man, including at least three separate stories of drama at the office, seemed to be his sole focus besides his new bride. I think it was three. It's difficult to separate stories when Jimmy tells them. He repeated stories he'd told me about Estelle and their communal living situation in the tower at the end of the block. The thought of an entire community of sprites living in one space sounded like a personal hell, but Jimmy seemed more than content with the arrangement, so I was happy for him.

Rascal, the neighborhood cat-sith, raced from an alleyway, chased by a couple of brats. Their hand-me-down clothes told me that chasing the giant cat was likely their only form of entertainment today. The young snob on the unicorn in the Eighth Level flashed through my mind. The polish she used for her unicorn's horn probably cost more than the clothes all these boys wore.

Rascal was never truly at risk of them catching him. He enjoyed torturing the angels on the block. As big as a German Shepherd, I hoped for the kids' sake Rascal's disposition never changed. I wouldn't rescue them if the cat-sith suddenly decided he didn't like being tormented. As much as I dislike entitled Nephilim and demons, I dislike anyone who abuses animals even more. In a way, I was rooting for Rascal to turn on them and teach them a lesson in humility, complete with fresh scars from his three-inch long claws. See how many cat-siths they chased afterward.

"That thing is still alive?" I shook my head.

Jimmy's dark orb eyes watched Rascal race by. "Good thing I can fly. I don't trust that Rascal."

"Nor should you."

After that, he explained, in far more detail than anyone needed to know, how he and a few of 'the guys' in the tower were working on a five-thousand-piece puzzle that was supposed to be a picture of pencils.

"Fascinating," I said, hoping I sounded as if it was. I nodded at the sign hanging over the door of The Abyss. "Want to finish up in here? I'll buy the first round."

"Sure," he said, beaming. "But I can't stay too long. Estelle is cooking tonight. Spaghetti. I love spaghetti. All sprites do. She does this thing with the pasta and something with butter that is just—" He connected the tips of his forefinger and thumb, brought them to his lips, and made a smacking sound. "Magnifique."

I chuckled. "No worries, buddy. I won't keep you long. I have things I need to discuss with Abaddon, anyway."

"Oh, like what?"

"Boring stuff. Relationship stuff."

"Are you getting back together with Alisha?" He zipped around in a loop again, this time with his hands stuffed in his pockets so nothing fell out. "Oh, that's wonderful!"

I shook my head. "No, I'm not. Sorry, buddy. We're not."

His little face crinkled. "Then why are you home?"

Boundaries. Jimmy recognized none. "Come on, let's get that beer."

We stepped inside The Abyss, another step toward the goal Billee helped me define.

A dim place, the bar isn't the big draw. It's not even a hot spot in the neighborhood. But it's close to my Upperworld home, relatively clean, and the owner is absolutely amazing. A place you'll never find a tourist or entitled jerk holding a business lunch with colleagues. This is a safe place for angels to be themselves.

Behind the bar, a red-haired woman mixed a cocktail. When I say her hair was red, I mean red. Not auburn. Not copper. Nor was it strawberry blonde. Not burgundy. Abaddon's hair was the color of blood. Just the way she liked it, I imagined. It set her apart from most angels in the Third Level. Hell, it made her stand out from the entire Upperworld. Abaddon was unique like that. From her hair to the way she painted her face, being different didn't bother her. Today's face paint was conservative by her usual standards. She still wore the full-face white foundation, but she only decorated one side of her face with a unique design. Today's selection for the other half of her face? Cracked dirt. I don't know how she pulled it off, but from her hairline to her jaw, the entire right side of her face was pale brown, with jagged lines of black to replicate parched, split soil. Seriously talented, this bar owner was. I swear, even though I knew it was a passion of hers, Abaddon's creative talent was an effective marketing tool. I'd bet a good portion of her customers patronized the bar just to check out her latest creation.

I pulled up at the bar. Jimmy settled down on top of it next to me.

"Revelation Carver," Abaddon said, shaking the concoction she was making for an older man sitting in the far corner, "do my eyes deceive me?"

"They do not," I said with a smile. "Miss me?"

Abaddon's lips scrunched, screwing with the illusion her face paint created. "Not really. I just saw you a few days ago. Do we need to be worried? You never come home twice in a year, never mind twice within a few days."

"I'm not that bad."

"Yes, you are," she and Jimmy said simultaneously.

"Get me a beer," I laughed.

"What are you having, little man?" she asked Jimmy.

"Bourbon. Straight, please."

Abaddon finished the old man's drink and dropped ours off, leaning an elbow on the bar. She could have passed for a saloon bartender from the Old West if she wasn't an angel, a woman, wearing face paint, and lacking the white dress shirt, arm garter, and curly mustache. "So what's really going on? Why are you back so soon? Did I guilt you with my comment last time, or is there something you need? Or something we should be worried about?"

"Nah, nothing like that. I'm here because, if I didn't come back, my partner would kick my ass."

Abaddon quirked an eyebrow. Well, at least I think she did. Behind all that paint, it was hard to tell, and I was just going off the distortion of that side of her face from the possibly perceived movement. "Oh? Why's that? Don't you have mortal partners?"

"I do. We're on a case and we shared stuff partners share. She's a counselor, so—"

"She has a way of getting you to talk about things stubborn people like you don't enjoy talking about?" Abaddon's rusty voice lightened.

"Exactly. Pain in my ass, I swear."

"Yeah, people who spend all their time taking care of others typically react like that when someone tries to take care of them," Abaddon said. Her throat made a grinding sound. I think it might have been a laugh. Who knows? "So, what did she finally get you to open up about? The job? The fact the Order won't let you quit? Alisha?"

That last one landed hard.

I must have delayed for too long because Jimmy piped in. "I think he's still in love with her and that's why he's here. Do you think they'll get back together? Estelle and I were talking about the couples we root for on those reality shows. We were watching an episode of Lovers In Paradise the other night, and I pointed out one couple. I told her, 'they remind me of Rev and Alisha,' I said. I swear it. They were just like you two, Rev." He glanced at me, frowning. "Except his hair was nicer."

Abaddon gave a grating laugh at that. "You mean he brushed it?"

"Ha ha," I said, using a long drink as an excuse to figure out how to answer the bartender's inquiry. I didn't want to uninvite Jimmy from the conversation, but there was one truism of the Third Level. That was, if Jimmy knew something, he was going to tell others. The question wasn't 'if,' but 'when' with the sprite. "Actually, it does have to do with Alisha."

Abaddon purred, a sound like metal gears cranked for the first time in years. "I knew it. This counselor of yours, she's good."

"She's my familiar. My partner. Not my counselor. Though she probably could be, if I'm being honest."

"Sounds like a good friend."

"She is."

"So when do you see Alisha?"

I lifted my beer. "That's why I'm here."

"You won't find her in a place like this," Abaddon said, tilting back and cocking her head toward the ceiling so her voice carried. "This place is full of degenerates."

The patrons returned a spate of good-natured grumbles and gripes.

Now I tipped the mouth of the beer bottle at her. "And that's exactly why I came here first."

"Why?"

I shrugged. "Hoping you'll talk sense into me."

"I could go fetch her," Jimmy said, swirling in the air just to my side. "It's not that far. I still remember where she lives and see her all the time. She's still as lovely as ever, Rev. Just in case you were curious." He stopped talking, blessedly, for a second to check his small watch. Pulling it to his ear, his face screwed up, and he pulled it away. Tapping it, he scowled. "Well, isn't that just grand?"

"It's okay, Jimmy. Really. Thank you, though. This is something I have to do on my own."

"Again, so why are you here?" Abaddon said. "You're out

of your mind if you think for one second that I'm going to stop you. You're lucky if I don't kick everyone out, close this place up, and escort you there myself."

"You'd have a revolt on your hands from them if you did," I said, tipping my head to indicate the smattering of daytime drinkers spread throughout the bar.

"I can take every single one of them," she said, and I believed her. She locked her gaze on me.

Most angels don't meet Abaddon's eyes. She has heterochromia. One eye is sky blue, the other blood red. No contacts used. It's a tough look. One that requires empathy and exposure. Abaddon, being the wonderful woman she is, never puts someone on the spot. Using her duties as the owner and operator of the bar, and her emotional intelligence to read any situation, she ensures her eyes never make someone uncomfortable.

Right now, she was giving me no such allowance.

"And I can take you if you don't get your ass out of here and go see her while you've got the balls to do it."

I didn't doubt she meant every word.

"I don't know what to say."

Abaddon placed her other elbow on the bar, fully leaning over it and toward me. "Say whatever is in your heart, Rev. Jimmy cares about you." The sprite nodded vigorously. "I care about you. Alisha is a good woman."

"She is! She's awesome," Jimmy chirped. "Just the other day, I saw her helping—"

"She won't be put off if you stop by to open your heart," Abaddon said, cutting the sprite off. "A quick visit. Nothing more. A touchstone, for both of you to know the other is okay. No overstepping. What's wrong with that?"

The thought of seeing Alisha again, of being so close, in proximity and readiness, was utterly frightening. "Nothing."

"Exactly." Abaddon squeezed my hand. "Go see her. Settle your soul."

12

THINGS LOST

I KEPT THE HOUSE IN THE DIVORCE. NOT BECAUSE I'M AN EGOIST or fragile man who believes he's entitled to all the goodies because of the split. Hell, I was only the breadwinner when we were together because I was good at killing demons and monsters—and angels—and the Order pays assassins well. Alisha was, and is, smarter and more talented than I could ever hope to be, and she did pretty well for herself throughout our marriage.

Now, standing outside her new home, appearances said she was still kicking ass. That made my crusty, jaded heart swell.

A white stucco wall, six feet high, surrounded the property. A black wrought-iron gate separated her yard from the street. No lock, no security system—she wasn't one of those types of angels. Knowing her like I had, Alisha chose these features for aesthetic reasons only. A nice touch.

I don't think I swallowed when I pushed the gate open and stepped into her yard, climbing the red brick steps on shaking knees.

My finger most definitely quivered when I extended it to ring her doorbell.

I shook my head. Middle-aged and acting like a boy with his first crush.

The convivial chime sounding within Alisha's home hit me like a gong. A moment later, soft footfalls sounded from deep within the mysterious realm on the other side of the door. My heartbeat doubled its rhythm.

I breathed—look; it required concerted effort at this stage.

From the other side, the lock clicked open. My breath caught.

And then she was there. Alisha Rosi, formerly known as Alisha Carver, better half to Revelation Carver, smiled at me.

Everything moved in slow motion. The Upperworld disappeared. The sounds of laughter and sidewalk conversations. The carriages rumbled over cobblestone. Kids playing. All of it zipped away the moment she peeled back the door.

Standing at five-foot-eight, Alisha looked as good as ever. Older and far smarter than me, she could have passed for five thousand years my junior. Her auburn hair would never match Abaddon's vibrancy, and it didn't need to. It framed her lightly freckled face in the most perfect of ways. Her blue eyes sparkled today as they had when she said goodbye, as if the life that had beaten me down since hadn't visited her. If that was Yahweh's doing, I would thank Him if I ever saw him.

"Rev? Oh, Yahweh, hi!" She strode forward, throwing her arms open as soon as she was clear of the doorway.

All trepidation, all apprehension, evaporated. Damn, her arms wrapped around me felt... transcendent. Her soft smell. Her height was perfect for pulling in and holding, for eternity if necessary. All of it, right. All of it, perfect. And all of it, over too soon.

Alisha stepped back, worry rippling her temple. "What are you doing here? Is everything okay? Oh no, did someone get hurt? Is it Pher?"

I laughed, standing in the same spot since ringing the

doorbell, feeling completely awkward. Not because she made me feel out of place, but because I wanted to dump on her. I wanted to tell her I was sorry. To share every regret I had, from this second and going back to the day I made the worst decision of my life and agreed to the Order's creed that ultimately led to our marriage dissolving. But that's creepy, and I wasn't going to re-introduce myself to the most important angel in my life that way.

"No, no, everyone is fine. Everything is okay," I said. "I was wondering if we could chat. I should have called ahead and I'm sorry. This was a spur-of-the-moment decision. Well, sort of. Do you have time? Absolutely cool if you don't, since I'm imposing."

What was probably a fraction of a second felt like an eternity while I waited for her answer.

"For you?" she said, crossing her arms. She stood that way for a moment and I wanted nothing more than to leap from the steps and run through the yard, squealing like a pig. I know. Really impressive for the Upperworld's assassin. I get it.

But then she dropped her arms and laughed, waving me inside. "Of course. Come in. Let me put on some coffee."

"That would be wonderful," I said.

Alisha's home was exactly what I expected. Cozy, warm, and welcoming. Soft colors abounded, from the throw pillows on the large reading chair tucked in the corner—that also matched the color of three large pillar candles on the coffee table—to the light fixtures she must have had custom-made. Light, melodic music came from the back room.

Past the cozy front room, the house was one long, open space to her kitchen. An island, complete with stove and sink, stood sentry. Three bar stools lined it. Alisha stood on the other side, near the counter that was so spacious popular restaurants would have been jealous. The crackle of grinding coffee beans provided an excellent opportunity to think through my approach. Or lose my nerve.

"Sorry," she yelled over the racket. "I fresh grind every time. I have become somewhat of a snob with my coffee in the last few years."

I waved away the apology with a hand and a warm smile. "Just remind me to not invite you by for coffee, then. I get cheap bags of the pre-ground stuff."

She grimaced, sticking out her tongue. "Gross. How do you even stay caffeinated?"

"Drink a lot." I winked. God, this was so easy. Years had passed, yet when I plopped down into her life, we seemed to pick up where we'd left off.

"Well," she said, turning back to her artistry, "don't think less of me because of my new preferences."

"Just as long as you've restricted your snobbery to coffee and music. Nothing worse than someone with poor taste in music."

Alisha's back was to me. She had her hair pulled up in a ponytail, exposing her thin neck. Her skin was pale and smooth. Memories of the thousands of times I'd lightly run my fingers along her neck, from her tiny earlobes to her shoulders, bombarded me and I gave my head a shake to dislodge that runaway thought train.

"Your place is really cozy. I like it," I said as I looked around the open floor plan, from my place at the kitchen island into the living room. When I'd walked into her reading room, I'd seen no clue of anyone else in Alisha's life. Though I didn't expect her to have pictures of some guy in her kitchen, I was pleased to see the living room was also barren of them. Unless she had the pictures tucked away in the bedroom, the outward signs said she didn't have someone else in her life. "A little too girly for me, but very comfortable."

Alisha laughed, her sharp cheekbones peaking as her mouth spread. "Rev, if you had it your way, everything would be black." Her hand dropped from the grinder. "Oh, Lord. Please tell me your place has at least a little color."

"Splashes here and there."

She rolled her eyes, filled the reservoir with freshly ground beans, and turned the coffee maker on. "Women aren't fond of bachelor pads. Especially in old men."

"Hey, you're older than me."

Alisha put a hand on her chest. "You dare talk about a woman's age?"

Damn, I missed this.

"Plus, I'm not bothered trying to impress women with my interior decorating. If they don't like men with guitars, stacks of magazines on the coffee table and socks draped over furniture, I'm not for them."

"Not on the market, huh?"

Ha! She asked first. I was only happy to answer. "No. I'm so wrapped up in things, I don't have time to figure out how 'the market' works anymore."

Her sparkling eyes widened. "Isn't that the truth? An entirely new game, I swear."

My heart felt ten pounds heavier. "You've been dating?"

"Recently? No." She turned away to the cupboard and retrieved two mugs. Setting them next to the brew, she grabbed the creamer from the refrigerator. "You still do sugar?"

She had been dating? Ouch.

We'd been living separate lives for years. Why wouldn't she? Alisha was beautiful and intelligent. A go-getter. A confident woman who knew what she wanted and went after it. Secure in the sexiest of senses.

Coffee. I needed to focus on coffee, and not my ex-wife's love life. "I'm cutting back, but yes."

Alisha nodded. "Try to keep cutting down. Sugar is terrible for you. Especially the mountain of it you used to load into your coffee."

I smiled in the safety of knowing she could see sentiment plaster itself all over my face. Why in the world had I waited so long to see her?

Because she's moved on, and you should too, dumbass. A long time ago.

"You'd be proud," I said, trying to shut down the inner monologue. "I actually have more coffee in my coffee than sugar nowadays. Of course, I replaced it with drowning the coffee with creamer."

"You're impossible." Alisha laughed lightly. "But progress is progress. We need to keep you around for as long as possible, so it's nice to hear that you're cutting out one bad thing."

When she wasn't an amazing woman, Alisha was a family practice physician. She was in the business of taking care of angels, most of whom were, like me, incapable or unwilling to take care of themselves. Unlike me, she didn't seem jaded by her job because here she was, making sure she snuck in morsels to reinforce healthier habits.

"Trying, at least," I said. "Now, if I could just figure out how to cut back on the truly unhealthy shit in my life."

She threw her head back, her ponytail swaying. "There it is."

"What?"

"The raw language. I was wondering if you were trying to impress me. You've been here for ten minutes and haven't sworn. I was starting to worry."

"And what if I was trying?"

"To impress me?" she said, closing the refrigerator door slowly.

"Yeah."

The corners of her mouth turned up. Slightly. But they went up instead of down, and that was the important observation. "I'd ask why."

I took the coffee from her. "Thank you. Why wouldn't I want to impress you?"

"Do you make a habit of going around the Third, worried about the mark you're leaving?"

"Hardly."

"So, why me?"

I couldn't tell if she was messing with me or flirting. Alisha was at her best, now as she'd always been. This part of her personality, so much like a guy's in that respect, was one thing that attracted me to her in the first place. She had this knack of constructing an edge and having me walk along it voluntarily. I'd seen her do it to close friends at dinner parties or game nights, too. Alisha didn't do it because she was an asshole or manipulative. She was smart and enjoyed intellectual play. Angels who got what she was about were as stimulated by interactions as she was. Angels who didn't understand her eventually became intimidated and usually drifted away. To me, there was never a dull time. Beauty. Intellect. The ability to captivate a room.

She's hot like that.

"Because you're you."

Alisha lifted her cup, blowing on the hot concoction of premium water run through ground beans. "Interesting."

I made a sound that came out like a cat's purr, not meaning to. I covered the sound with words. "Because I respect you. And even after everything we've been through, you're still important to me."

"As you are to me." She sat the cup on the island, wrapping her hands around it and leaning forward. "So why don't you tell me what this visit is about? You're here for something more than getting a lesson on why you don't scrimp on coffee. What is it?"

Did I hear an eagerness in her voice? Was that simply my imagination? Why did I worry? This was why I'd avoided conversations with her that didn't center on our divorce and splitting up our communal property. Why I hadn't visited her or asked her to dinner in years? When you keep feelings stuffed deep inside, you don't have to deal with them.

"Give me the real deal," she said, prodding.

After a second to make sure I didn't sound like a school-age boy being broken up with, I said, "To be completely honest, I wanted to talk to you about the Reapers."

"The Reapers? Really?" she said, pulling back and her face lighting. "What about them? Did you finally get a promotion?"

I snorted. "I wish. I'm still doing the shitty stuff they've had me doing for millennia."

"Oh. Sorry. I was really hoping you got a break, and that's why you were here. To celebrate."

I stared at my coffee cup. It was easier than looking into her captivating eyes. "I don't see them changing. Sadly, I'm stuck."

"Then how can I help? You know I tried to stay away from that—" She caught herself, pinching her lips closed.

Many of our arguments centered on the Reapers and the dirty deeds they assigned me. A quarter of our marital problems originated from me being gone so often. The other seventy-five percent was 'the why' of why I was away. Alisha had always been a fan of mine, my biggest cheerleader and supporter. But she most definitely was not a fan of what I did for a living.

"Mess." I smiled, relieving her of the duty of categorizing what the Reapers were and the result of their impact on her life and mine. "It's all a mess, and it's getting worse. Bad stuff is going down."

"I don't want to know," Alisha said, her voice going flat and reminding me of what she sounded like, more times than not, toward the end of our marriage.

I nodded. "I know. The last thing I wanted to do was bother you with that, anyway. Really? I just wanted to say I'm sorry and catch up with you." I sat straighter in the chair, trying to summon the courage to say the two words I needed to say. Why was 'I'm sorry,' harder to say than staring down the barrel of a gun or facing a beast of legend? My pulse was a chaotic mess, speeding and jumping in rhythm. The world outside narrowed around this kitchen. I forced the words out. "I'm sorry, Alisha. Sorry for all the shit the Order put us through when we were together, and for how I reacted to it. I'm sorry you became my verbal punching bag when I couldn't deal with the shit I had going on. I feel horrible that I blamed you for what they were putting me through. Sorry, I yelled every time I was mad at myself for being dumb enough to get suckered into agreeing to their deal. And for being too stupid to know how to get out of it."

"You never had a choice, Rev," she said softly. "They've been around a lot longer than any of you. They know what they're doing, and how to manipulate situations. It's so gross, how they make victims out of Reapers. But especially you, because you have all that." She stopped, clicking her nails on the handle of her mug. "Other stuff they dump on you. I hate it for you."

"Thank you," I said, feeling worse than when I opened my mouth. "But this isn't about asking you to feel for me. For too many years, I've kept shit bottled up inside. About you. I was hurt and, honestly, despondent after the divorce. For a long time. Too long."

"Why? I thought we handled it pretty well."

"We did. Far better than Jakeb and Tammi. Remember them?"

She giggled behind her mug, which she'd raised to her mouth. "Oh, God. That was a mess. What drama. Compared to them, we should be proud of ourselves for handling a divorce like adults."

"Compared to anyone, we should be."

"Here, here." She raised her cup.

I raised mine, and we clinked them together over the

island counter.

In that quiet moment, I made my next mistake, but sometimes men, when driven by emotion, say stupid things. "We should have never gotten a divorce."

A moment of vulnerability. Something I'd meant to mumble into my empty brain chamber. Not something for this semi-public consumption.

But it was out now, hanging in the air. Dangling between us awkwardly. Drawing attention like a couple trading nasty insults over dinner at an expensive restaurant during what was supposed to be a delightful night out.

Alisha relieved the pressure with soft words. "Rev, I couldn't be around that anymore. You weren't you toward the end, and I... I was no good at helping you. No good for you."

"You were always good for me."

"I couldn't save you."

"I couldn't save me, Alisha. That wasn't your failure. It was all mine. I'm to blame."

Her face was blank, until it wasn't. Her lips cracked. "Well, Pher too, for getting you into this mess."

"The bastard."

Alisha slid sideways down the island until she stood directly in front of me. "Can I ask something and have you answer honestly?"

"Of course." My throat tightened.

"Have you been beating yourself up over this for all these years?"

"Worse." Try as I might, I couldn't meet her eyes. "Believe it or not, what you're seeing is the result of a lot of self-talk and friend therapy. I was worse for months after the divorce. For a couple of years, actually."

She reached over and took my hand, squeezing it. The world never felt so right. "Don't do that to yourself. I never blamed you. Well, except those few times you were a real ass."

We snickered together. Two voices lifted as one. Just like old times. The good times.

She squeezed harder. "Seriously. We both gave it our all. Neither of us cheated on our marriage, emotionally or otherwise." She stopped, breaking the hold she had on my hand and standing straight, looking around her home as if it held the answers. "Sometimes, life just happens. Being immortal isn't easy, but being the Reaper Minister proved impossible for me as his spouse. What happened, happened. Neither of us should look back with regrets, because we did the best we could, for as long as we could. Life just beat us." She spread her hands, smiling. "But look. We're here, together, chatting as if no time has passed. And that's important. Life may have won the battle, but it didn't win the war. I have my patients. You're still making a massive difference in the lives of the mortals you help. You're filling a great need that no other angel can. Rev, you're special."

"So are you," I said quietly, meaning it in a completely different context than her comment.

"They're lucky to have you."

"Damn right they are."

She chittered. "You're doing important work and have been. If you feel you need to apologize to make peace with yourself, then I accept. But please don't feel as if I needed any apology. I never did. I just wanted both of us to be happy."

"I wish we could have been happy together."

Alisha's lips pinched so hard, small dimples appeared. "Me too, Rev."

A moment of thick silence passed, both of us finding our attention drawn to different things. Alisha's home received my scrutiny. She analyzed the contents of her cup. Neither of us said a word. But when I looked her way, it pleasantly surprised me to see her now looking at me. And we burst out in unrestrained laughter.

After the spat passed, she wiped the corner of her eye. "Oh

God, it's so good to see you again. We should do this more often."

"Sure, if your boyfriend doesn't mind."

She was halfway through a drink of coffee and nearly choked on it. She coughed, setting her cup down quickly. "You're terrible at this. Just ask next time, if you're curious. No. I don't have a boyfriend. No. I don't want one. I'm too busy with the job. Who knows how much asking around you've done? Maybe Jimmy or Abaddon gave it up, but in case they didn't, did you know I'm looking at starting my own practice?"

"Really? That's amazing. I'm happy for you."

"Thank you. There's a lot of work to do, but I have the foundation set and even have a lawyer combing through the leasing agreement for a space. I'm very excited. Sadly for the men of the Third Level, I lack the time or inclination to entertain them."

"Suckers. Their loss. But seriously, that's awesome. No less than you deserve."

"Here's to hoping you get what you deserve too," she said, raising her cup in a toast. We clinked cups one last time.

"The wheels might be in motion," I said.

"Oh?"

"I'm on a big job right now, so I used it as an excuse to set someone else up to be the Interim Minister."

My ex-wife read my devilish smile. "And you're hoping this Interim proves themselves to the Order and you'll make your move to be removed?"

Goofy knew no bounds like it knew me at that moment. Over the course of a single conversation, Alisha had wiped away years of melancholy. Thankfully, she didn't have a mirror nearby for me to confirm that as the truth. "Am I that transparent?"

"Only to me. That's how well I know you."

Yes, she knew me that well. Better than anyone in the

Upperworld, now or ever. That's the way it was. The way it would always be because she was the only one I'd ever fully open myself to.

We talked until we both realized we could pass the month catching up. Both of us had other things to do, and unless I'm completely losing my mind, she seemed as resistant as me to ending the visit. But demands called, because they always did.

As we said our goodbyes, swearing we would catch up again when things settled down for both of us, I kept that thought close. My steps were lighter, freed from the burden of carrying decades of guilt over ruining such a solid love. Freeing me from shouldering the responsibility. Now I could focus on what needed my attention.

No one might ever understand me and my reasoning, but Alisha could. She had and even did now, even though we'd lived separate lives for far too long. I didn't have to justify anything to her. I didn't even have to explain my motivations. She just got me.

And in that, I found a peace I hadn't known in a long, long time.

Anapheil was the Interim Minister. Alisha didn't hate me or even blame me for ruining what could have been a lifetime of special memories. For the first time in a decade, I saw a light at the end of the tunnel. As an angel, I promise, it isn't a white light. That's a jaded stereotype. But this was a glimmer of hope.

Calm wrapped around me for the walk home. I would have hugged it back, but that would have just looked weird. Don't think for a second I didn't hum a tune all the way back to my Upperworld place.

The behemoth better bring its A-game because, after this reassuring visit with the only woman I ever loved, I was ready for a fight.

13

STING OF THE BUMBLEBEE

"You look different," Billee said from the passenger seat.

"Huh?"

She dangled a finger in the air, looping it to ring my face. "This. You're, I don't know. Different. What happened?"

"I took your advice," I said, almost proudly. Which was strange. I'm a private man. Personal business is supposed to remain personal. Not surprising for someone who doesn't like to be touched, I also don't subscribe to the whole 'my business is everyone's business' concept. Too much emotional touching.

Billee slapped my arm lightly. She didn't know about my boundaries. My fault, not hers. "You went to talk to her?"

"Yep."

I'd never tell Billee outright, but I'm sure she could guess from my grin, that I was still floating from my visit with Alisha.

My partner guffawed. She didn't chuckle. She didn't laugh. It was a legitimate guffaw. "You should see your face. You look like a teenager."

"Yeah, well, I have you to thank for it. Or blame, if this goes to shit."

"Hey, I'm only responsible for getting you to talk to her. What the two of you discussed is on you." Billee's voice changed, sounding more serious, her counselor persona coming out. "How are you doing with it? Are you okay?"

"Very. It's weird."

"How so?"

We were at a stoplight, so I had a moment to face her. "It's not like we agreed to try again or anything. Just knowing she's okay. Knowing her and me, whatever we are, are on good terms. That I was wrong about how she thought of me. I don't know, Billee. This is strange."

"Yes, I can see how experiencing your feelings would be weird. A lot of my male clients are like that too. Stubborn. All of you."

"Don't blame us. We're trained to be tough."

"Feelings are for wimps, right?"

I winked at her, and the light turned green. I took us across the intersection. The old brewery hovered a block away. "Good to know there's a woman out there who understands our plight."

"Impossible," she said with a chuckle. "But I'm glad you did it. I hope you are too."

"I am."

"Good." She pointed at the section of the aged structure poking up from the buildings around it. "Is the entire group going to be there?"

"They better be. I told Bolt to bring them."

"Bolt?"

"The kid with the long hair. The ones we caught cutting the locks at the storage units."

"Ah, with bolt cutters? Thus his name?"

"See? You get me."

"Very creative. Are they coming willingly?"

"As opposed to?"

"Rev," she said brusquely. "Are they, or do you have them

under the influence of the stone?"

I shook my head. "The stone doesn't work like that. Its effects aren't forever. Whatever influence I put on them, it wears off. Sometimes only a few minutes. Sometimes, hours or days. But whenever they come out of the influence, they're always confused. Disoriented, too, depending on how much effort I put into it. They remember only what I want or tell them to recall."

"Nothing slips through?"

I bobbed a shoulder. "No. Plus, since most of my business would be considered crazy talk if they could remember afterward and shared with someone…"

"They wouldn't share at all?"

"Bingo. So, no, they're not under the influence of the Soul stone. They're coming of their own volition and the fact I promised Bolt I'd pay them. Seems teens still like money."

"Go figure," Billee said. "Well, I'm glad they're not being controlled by that thing. You know I don't like it. It's as gross as this." She lifted her arm. The gold bracelet, the trinket I'd gifted her to lock her into my service, dangled just below her glove. "At least I can cut off mine. They don't get that choice when you put them under the spell of that stone."

I chuckled. "Have you tried to cut the bracelet?"

Billee blinked. "No. Why?"

"Because you can't. Try if you don't believe me, but you could take an industrial saw to that thing and it'll still be on your wrist long after the blade dulled. You and it are one. Partners for life."

Her arm dropped. Her gaze locked on the rotting building.

We pulled into the parking lot. I parked and shut off the car, turning to my silent partner. "Billee, you're going to have to get okay with the ambiguity of morality on this job or it'll drive you crazy." Something flickered across her face as her expression darkened. "No, that's not right. Crazy isn't the end state. It'll kill you if you don't accept that this," I stopped and pointed at her wrist, "is your reality."

She stared out the window at the dilapidated building. "I thought the Rev who came back from his conversation with his ex would be a kinder Rev."

"Do you want that guy to disrespect you and fill your head full of shit, or do you want him to show he truly cares by being forthright and honest?" She didn't answer. Of course not. We both knew why. "That's how this Rev shows he cares. He doesn't lie. He doesn't pull punches. And he most definitely doesn't put those he cares about, and even those he doesn't, at risk by letting them think this is anything less than what it is."

I swear I could hear her teeth grinding. "How long?"

I slowed my breathing. A few months in the job wasn't long enough to get accustomed to all the unfairness of the gig. "How long for what?"

She looked at me, her bottom jaw jutting out. "How long did it take your other familiars to get used to this? To come to terms with the fact that they're slaves to an angel, their autonomy, lost forever. How long before I'm okay with this?"

I rocked my head, softening the blow the best I could, in tone and words. "Everyone is different. Most take years before they're fully okay with their fortunes. Some never come to terms. A lot of them never got the chance."

"This sucks."

"Yep. Stings, doesn't it?"

"Like a bee." Her hand was on the door handle. She looked out the window but aimed her words at me. "Thank you, Rev."

"For?"

"Respecting me enough to tell me the truth, even if I don't want to hear it."

"You're welcome."

She got out and walked to the building without waiting.

True to his word, Bolt had brought in the entire storage unit crew. They waited inside. Some of them sprawled out on dusty pallets, staring at their phones. Small clumps of teens hung in the corners, talking quietly. A few of the more rambunctious teens passed the time banging on the walls or trying to see who could throw a stainless steel pot onto the second-story mezzanine.

"Hey guys," I called out, drawing nearly sixty gazes. "Roundup."

The teens gathered around. A smattering moved more hurriedly than others. One tall, thin kid, in particular, hung back, pressing his phone forcefully with his thumbs.

"What's his deal?" I asked Bolt.

The leader of the teens flipped his long blond hair out of his face. "Oh, Gary? He's in a fight with his girlfriend."

"Good for him," I said, then pinched my finger and thumb between my lips and sent a piercing whistle shooting through the abandoned brewery. "Gary. On your feet. Let's go. Everyone's waiting on you. The quicker we get this over, the quicker you can get back to important things in your life."

The kid moped, but he complied. He threw in a stomp or two of petulance for good measure.

"Okay guys, any news? Has anyone seen anything out in the Olympics?"

The teens either shook their heads in negative response or looked at each other with partially confused expressions.

"Nothing?" I asked. "No one has seen or heard a single thing out of place?"

"I haven't been out. Got grounded last week," a redhead in the back said. A few of the boys near him chuckled.

"That's because you got busted drinking," a kid with a pock-marked complexion said, giving the first a shove for good measure.

The red-hair smiled. "Yeah, I did. But that party was awesome. And I got laid."

That brought more raucous laughter.

I rubbed my face. "Who has actually been out to the Olympics this week?"

Two hands went up.

"Guys, I need eyeballs out there. Did you not hear that I'm paying or does your generation not appreciate cold, hard cash?"

"I told them," Bolt said, with a half-shrug. "But it's tough. A lot of us have stuff after school. A bunch of us don't even have cars."

"Go together with someone who does," I said.

Billee leaned in. "They're teenagers."

I kept my groan to myself. "Guys, this is important work. You guys pull this off, and I'll see what I can do about bumping that pay. Sound like something that would help you make this a priority?"

Their shared smiles told me it would. The Order was going to have to figure out the reallocation of funds to pay these kids more than the going rate. All I cared about was getting solid leads and each one of them home safely.

"Good. I'll see what I can do. It'll be a handsome payday. Might pay for school for those of you who are smart enough to get into a trade school, college, or university. But the clock is ticking, and this is a time-limited offer. So get to work."

"We're still just looking for any signs or word about this big animal, right?" Bolt asked. "Nothing else?"

"Bingo."

"And you'll pay us just for that?" a handsome kid standing next to Bolt said.

"That's the deal. Paid on delivery once I get eyes on the animal. That's all." The enticement of a payday brightened their diverse expressions. Still, they were innocent mortal civilians, I reminded myself. "But, and I'm not joking. Don't do anything more. See if you can find tracks, a nest, rumors about a sighting, or anyone who has. I need an area of the forest. That's it. None of you, and I mean this, none of you are to go after this thing. Don't follow it. Don't hunt it. I don't care how good of a shot your daddy claims he is. I don't care if you think you're the biggest badass in your school." My gaze fell on Bolt. "You shared what I told you to?"

"Yeah," he said with a nod. "Just like you said. It's gonna be humongous and that it'd scare the shit out of us if we saw it."

That brought a round of juvenile chuckling. I let them have it and waited until it faded.

"Good," I said, swaying my gaze over the crowd of teenage boys, "because this isn't a joke. If you are unlucky enough to come across it, you better hope you're far enough away that it doesn't notice you. You won't come home if it does. I promise that." More than a few Adam's Apples bobbed. Good. "Ask around and see what your friends know. Maybe someone in school has already seen something and you'll be the key to them opening up about it. Be smart. Be careful. Going around school, talking about giant animals is a good way to ensure you never get a date until you graduate."

"A few of us are going out snowshoeing this weekend," Bolt said, pointing at a big kid across the crowd. "Rick said he and his family are going hunting."

I nodded at Bolt, then at the kid named Rick. "Good. All of you, be smart and safe. Rick? Make sure no one in your family fools themselves. I don't care what you're packing. You won't bring this thing down. Trust me. Don't make this be the last time I see your smiling face."

"Yes, sir," Rick said, his chin wrinkling as he swallowed.

"Alright boys," I said loudly, "you'll hear from me through Bolt." I got confused looks, so I pointed out their ringleader. "My nickname for him. A term of endearment. I promise. Anyway, he'll spread word when I want to gather again. If any of you get information for me in the meantime, message him and he'll get us together. Understood?"

I got head nods and uh-huhs from the group, which was about as much as I could expect from teens.

We left, but the boys hung back. When we were back outside Billee's place, she paused when getting out of the car. "Do you feel dirty involving teens in this?"

"Yep."

Her face scrunched. "Then why are we? There's got to be another way. The Upperworld could do something."

I shook my head. "They can't. Not without risking a reaction from demons. Sorry, Billee. This is on us and whatever resources I can scrounge together. I'll do everything I can to protect these kids, but I need help. The kids aren't the only ones I've got working to find the behemoth."

"Oh?"

"The group we stopped from beating the man in the park?"

"They're involved too? Jesus, Rev."

"No, he's not helping. Though I wouldn't mind. Sorry, but it's just you, me, and a bunch of civilians I'm putting in harm's way. Welcome to the life of being a Reaper's familiar. Remember what I said about the ambiguity of morality?"

She rolled her eyes and sighed. "Yes." After a moment's pause, she asked, "Does it get easier?"

"Nope."

"This sucks," she said, and not for the first time.

"Yep. I'll see you later. I'm headed to a couple of towns bordering the forest to see what I can dig up. Can't have the kids doing all the work."

Billee leaned down to look at me across the car. "You are? Do you want me to go with you? Make sure you don't piss off demons with your work or something?"

"No, I'll be careful. Go have a good rest of your day. I'll kick up this bee's nest on my own. That way, maybe I'll be the only one stung."

14

HITTING THE JACKPOT

HOODSPORT IS A SMALL TOWN YOU'D MISS IF YOU SNEEZED WHILE passing through, driving the speed limit—which I rarely do. It's one of those places that makes you nervous to visit if you're not a local. They've got each other's faces memorized and they don't trust those from the outside world. Secluded, rural communities can be like that, regardless of where in the Overworld you are.

I imagine I set several expectations when I walked into the bar and grill in town—literally the only place of entertainment for the entire community. At six feet and still in decent fighting shape for my age, donning my black leather duster, and with long hair that would make the more conservative community members squirm, I stood out.

But I had a job to do. They could drown their preconceived opinions about me in their cheap beer if they had a problem with non-conforming appearances. Plus, one of the beautiful revelations about the aging process for angels—and I've spoken with enough mortals over the years to know it rings true for them as well—is that the older I get, the less I care about what people think. The less I care about politics too. World affairs, pop culture, and most definitely, perceptions about me were included in that mix.

If anyone was going to embrace the whole 'aging rock star' vibe, I was that guy.

Eight heads turned my way. Seven remained on me while I took a seat. Only a woman, sitting by herself under a wide rectangular mirror displaying a cheap corporate beer company's logo, looked away. I ignored the other seven, keeping my third eye tempered for now. I was here to ask around about strange sightings, not to get flooded with the life stories of these small-town folk.

What lingered in the air inside the bar made me think no one had cracked a window since the nineteen seventies. Added to that gem, I was pretty sure patrons smoked in here whenever they thought an outsider wouldn't call the Health Department on this "fine" establishment.

"Whatcha havin'?" the husky woman behind the bar asked. She was missing a front tooth.

"Whiskey sour, please," I said, pulling up on the stool. The red plastic seat cover had split open so long ago that the cushion inside was rubbed, or scooped, away in small divots. Instead of trying to get comfortable on the stool that looked as uncomfortable as the looks I was receiving from the men on either side, I stood while she made my drink.

When the bartender finished, she said, "Eight bucks."

I slid my card to her. "Keep the tab open. I'll be here for a bit."

She snatched it like I'd stolen it from her and walked away to chat with another patron who might have been her husband.

I found a seat closer to the front door that also placed me behind anyone coming in. The spot would give me a slight advantage, putting any new entrant in my targets before I could fall into theirs. The things you pick up after spending thousands of years hunting and stalking demons, monsters, and rebellious angels, I swear.

Did I expect trouble? No. I had already stopped at a few spots around town, which meant I'd already covered the entire community so many people spent their entire lives in and around, and I detected nothing untoward or unsettling. At each stop, I'd used my third eye. My visions are limited to a half-mile radius, but in a small town like Hoodsport, that meant I could canvas it in a single visit. That was the plan, and this was my last stop in today's execution of it. With this being the town's only drinking hole, I figured I'd camp out and see what came in.

Communities like these are perfect for hunting a behemoth hiding in the thousands of acres of wilderness the beast supposedly called home. Unlike city people, these hardy mortals spent a lot of their time outside, in the surrounding woods and trails, either hunting or tearing up the beautiful planet with recreation vehicles. Towns like this one might be small in population, but they were huge in potential, and even though I'd come up empty so far, I had hope.

The six-hundred-thousand acres of mountainous national forest was looped by Highway 101—a misnomer, really. For vast stretches, it's nothing but a two-lane road. But it circum- navigates the peaks and valleys of the forest hiding the behe- moth, dotted by small towns such as Hoodsport. Given enough time, I was going to hit the jackpot in one of these rural communities. I simply had to keep playing the numbers game.

Everyone in the bar might be from the same community, but they still acted like city dwellers. Broken off into clusters of two or three, few interacted with anyone outside their group. An old man who looked more at home on a farm sat by himself. The only woman in the place, the only one who didn't care to stare me up and down when I'd entered, was the only other person sitting alone. Neither looked bothered by that fact.

The whiskey sour was tart. Around these parts, I didn't imagine anyone tested the bartender's skills beyond having her pop cheap beer cans open. This place shrieked that it hadn't evolved to the stage of stocking bottled beer yet.

I grimaced through another sip of my drink. In case a break fell in my lap and I needed to stay long enough to outlast the whisky sour, I was going to have to go with beer and avoid asking her to stretch beyond her capabilities by making a second mixed drink.

I winced and set the expensive drink down, opening my third eye.

The rush of information was as intense as always, a reason I kept the third eye suppressed most times. I don't need that kind of bombardment of stimuli normally.

My vision is a special treat. Something I alone possess, at least as far as I know. No other Reaper has ever mentioned being able to do anything of the sort, and even my personal conversations with Pher haven't hinted at him or anyone he knows having a third eye. With it, I can see the past and the future of those around me. I don't always need to have eyes on them, either, which can be a powerful advantage or a terrible burden, depending on the circumstances or need.

The dirty secrets. The funny teenage mistakes. First heart-breaks. Devastating losses. Inexplicable joys. All and every-thing. When I opened my third eye, I knew all there was to know about the mortals around me. I knew what they'd done and what they were going to do. I saw the loves they had and the ones they were going to lose. The ability allowed me to see how they lived, were going to live out their lives, and also how and when each one of them was going to die.

Sifting through the personal histories and futures of one mortal is a lot of work. Doing it for nearly a dozen was a headache. But if I was going to find this cursed behemoth, I was going to have to use every tool in my toolbox. Thankfully, thousands of years of practice made me adept at focusing my attention.

The old man sitting alone at the bar better enjoy his drink. This was going to be his last visit. Next week, he'd die of a heart attack, alone in his kitchen.

The pair of gruff guys dressed in camouflage, looking like they'd just come from a hunting trip, were actually lovers and hid that fact from their friends and family. From a neighboring town, they came here for drinks and to get out of the house, where they were safe from suspicion and criticism from anyone who suspected and refused to accept them. They'd get married, even though it would be another ten years before the stars aligned and they could pull it off. Serious trials and tribulations lay before them. They'd end up happy and spend long lives together, outliving many of the people who'd reject them when they discovered their relationship. Love would trump hate in the end. The bartender would go on making lousy mixed drinks for another twenty-something years before she'd stop to live off her social security check in a trailer on the outskirts of town, kept company by seven cats and a goat. I didn't bother to look further into her story. I doubted it would be one with a satisfying ending.

None of their stories revealed anything of interest or use. Not until I sifted through the life of the woman sitting by herself underneath the mirror emblazoned with the beer company logo.

She was divorced, wouldn't remarry, and would actually live a fulfilling life, embracing the experiences domestic freedom provided her. At the moment, she was struggling with her sexuality, being raised in a conservative Christian family. Within a few years, she'd come to peace with who she was and find fulfillment. A broad woman, she'd learned to present an over-confident persona because it kept assholes away. The third eye wasn't required to tell this woman experienced some bad times in her past.

As interesting as her life was going to be, she was struggling right now. And I knew why. And, no, I don't feel bad that it excited me. She had seen the behemoth.

Last week, she was snowshoeing in the Olympics. When heading home, she drove one of the forestry roads, taking her time and enjoying the experience. The sun sets early in this part of the world at this time of year, and even though she'd gotten a proper start on the drive, to ensure she was out of the mountains, dusk was already falling. In the gloom, the behemoth was tromping across the open face of a hill. This witness nearly drove her truck off the road.

That's why she was here, now. The sight of the behemoth had, understandably, upset her. Spending time alone in her isolated house was not something she was crazy about, so she'd spent the last few days in town, around people, in any business with open doors. At home, she was a wreck until the next morning, when she could go out and be around others again.

I had to talk to her.

In a lot of ways, men have it easy. We don't face the same challenges as women, and we often get a pass to do things they're not allowed to do, by contemporary standards—but trust me, those things have changed little since mortals invented religion. But we don't have carte blanche or full privilege either. In some ways, the roles are reversed. In public, any woman could walk up to any man and start a conversation, and no one would think twice. But when a guy does, especially to a woman on her own, in a bar, he falls under immediate suspicion. From everyone. Not just the woman he's trying to talk to, but any observer. Most question his motives, and those who don't question him don't bother because they've already filled in the blanks in his storyline.

I'm well aware of that reality, so I approached the troubled woman with caution.

Her eyes flicked in my direction multiple times as I approached. She was very aware of her surroundings and good at disguising that awareness.

"Hi," I said with a friendly smile. She kept her head directed down, not recognizing my arrival. "Do you mind if I ask you a question?"

"I'm not interested in a drink. Or company." Her voice was husky as if decades of cigarette smoking had rotted away her esophagus. Untrue. She hadn't smoked since her last experiment with nicotine in high school.

"I'm not interested in buying you a drink. They're overpriced and shitty."

One of the pair of future lovers at the nearby table chuckled, unable to hide his eavesdropping.

"What do you want, then?" she said brusquely.

"A question about something, if you have a moment?" I wanted to do this here and now, but the topic was tricky. After all, I wasn't after her opinion on local or state politics. This wasn't something you could just drop in her lap with a dozen prying sets of ears in such a small space. It didn't help that she wasn't exactly the welcoming type offering the empty chair on the other side of the small round table.

"I'm busy."

I pointed at the cell phone on the table, next to an empty glass, the remains of her drink. "You're surfing the internet. Researching what you saw the other day, out in the forest. But you're not finding anything, because no one has seen what you saw. Or, at least, anyone who has seen what you did hasn't been crazy enough to blog about it. Research all day, but you're still going to go home, scared out of your mind, and none the wiser. Unless you give me a few minutes."

Her mouth fell open.

"Hey Stacy, is that guy bothering you?" one of the lovers disguised as a hunter asked.

Behind me, a chair scraped. I almost turned to face whatever tough guy was going to play white knight in this scenario, but the woman snapped her head. "No. I'm okay. Thanks, Larry. If he gets out of hand, I'll kick his ass."

A few chuckles later, everyone went back to their own business.

Gesturing with an arm at the chair, I said, "Can I sit?"

In a restricted tone, she said, "Yeah. Go ahead."

As I took a seat, she adjusted on her chair, scooting closer as she shot glances around the bar.

"I promise, I won't say anything to anyone," I said. "I know you're questioning yourself. Questioning if you really saw what you think you did. But you did, trust that."

"I thought I was going crazy."

"You weren't. You're not."

"What is it? I've tried looking it up, but I'm not finding anything. It's almost like..." She looked around again, tucking her chin to her chest as if she hoped to disappear into herself. "Almost looks like a dinosaur. But that's crazy. Right?"

"Here's the thing," I said, approaching the topic carefully. She already thought she was losing her mind, and she'd lived every minute of her life after seeing the behemoth in fear. I didn't need to add further incomprehensible things to the mix. Stacy had enough to deal with. "I know this might sound suspect, but trust me. You saw a giant animal you don't understand. Something that keeps you up at night. Right?"

Her fingers rolled in toward her palms. "Yes."

"Listen, I have no desire to expose you. I'm actually here to help. Though I probably don't look the part," I said, and ignored her instant assessment of my appearance, "I'm hunting it, and I need help."

She scoffed at that. "Hunting it? Good luck with that."

"I need luck, yes. But I need information too. I don't know

where it is or what it, specifically, looks like. Maybe you can help me?"

"You're hunting it, but don't know what it looks like?" Another scoff, and a quick look toward the logo'ed mirror. "What? Did someone hire you or something?"

She was prying for information, wanting to believe my message and hoping I could make sense of her recent experience. To her, I was a lifeline. She just didn't know if I'd snap when she was halfway to safety, so she exercised caution. I couldn't blame her.

"Yeah. Something like that. Can you help? I need to know what you saw and where you saw it. Then I'll get out of your hair. I promise."

"You won't believe me," she said to the wall.

"I will," I said, putting emphasis on the words to help her hear my conviction. "Nothing you say will sound crazy. Come on, help me help you. What other choice do you have? Once I walk out of here, you'll never see me again. Do you want me to leave? The one person who can help squash your nightmares? Or do you want to see the back of me, knowing that every night, from today forward, could have been different but won't be, because you chose not to trust me enough to talk about what you saw?"

Stacy clenched and unclenched her jaw, still staring at the wall. A thin pool of tears formed in the corner of her eyes. She inhaled stiffly and faced me.

Reaching for her cell phone, I feared I'd pushed too hard, and she was about to run from the bar, leaving me behind to deal with the local country boys who looked more than ready to defend a lady's honor.

Instead, she unlocked the screen, flipped to her photo gallery, and scrolled down a few rows. I don't make a habit of looking at other people's phones, especially when they're scrolling through their pictures. Usually, that's a good way to learn something about someone you never wanted to pull back the blankets on. But Stacy wasn't making a secret of what her phone contained. She was putting it out there like it was a mechanism to keep her committed to accepting my offer of help.

"You want to know what I saw? Here." She clicked one of the small tiles.

That's when I noticed she hadn't chosen a picture for me, but a video. When it began playing, the sound of Stacy breathing heavily blared from the phone and she scrambled to turn it down. None of the other patrons noticed, and she visibly relaxed and placed the phone between us again, turning it just enough to give me a perpendicular perspective.

"This is by Upper Lena Lake," she said. "There's a hiking trail, but I don't always stick to them because I like to find out-of-the-way places to camp and explore."

"You camp out there? Alone?"

"I can handle myself," she said as if I'd offended her.

"I meant because it's still winter. That has to be miserable."

"Not if you're prepared and you know what you're doing." She tapped the video. "Plus, I was out doing a day hike. I don't enjoy being around people, and I know the trail system well. I spend a lot of time out there." Her fingernail clicked on the phone's screen. "That's when I shot this."

She was watching for my reaction.

She'd shot the video from behind a boulder. Stacy had been standing too close and kept ducking down behind the gray stone. At first, I only heard her breathing, and all I saw was her constant up and down as she hid and then peeked above the rock.

"Keep watching," she said, sounding haunted. "It's coming."

Before the camera's perspective rose above the boulder, I heard what I wanted to hear. The rumble of a behemoth's footfall shook the world. In the video, Stacy gasped. Sitting across from me in the bar, she inhaled a shaking breath.

The distance from her hiding space to the behemoth was difficult to discern from the video, especially with dusk obscuring details. It could have been three hundred yards or half a mile. Phones these days are impressive creations, capable of so much, and improving so rapidly that I can't keep up. The video she shot was clear enough to convince me she'd tripped across Yahweh's creature. Regardless of how far away it was, the behemoth was prominent. The blasted thing's girth filled the screen.

"Good God," I said. I couldn't tell the exact size of the beast because it had just gotten to its feet, and the valley was clear. From the lake to the line of trees in the near distance, I had no reference to compare it against.

Each time it stepped, a boom rumbled in the phone's tiny speakers.

The beast looked reptilian. Two horns jutted from its head. Its face resembled that of a crocodile, but its body was more like a dog's. Except spiky scales covered its body that was taller than a 757 airliner. Scale was impossible to determine, but a wild-ass guess led me to believe its tail was at least twenty feet long. That would take the total length of the behemoth to a minimum of forty feet.

On all fours, the creature was so heavy its clawed feet sank into the valley floor as it moved to the lake before walking out into its waters. The behemoth stopped halfway across.

"That lake is about thirty-five feet deep at its deepest. Pretty shallow, but what does that say about that thing?" Stacy said.

"It's fucking huge."

She extended a finger, just about to pause the video, when I noticed something else in the small frame.

"Wait!"

She jerked her hand back and almost snatched the phone.

I grabbed it first, holding it up for her and trying with all my might to keep my voice down. "Did you see that?"

She looked from her phone in my possession to me, and back again. "What? I told you it was crazy." She scowled. "You said you were going to help. Give me my phone."

"No. Here, I mean." I paused the video and pointed at a spot on the screen near the lake's far bank. "What's that? Did you shoot another video or zoom in?"

Stacy squinted at the spot. "No. I didn't. I didn't see that when I shot the video. The—the..." At a loss for words, she flicked her hand at the screen. "I was focused on the animal. I swear, I didn't even see that person."

Well, shit. Just when I thought I'd gotten a bigger break than expected. Yes, it was wonderful to know what the behemoth looked like and its rough location in the vast forest. But the tease of seeing someone in the video, close to the lake, was frustrating. Stacy was too far away to capture who it was, and even if she'd noticed them and thought to zoom in, the resolution wouldn't have provided an identity.

Still, the video was enough. Whoever stood at the lake wasn't running from the behemoth. Instead, it almost looked like they were watching the beast recreate in the mountain lake's depths. No fear. No apprehension or revulsion. Whoever it was, they were comfortable being close to the monstrosity.

Which meant someone was controlling the beast. And that meant someone had a purpose for the behemoth.

I snagged a napkin, making Stacy jump. "Sorry," I said, handing her phone back. "Do you have a pen?"

"Yes." She reached into her jacket pocket and handed it to me.

I scribbled my email address on the napkin and slid it to her. "Please email me that video. I swear I'll leave you alone. I won't forward your information to anyone. But I need that video. Can you do that?"

"Yes. Of course." She stopped and swallowed. "Are you really going to go after it?"

"Yes, I am." Standing, I stopped myself from racing out of the bar, remembering I was dealing with a scared mortal who didn't understand what she'd witnessed. Life as an angel assassin can be strange, especially when you have to deal with the supernatural constantly. Sometimes I forget I'm dealing with mortals, and the things they have witnessed are things no mortal should ever witness. "And if I do my job, you won't have to worry about having nightmares about that thing anymore."

"And if it attacks you? What then? Is there anyone else who is going to help?"

"Fat chance. I'm your only hope." I tapped the napkin. "Please email me that video. Now, if you can."

I was halfway to the bar to retrieve my credit card when Stacy called out. "Good luck!"

Without looking back, I gave her an appreciative wave, knowing I was going to need more than luck to take down the behemoth and its beastmaster.

15

AGAINST THE ODDS

THE PROBLEM WITH POLITICS IS POLITICIANS. WITHOUT THEM, politics might be productive, maybe even enjoyable. Sort of like a healthy debate, just without all the lingering bullshit that harms others' lives.

Probably one reason I was never successful in removing myself from the Reapers. I suck at playing politics.

But that didn't mean I didn't have my own game to play. Just because I'm no good at the elitist game doesn't mean I haven't cut my teeth on a more rudimentary level. That's why, without breaking for sleep, I was back in the Upperworld, calling on Anapheil and the Reapers.

It took a few hours to round everyone who could show up. Even with billions in the Overworld asleep, the Reapers are still stretched thin at the best of times. Rounding everyone up is impossible. Getting as many together at one time, in one place, is the best the Reaper Minister or the Interim Minister could ever hope for.

But this was necessary, and Anapheil Icogto proved to have an effective hand on everyone's whereabouts.

She glided in my direction when I approached the door of the small arena. "This is bad."

"Yes, it is," I said, looking up. "Impressive place. How'd you manage this?"

She turned to take in the gray facade of the arena. "I have connections."

I gave her a quizzical look.

"Family. They're in real estate. This is only a lease, but I negotiated friendly terms for the Reapers." Along with her tone, her smile displayed deserved pride.

"Nice. What did the Order say?"

"They were thrilled."

I nodded. "Good to hear."

"What did they say about your desire to share this with us?"

"They don't know."

Anapheil sucked in her breath. "Risky."

"Yeah, I live on the edge. Plus, this is serious shit. I'm not sure everyone will get out alive, so the more trusted Reapers we have in the know, the better. In the end, it might be the only difference-maker." I looked up at the ridge of the roof line of the arena, focusing on how my replacement was taking the Reapers forward instead of how I was about to dump a load of trouble in everyone's lap. "Let's get this over with."

The interior was less impressive than the outside. Cost-saving where you can, I guess. Gray concrete pillars. Gray concrete floor. Dormant food stands were covered in purple, form-fitted tarps and pushed against the walls. In the air, I smelled a mustiness that large concrete-filled buildings always seemed to hold.

A buzz sounded from behind a pair of heavy metal doors, painted orange.

I looked at the Interim Minister. "Sounds like you got a good crowd together."

"I don't play around," she said, pushing her glasses up her nose with a single shove.

"Good." I started for the door and her warm hand around my wrist stopped me.

"How are we walking in there?"

"One foot in front of the other."

"I'm serious. How do we do this? I just took over as Interim Minister. There's going to be a lot of confusion, now and after this meeting, if you roll in there acting like you're still the Minister."

"I am. Just not the Acting one."

"Yes, and I understand that," she said with a super-sized dose of patience. She pointed at the obnoxious orange doors. "But they won't. The old ones will assume you're back in command. The new ones won't know what's going on."

"Gotcha. Well, this is your show. I'm just the eye candy. Take the lead. Do what you need to do so they know it's your meeting. Then introduce me. Use the draftees as an excuse, if that helps. I'll say my piece about the behemoth and Beelzebub and then get out of your way."

"Thank you," she said, her dark eyes dancing back and forth across mine. Anapheil nodded stiffly and led me through the double doors.

An eight-foot-high wall surrounded an open floor. A small stage with a podium stood, centered, in front of the stands twenty yards out onto the concrete. Angels filled each seat on this side of the arena, but the rest of the space was empty.

"Wow," I said, taking in the crowd of Reapers. "This is impressive. Nice work, Anapheil."

"Thanks."

Eyes tracked us across the floor. The consistent murmur I heard when standing outside the doors quieted when we walked in and steadily diminished the closer to the podium we got. The air filled with expectation and nerves.

By the time we stepped onto the stage, you could have heard a sprite's wings flap.

"Thank you for coming," Anapheil said. The acoustics in

the arena were amazing. Her voice carried to the rafters. "As always, we're going to keep this short." Someone near the rafters whooped at that. She lifted her arm in my direction. "For those of you who are new and don't know, this is Revelation Carver. Though you've mostly dealt with me, he holds the Minister's seat, though the Order of Thirteen has currently tasked him to conduct other operations. Rev has something he needs to share. Rev?"

She stepped aside, allowing me to take center stage. I looked into the sea of faces, the wide eyes, the set jaws, the ringing hands. Grim, apprehensive expressions. Even the familiar faces in the crowd seemed edged. These Reapers already sensed something disconcerting was coming, and I hadn't even opened my big mouth yet. Wait until I did. But before I put pressure on them to help in a bigger cause than what they signed up for, or were signed up for, I needed to ensure they knew where I stood and how Anapheil served the organization. Some of them had worked for me for thousands of years. To them, Anapheil would be second fiddle, at least for a few decades or so, until opinions changed. Being immortal meant we saw time on a different scale than mortals, and that sometimes extended to our mindset and routines. When you're immortal, things tend to move and change at a creep. This was one matter I didn't want moving slowly.

"Thanks for having me, Anapheil," I said, making a show of turning to her while I expressed my gratitude. "I appreciate the time because I know you're busy." Turning to the crowd of Reapers, I said, "All of you are. So, I won't waste your time. However, before I get to the problems facing us, I wanted each of you to hear something from me. I am very pleased Anapheil has agreed to step in as the Interim Minister to allow me to take care of business. I'm fully confident she will manage you effectively. Those of you who have served in the Reapers, even if for only a few months, are already aware of how good she is at what she does. Those of you who were recently recruited into our ranks will learn this about her. Make no mistake." I faced the Interim Minister once more. "She has my full confidence and I'm excited to see the heights she takes the organization to in my stead."

Long may it last… and maybe become permanent.

"I'm going to ask all of you to support her as you supported me. What I'm asking of her is unfair. She's had no time to prepare. There's no transition plan. But the circumstances call for it. Give her everything you've got. The best of you. The Reapers need it."

"What's going on, Rev?" Diniel asked from the front row. One of the more senior Reapers, he'd always been a straight shooter, and I appreciated his style. If he and Anapheil didn't butt heads too often, they'd make a great higher echelon of the Reapers, one for the less experienced to follow.

"Let me give it to you straight," I said, moving to the front of the stage to be as close to this crowd of Reapers, hundreds upon hundreds, as I could. "I've been tasked with finding and killing a behemoth."

A collection of groans and gasps flitted across the crowd.

"Yahweh has manifested a new behemoth. I've seen it in a cell phone video, and it's as ugly as the current music scene." That received a snicker or two from the younger angels in the crowd. "I'm going to stop it before it gets to population centers around the United States. Right now, it's restricted to a small mountainous forest in the Pacific Northwest, but it won't stay there forever. In fact, I believe it's very close to moving out." I briefly hit on Stacy's video of the behemoth and the figure in the background. "Someone is handling the beast, and I intend to find out who and put an end to this thing before it wreaks havoc and takes lives. If I fall, each of you will be far busier than you are now. So if you're not already, root for me and send a request or two to Yahweh, asking Him to guide my hand."

Across the stands, angels leaned toward each other to whisper. Even the experienced Reapers, those who I used to share a conference room with, and who essentially formed my inner circle of trusted confidantes, murmured. From thirty feet away, I felt their nervousness.

A handful of the angels had dealt with the last behemoth Yahweh manifested. They would remember what a problem that thing had been. They would also do quick math and realize the mortals had germinated the entire planet, their numbers exploding since the last iteration. The potential devastation was mind-numbing. In the faces before me, I saw that realization dawning and felt the turmoil it heated in their guts.

"That's not all," I said, loudly enough to draw attention back to me now that I'd given them a chance to process the near future. "While I was in the Overworld carrying out investigations, I also saw Beelzebub. For those of you not up to speed, he's one of Lucifer's Third Council members. He was in a city not too far from where the behemoth is."

"What was he doing there?" Inian Paltoon asked, her freckled face stretched in stress.

"Without sounding callous, I don't know and I don't have time to pursue his actions," I said. "That's for someone above my paygrade to decide. The Order doesn't want everyone in a panic, so I wasn't supposed to share that with you, but they don't travel to the Overworld and put their lives on the line. Reapers do. If you haven't had the pleasure yet because you were drafted and are still in training, trust me. You will. They'll have you all over the Overworld soon enough, and you need to know what you're walking into. Never forget, you can be injured or killed there."

I felt Anapheil slide closer way before she whispered, "Actually, I'm handling assignments again, Rev."

I blinked in surprise. That was news to me. "Oh. Okay."

I didn't like that, especially if I wouldn't get away with

staying out of the Minister position. This would add to an already packed daily slate as Minister. We'd have to circle back to the issue if I didn't die underneath the oversized paw of a ten-ton monstrosity.

"Even if you know what you're walking into," I said, read-dressing the captivated throng, "you're still in danger. Anyone who enjoys living in the Upperworld, especially the Eighth Level, cannot possibly appreciate what you do to get the job done. You need to be aware. You need to know the risks." I allowed that reality to sink in, dropping my voice an octave. "This stays here. With the Reapers. No one goes out and stirs up a panic. Don't tell your momma, your girlfriend, or your boyfriend. Don't even whisper this to your dog. I've shared this to protect you, not to stir up controversy or make you the center of attention at cocktail hour. I am a good subordinate to the Order, but my first allegiance is to the Reapers. Yours better be too. Reapers stick together." That was more for the newbies. Old news for the veterans. Based on the reactions I saw at the news of the behemoth and Beelzebub, the message hit home regardless of the length of service to the Reapers. "Something is changing. I don't know what, how, why, or who. Basically, I don't know shit."

Diniel shouted, "No big shocker there, Rev."

I smiled, keeping it conservative. "If Beelzebub is brazen enough to walk around the Overworld, you know he's up to something. Something that will impact the Balance. There's can be no doubt. With him being on Lucifer's Council, he can't take a shit without the Balance shifting. That's above our pay grade, but it still impacts us. Whenever you're back in the Overworld, be aware of your surroundings at all times. This ain't child's play."

"Do you think we're at risk or being targeted?" a tiny voice said from the back rows.

I shook my head, not finding the angel who voiced the question. "Not explicitly. At least, not yet. But that doesn't mean you won't be seen as a threat if you're in the wrong place at the wrong time. That doesn't mean our mere presence won't be used as an excuse for the demons to pull some crap to shift the Balance to their favor."

"Doesn't even have to be the demons, Rev."

I scanned the crowd for the youthful, feminine voice. Inian raised a hand to help me locate her. "Right here."

"What do you mean?"

One of the youngest Reapers to sit in my circle of trust, she was not only intelligent and effective, but her zeal brought much-needed energy. I hoped Anapheil kept her close while she acted in my stead. Tensions were sometimes tight between the pair. But with Anapheil, that wasn't uncommon. It only dawned on me now that it might be a problem if Inian didn't prove herself at her first chance.

"I've got it on good authority that the Four Horsemen are involved in something," she said.

Gasps grew loud. Everyone knew about the Four Horsemen of the Apocalypse. They were virtual celebrities to angels.

"How so?"

Inian looked around, sitting slightly forward on her seat, seeming to second guess that, and finally standing. "Supposedly, the Lamb of God was ramping them up to increase fear in the mortals."

"Why?" Anapheil asked, stepping to my side at the front of the raised stage.

Inian shrugged. "The guy I was talking to didn't say. Not for sure."

Someone chuckled, obviously making a big assumption about how Inian came across her information. The chuckle dried up when Inian's head snapped around. Composed, she continued, as if the rude reaction had never happened. "Maybe to increase fear in mortals, so we're more influential?"

"That doesn't make sense," Anapheil replied, pushing her

glasses up her nose. "Why would this man share that? How could you possibly believe him?"

Oh boy. Did we really need to go there?

"Because I know what he does, and I know how connected he is," Inian answered directly. Challengingly. She cocked her stance just enough to focus on me, at Anapheil's exclusion. "He's a reliable source, Rev."

Double-oh boy.

I nodded with direct eye contact. The kind that communicates 'I hear you'.

"I heard they were trying to unsettle mortals," someone from the blur of faces said.

"Dumb," another, new voice chimed in.

"Why would they?" said another anonymous voice.

The volume in the three-quarter-empty arena grew, slowly at first, before erupting into debate.

I looked at Anapheil. "This is your show."

It took the Interim Minister a while to settle everyone, but to be fair, it was like wrangling sprites. Understandably, the Reapers, new and old, were upset. This involved powerful angels and one of the most powerful demons around. Even to those who had obviously heard rumors, it was upsetting. Drama does that, and it wasn't like any of us in the arena could stop angels like Hellion if she was leveraging the Four Horsemen for something. None of us had a prayer against the likes of Beelzebub.

After the buzz of chatter grew to an annoying din, Anapheil stomped on the stage, making it shake, and clapped her hands. The sharp sound was piercing. Even twenty feet away, two of the nearest attendees jumped.

"Enough!" she said, commanding the arena. Even I straightened a little. "We're not here to speculate. We gathered to hear what Rev had to share. You know about the behemoth now. You know Beelzebub made his way to the Overworld, and we know we have to always be aware and exercise extreme caution." Her tone grew harsher. "But none of us have the training or skills to get involved. It's not our role. We see. We report. Everyone understand?"

A chorus of 'yes ma'ams' fell down from the stands.

After a round of updates from the large team—I honestly had no idea how Anapheil kept it all straight with so many Reapers—and question-and-answer time with me, I was off. Taking a moment to thank Anapheil, she started walking me out as if she wanted to be rid of me. Part of me understood. She had sprites to wrangle. I was the old boss. My presence, a hindrance.

But before I left, I stopped to have a word with the Reapers I'd served alongside for thousands of years. It felt good to be grounded in relationships with those you could confide and trust in. I had that with Billee. I had that with Pher. And I had it with many of the longer-serving Reapers. Sometimes that's all an angel assassin needs to make sense of the world.

As good as the short re-unification was, I needed something more. So after I extracted myself, assuring Anapheil I could find my way out so she could focus on her meeting, I headed toward Yahweh's headquarters and the residence of my mentor.

Maybe he'd help me make sense of how I could pull this off without stepping on any more toes.

———

PHER CRACKED THE DOOR, AND I HEARD A GIRLISH VOICE CRY out in glee from his living room.

I smiled. "Is my favorite munchkin here?"

Pher backed away, pulling the door open, looking every bit of the goofy grandpa he turned into whenever his granddaughter was around. He waved to the living room. "What? Nooo. Do you see Juniper anywhere?"

A giggle came from a blanket that stretched from the loveseat to a chair, pinned to the coffee table by heavy books. I pointed them out. "You think that's smart?"

His face pinched. "She'll be fine. Supposedly, she's a snake who, for some reason, lives in a cave."

"I thought it was a snake in the grass?" I said as I kicked off my shoes.

"Me too." He closed the door behind me. "But you know how it is."

"Everyone knows Juniper is the real boss when she comes over," I whispered. Lifting my head to project my voice, I said, "Oh, well. I thought I heard my favorite munchkin's voice, but I guess she's not here. That's for the best. She has stinky feet."

The draped blanket tent exploded upward to a rounded crown, accompanied by a shout of "Hey!" in a tiny voice.

Juniper the Standing Snake tried to pull the blanket off, but got caught in it and almost pulled her grandfather's books and a plant to the floor. I saved the plant, but a book took a tumble and popped open, its binding mostly still in-place.

"It was like that before," Pher said, obviously lying.

I bundled Juniper into my arms, pulling the blanket down to expose her head of long, brown curls.

"Uncle Rev," she squealed, her face alight.

What is it about round cheeks that just make you want to squeeze them?

Dramatically placing the back of my free hand to my forehead, I said in my best theater voice, "Juniper, you had me fooled! I thought you really were a snake! Oh, my heart!"

She giggled. "You're funny, Uncle Rev!"

"Hey honey," Pher said in his friendly grandpa voice, "Uncle Rev and I have to talk business. Go get a snack. I'll be in there in a second."

I set her down, and she gave my leg a squeeze. I patted her back. "Save cookies for me, okay?"

"Nope." She smiled, her eyes twinkling with youthful quintessence before racing out of sight.

Pher was smiling when I looked at him. His lips stretched farther when the pantry clicked open in the other room.

"She's a handful. I've been here for three minutes and I'm already worn out. How long do you have her for?"

"The weekend," he said with a healthy eye roll.

"You going to make it?"

"If you don't hear from me at the next meeting, you'll know where to find me. But I can't imagine a better way to go. I enjoy grandfather duties and would never hand them over to someone else."

Busted. Pher, in his way, wasn't happy about me promoting Anapheil. I wagged my finger at him. "I was wondering when you'd give me a hard time about that."

"A smart move, my boy. Hope the results are what you anticipate."

"Me too," I said, running a hand through my hair.

He watched me. "You look like you need a chat and drink. Let me scoop ice cream for the little one and pour us a stiff drink."

"Now that sounds like my kind of snack."

I waited for him to fulfill his grandfatherly duties. Juniper snuck waves at me while Pher covered her dessert with crumbled nuts and chocolate spread. He's brave, my mentor. After that much sugar, that little angel would be bouncing off the walls all night.

We moved to the side room, where Pher could keep an eye on his granddaughter while also protecting her from the bigger, badder world she wasn't old enough to understand yet.

I let him know about my run-in with the behemoth witness and the meeting with the Reapers. He'd understand why I told them, and wouldn't say anything to his peers on the Order. Pher was as safe as safe got.

"You do what you need to do with the behemoth and whoever is handling it," he said. He took a long sip of his bourbon, smacked his lips, and said, "I think we both know who is behind it. But if Hellion is involved because of whatever is going on with Yahweh and has access to Nephilim, the Four Horsemen, and the Council?" He tsked. "It's going to get very interesting around here. Take care of yourself in the Overworld. Keep your head down. There, and here."

"Here?"

"Jericho is a pain in the ass, but he's kicking up trouble. I think his mother is involved in the latest round, somehow."

"Maize? Isn't she happy in retirement? If not, shouldn't she be?"

"She should. But that doesn't mean she's not pulling his strings."

"Not surprised. Always knew he was a puppet."

"She's no joke, Rev," Pher said, in slight admonishment. "Ever since you busted her in that secret deal she was working with that crime boss. What was his name?"

"Went by Snide, remember?"

Pher smacked his hands. "That's right. Strange name."

"Stupid name."

"True. But Maize Judas is not stupid. Don't get lazy around Jericho. She's got plenty of something you don't have to make your life miserable."

"Oh, yeah?"

"Yeah. Time. Hers is bountiful. Yours is limited."

"More like non-existent."

One side of his face scrunched in a smirk. "Which means you need to be even smarter in how you plan, act, and react. And I don't like your odds."

16

ANGEL AT THE GATE

"You need to leave," the angel at the gate said.

"Not going to happen, my friend," I replied, glancing past him, side to side, analyzing the layout of Hellion's courtyard. "I want to see her."

"And that's not going to happen," he said, copying my tone.

"Funny."

"I thought so too."

"Listen, I know you don't get paid to think. You're one of those quiet-but-deadly types. Too full of muscle to pump much oxygen to your brain." He shifted, annoyed. So I did what all smart angels do when they're trying to get someone to do something they want. I push the issue. "But she's going to want to see me, and if you turn me away, she'll be pissed when she finds out."

"You're a real funny guy," the angel said, crossing his thick arms. Even though they were wrapped in a tight polyester blend long-sleeve shirt, there was no hiding the fact his arms were as thick as my legs. "But your comedy still needs work. Try brushing up on it on your way back to wherever you came from. You're not seeing Hellion."

I gripped the gate bars. Thick and solid. I could melt them with a nice dose of Angelfire, but escalating a confrontation with Hellion's security team was not the way I wanted to introduce myself to the Lamb of God.

As the saying goes, a funny thing happened along the way. I hadn't planned to see Hellion August. A perfect storm led me to this decision. I had to make sure the Reapers were in excellent hands. Check. I had to find peace with Alisha. Temporary check. I had to let Pher know about the undercurrents around the behemoth, the Reapers, Beelzebub, and Jericho. All sorts of checks. Thus, here I was.

I could dance around the sensitive issue of questioning the Lamb of God, but I have two left feet and a troubling lack of patience. Someone was on animal handling duties with the behemoth. In the Overworld, it's said that if you wanted to get to the root of a problem, all you had to do was follow the money trail. Well, the immortal realm uses gold, silver, and copper—we're slow to evolve our monetary system—and that's harder to track. But one thing any self-respecting assassin knows is that coincidences aren't worth the time required to think about them. There are no such things as coincidences, just meaning we ascribe to certain conditions. As far as I was concerned, the only thing worth my time was getting to the problem of the Upperworld's recent troubles. Few angels had access to the Safe. A Bowl of Wrath had somehow been stolen and poured on the world. Few angels could act as a handler for Yahweh's newest manifestation. Facts, not coincidences.

I didn't know what was going on with the current ruler of the Upperworld. That sort of stuff isn't in my job description. But with the blessing of the Order—and ostensibly the Council themselves—I was going to chase this lead. Sort of like a badass detective. Just one going rogue and poking a big ole political bear.

A massive iron gate and a stubborn security guy wouldn't stop me.

"Look at it this way, buddy," I said. "If I don't get to ask her a few questions, I'm going to ask friends what they know about her and her activities."

"You have friends now, do you?" he said. His billboard of a chest bobbed with a gratified chuckle.

"I do. Even have friends in the Underworld. Figured I'd start with them and see what they can tell me about Hellion's recent activities."

That was a lie. I didn't have friends in the Underworld. I didn't even have contacts there. As the Reaper Minister, that would be inappropriate and problematic in the best of circumstances. I was an assassin of demons. Not like any of them had me on their Christmas card list. But this walking mound of muscle didn't know that, and my threat got his attention, so I pounced.

"Tell her Rev Carver, the Reaper Minister, is here to see her and ask questions on behalf of the Order of Thirteen. If she seems hesitant, let her know I won't stop at this gate. If I don't get what I'm looking for, I'll go digging, and I just stopped at the hardware store and bought a lifetime supply of shovels."

The guard's chest bounced again, but he abruptly stopped chuckling and put his finger to his ear. I noticed the black earpiece, part of a radio system. Someone wanted his attention.

"Yes," he said brusquely. There was a distinct change in his posture. "Yes, ma'am. Of course." He dropped his arm and looked at me, suddenly a professional who wasn't interested in giving me a hard time. "Wait here. An escort will come for you momentarily."

With that, he turned and strode across the courtyard to the wide marble stairs leading to the mouth of the mansion.

Two oak doors stood twenty feet tall. He leaned into the

one on the right and slipped inside. It glided closed behind him.

I passed the time by ignoring the nagging thought that Hellion might have just blown me off with the excuse that an escort was coming. Maybe she and her staff and security team were inside the mansion now, looking out a few of the four gazillion windows facing the street, and laughing at me. Maybe taking bets on how long I'd stand outside. I wonder what the over-under was on that?

Pacing in front of the gate helped. But not much. Thankfully, before too long, a thin man in a black blazer appeared from the side, almost as if he'd been hiding in the tall shrubbery all along.

"Ms. August will see you," he said in a phantasmal voice.

The gate slowly swung in and I stepped through as soon as my frame could fit. I wasn't taking any chances for them to lock me out.

He led me to a side door, not the large double doors the security buffoon had retreated into. And here I thought I was going to catch up with my beefy friend on this side of the gate and see if he thought so highly of himself when unbending metal didn't separate us.

We entered a foyer that was as big as one of my empty Overworld side apartments. This room had about as much furniture too. A wide-open space, only interrupted by two pillars, six feet in diameter. The floor was black marble. Faint, thin lines of silver carved through the solemn expanse, adding a bit of reserved color. Mahogany shelves lined the far end and sides of the room, holding an array of books and a healthy collection of various glass figurines.

"Wait here. Ms. August will attend you momentarily," the wraith-like angel said and drifted away.

"There's nowhere to sit," I said after him.

He didn't even turn around. "You won't be staying long,

Mr. Carver. Consider yourself fortunate to get an audience with her."

And then he was gone, rounding the corner with all the properness and pomposity a place like this demanded.

I stood in the middle of the foyer and waited. And waited. And waited.

A power play, no doubt. So I shifted the dynamic and started snooping. I moved to the far end of the room and examined a handful of titles. Nothing of interest, if the book titles were any indication. No fiction at all. Apparently, Hellion was well-read, but not exactly one for escapism. Then again, who needed to escape when they were ridiculously wealthy and politically untouchable? The figurines were far more interesting than her book collection. Replications of ancient gods worshiped by mortals over the ages from cultures around the world. A striking choice of interior decorating for someone who owed their livelihood to Yahweh.

When I ran out of stuff to examine in this grand waste of space, I made my way to the archway leading into the adjoining room.

"I'd prefer it if you didn't walk around my home unescorted, Mr. Carver," a thick voice said behind me.

I turned to face the Lamb of God.

"Thanks for seeing me, Hellion."

Her wide mouth stretched in apparent displeasure. One peak of her lips' Cupid Bow was higher than the other, making it look like a permanent sneer, which did nothing for her appearance. Not an attractive woman, with eyes that looked like they were sliding to the sides of her face and a nasty demeanor, I'd never be captivated by Hellion, even from afar. Then again, I don't imagine that was much of a worry for her. "After your petulant scene at my gate, you left me with little choice. As you can probably appreciate, I don't have much time. So, what can I do for the Reaper Minister?"

So we were playing that game? That was fine with me. I'd

never had a one-on-one with Hellion, and never heard anything complimentary about her or the way she treated angels. From the first interaction, my welcome hadn't been welcoming—even though I was an unsolicited visitor, there's still a level of decorum and civility one would expect from decent angels. If she wanted to strip away the ceremony, I was more than willing to shrug off my chemise.

"I was hoping to sit and chat about your thoughts on recent events."

"Events such as?" she said stiffly.

"The break-in at the Safe. The theft of the First Bowl. Maybe even pick your brain about the behemoth."

The peak of her Cupid's Bow twitched higher. "Things I don't get involved with, Mr. Carver. Is there anything else you need?"

I tapped my lip. An irritating gesture, to be sure. Exactly why I did it. "Here's the thing, Hellion. I don't believe you." Thank Yahweh I wasn't expecting much of a reaction because I didn't get one at all. Standing before me, she might as well have been a breathing painting for as dynamic as she appeared. I pressed on. "You're as connected as they come. Maybe even more so than the Council. The asshole who poured the First Bowl on the Overworld was a Nephilim. You're a Nephilim. I'm not much into class warfare, but you higher-ranking angels stick together. Add the fact you have access to the Safe and the ear of Yahweh, and I'm interested enough to explore my options."

A grunt. A single, almost humored grunt. That's all she gave me to work with. I hadn't upset or even annoyed her enough to compel her to argue or defend herself. I was floundering here.

"I've even started hearing rumors about your involvement with the Overworld. Using your little pony men to stir up trouble."

"Childish." Her voice was so frigid I almost felt the first

tingle of ice scrape my skin. "You don't know what you're talking about, Mr. Carver. This is all very inappropriate. Did the Order approve this visit? Do they even know you're here, troubling me in my home?"

"I am conducting an investigation on their behalf. Oh, and on the Council's behalf."

"I don't answer to the Council."

The air chilled even more. Damn, she was intimidating.

"If I understand your position, you don't really answer to anyone."

"We all answer to someone," she said. I think she tried to smirk, but her elongated mouth didn't seem capable of curling upward. Probably too many eons of going unused prevented her from doing so. "That includes me. But one thing I do not do is answer to the Reaper Minister. You forget your place."

"I know exactly what my place is, Hellion," I said. "Unlike others, I don't abuse my power."

"Yet you stand in my home," she said as coolly as if she were asking her waiter for a wine recommendation. "You question me. And if I'm picking up on your attempted subtlety, you might even be accusing me of involvement in nefarious activities. Is that correct?"

"You're not far from the truth. I wouldn't be here if I didn't need to be. No one acts with impunity, and if the Four Horsemen are in the Overworld, causing trouble, I want to know why."

"As if it's your station to ask how and why I'm deploying them."

"I've got my orders, Hellion, and I'm going to see them out."

"Be very careful how you proceed," she said, cocking a quarter turn back toward the room she'd appeared from.

Behind me, I heard soft footfalls. One of her security goons, no doubt.

"I don't respond well to threats," I said, creeping my hand forward, just in case I needed to slip it into my duster for my trusty .327.

"Nor do I," she said with a reserved, almost undetectable sniff. "My men will see you out, Revelation Carver. Don't come back. I will report this unfortunate decision to invade my home to the Council and ensure they take appropriate action." She stopped, partially angling her face in my direction as three security angels, each dressed identically in those black, long-sleeve shirts and dark pants, stepped closer.

A show of force, nothing more. Hellion didn't want this to go down here. I didn't want this to go down here. Hell, I didn't want it to go down anywhere, any time that wasn't absolutely justified. Killing might be my business, but it's a job full of dirty deeds, and I didn't feel like soiling myself. A fight here in the Upperworld meant no one would die as a result. But engaging would cause a firestorm of controversy, draw too much of the Council's attention, and maybe force Yahweh to step in. In a time when the Safe had been breached and a behemoth was loose in the Overworld with someone controlling it, the last thing anyone needed was this drama. Well, except whoever was behind all the recent problems. That angel would love a significant distraction like me throwing down with the Lamb of God and her goons so they could further ensconce their activities and aims in secrecy.

I put my hands up to show the muscle heads I didn't want any trouble and moved toward the door. "I'm leaving, Hellion. But I'm not done poking around. If I find out the Four Horsemen are creating problems, I'll take care of them. Myself, if I have to."

"Don't threaten my Horsemen."

On top of her comment, I said, "And if I find out you're involved in this mess with the Safe and the First Bowl, I'll make those who can hold you accountable, do."

She said nothing.

A goon behind me gave me a light, but direct, shove toward the door. "Move."

"I'm moving," I said over my shoulder, dropping my hands, ready for anything they might try.

The air was no longer chilly. It crackled with tension.

A goon stepped in front of me and pulled the door open so I wouldn't have to stop on my way from being kicked out of Hellion's mansion. Just as I reached the breach, she spoke one last time.

"Beware the carnival of souls, Rev, for it has already begun."

Someone shoved me out into the day before I could ask just what in the hell she was talking about.

I didn't expect an invitation back. Whatever would come from this visit, one thing was for sure; I'd taken a big ole stick and drawn a line in the sand too deep to step over now that I was on the other side.

17

BEFORE THE SUN

THERE'S NO REST FOR THE WICKED. NO PEACE FOR THE UNSETTLED mind.

My doorbell rang, breaking me out of the alluring reverie of three hours of sleep.

I rolled over, seeing it was three in the morning, rubbed my eyes, and readied myself to kick someone's ass. Especially after I stubbed my toe on the footlocker at the end of my bed. "Someone has a death wish."

I grabbed Maggie and headed to the door to see who ruined a perfectly good, and far too short, rest.

The nice thing about spending so much time in my Overworld apartment was how familiar I was with it. I could navigate it with my eyes closed. Well, once I was coherent. An additional bonus was that I could do it with a decent amount of stealth as well. Without making a sound to give away my state or location, I reached the peephole to spy on my nighttime visitor.

She was short. That's the first thing I noted through the warped view the peephole provided. Behind her, a Rift rippled in the hallway. The last thing was the air of nervousness. As she waited, she fidgeted constantly.

"What do you want?" I said through the door.

She stepped back, staring at the barrier, looking intimidated.

This was someone who knew who I was. You pick up on these things when you've had to rely on your survival instincts for thousands of years.

She moved closer, the curved peephole glass making her face seem to stretch and her body shrink. "Rev? Is that you?"

"Who are you?"

"Uziel sent me," she said, but it sounded more like a question.

It was my turn to pull back. A member of the Order sent a runner to the Overworld? Oh, damn.

I flicked the light switch, opened the door, and invited her in.

"Thanks," she said, looking down. She didn't look up until I closed the door.

"What can I do for you? It's the middle of the night."

"Uziel said to tell you she wouldn't have bothered you if it wasn't important. She asked for you to come by her private residence."

"When?"

"Now."

"Now? It's three in the freaking morning."

The unknown angel shrugged. "I know. She wanted me to send her apologies in advance but said she has to talk to you. Here's the address."

I took the small piece of paper from her and unfolded it. "The Sixth? Okay. I'll get ready."

The angel slipped out after a quiet 'thanks,' and was stepping through her Rift before my door closed.

I got dressed and opened a Rift to a transfer station in the Sixth. After a series of sub-stations that were immaculate enough to take a stroll through with a special lady, I was in Uziel's neighborhood.

Evening had a firm grip on the Upperworld. Dusk was fast-approaching. I hoped I wasn't interfering with dinner plans, but the Order's Chief of Ethics had called me to her place, so any interruptions had to be placed squarely on her shoulders.

The homes here were packed together tightly but still held an air of exquisiteness. Like a neighborhood in San Francisco, just a lot nicer. That's not a slight on good ole San Fran. It's a testament to the money in Uziel's neck of the woods.

The rosewood bushes bordering the flight of stairs leading to her front door were manicured into the shape of doves. Not a branchy beak or wing was out of place. The doorbell plate was polished enough that I could have checked if I had any food caught in my teeth. Its chime was something you tipped extra for at the lounge while enjoying overpriced cocktails.

Through the panes of etched glass, the silhouette of someone shaped a lot like the Order member appeared and moved toward the door, opening it. Uziel's mouth curved in a self-satisfied way, like my compliance had confirmed something for her. "Hi, Rev. Thank you for coming on such short notice. Please, come in."

As I stepped inside, she locked the door behind me. I noticed she had stayed out of eyesight of the street when she opened the door. That, and the immediately locked door, made me uneasy. Not that I couldn't bust through it or had anything to worry about from Uziel. As more and more mysteries swirled around the Upperworld, I was growing more guarded with everyone who wasn't my familiar or named an ancient angel named Pher. Maybe Puriel. After all, she had gifted me the mana stone that would keep me on the right side of above ground after my fight with the behemoth.

But Uziel and I weren't close. Never had been. We'd never been antagonistic. Ours was an extended relationship, but cordial, and dare I say, friendly most of the time.

"Uziel, what's going on?" I asked as she led the way into

her living room. On the far end, the space narrowed into a dining area.

We were alone. The furniture was an explosion of white. I didn't want to sit. Anywhere.

She walked to the dining table. A chair was already pulled out, giving away the spot where she'd been waiting for my arrival. She sat, gesturing to the closest chair. "Considering what you do for a living, I don't imagine you want your back to the door. I figure that's the most practical seat for you. Please, sit. I need to share something I'd never put in writing, and there was no way I'd attempt to talk about it at the head-quarters."

"Okay," I said slowly and took the offered chair. Kudos to her for her level of awareness. I didn't want my back to the door, or any window, and this spot was the only one at her table that provided me that comfort.

"Some in the Order may see this as a betrayal, in case you're wondering," she said, whirling her finger in the air. "This. What I'm doing."

"Well, you know how to get my attention."

"Good. Because I don't want you being fooled."

"By?"

"Jericho held a sidebar chat earlier today," she said, and I groaned. Her face twisted. "Not everyone. He doesn't have the guts for that. But he's a conniving brat with the force of his stubborn mother behind him, pushing him forward. One who has plenty of pull because of that silver spoon wedged up her ass."

Okay, that caught me off guard. I laughed into my fist. "Excuse me."

She winked. "Anyway. I won't name who was in this informal council of his, but I was there. By invitation, I'll say. Not everyone was allied with him, but I think he believes we're aligned, if you catch what I mean?"

"So no Puriel or Pher?"

"Exactly." She rocked her head, her short, dark hair swaying. "Others were missing too, but I figured you'd guess who Jericho wouldn't risk involving. Though he wasn't exactly smart making the assumptions he made." She spread her hands. "But his miscalculation allows the two of us to have this conversation. I know we haven't been close. But I do that on purpose, Rev. It's nothing personal. Nothing against you. I'm just not one to mix business with anything. I take my duties seriously."

"What did he share with this close circle?"

I was expecting her to say that he was pushing to have me fired or for voting Puriel out in some emergency measure. I hadn't her expected her to say, "He told us you were blackmailing him."

I coughed for real this time. No laughter. "He what?"

"Yes. Very concerning allegations. The Reaper Minister blackmailing a member of the Order of Thirteen." She let her sentiment drift away.

I pushed the admonishment aside, too focused on my irritation with that asshole for exposing what I'd done in the name of stopping the spread of the virus. The very one that was created when his ex-schoolmate buddy poured the First Bowl on the Overworld. This was about context, except, apparently, Jericho didn't want to provide that for the Order.

"They're definitely concerning allegations. If they were truthful," I said carefully. "Did he say what I was after from this supposed blackmail?"

She watched me before answering. Her short black hair barely fell below her earlobe. She tucked one wedge behind her right ear as if buying time. When she spoke, her tone took on an aloofness as she mimicked Jericho, swirling her hand in the air as she re-told the incident. "Oh, it was grand. That you were demanding your release from your Minister obligations because you were in love with a mortal and wanted to be with her, free of the Upperworld's influence."

"Oh, really?"

"Definitely."

"And if I wasn't released? I mean, it can't blackmail him without explicitly detailing the consequences if I don't get my way. Right?"

"Truly. He said if you didn't get what you wanted, you were going to kill immortals."

"This gets better and better. How was I going to do that? We can't die here. I expected more of him if he was going to bother fabricating trouble. Unless I'm dragging angels into the Overworld to assassinate them?" I cocked my head with a smirk. "Not that I haven't done that before. But that was with bad guys, not innocent angels or members of the Order of Thirteen."

"You'll be happy to know that's exactly what he claims. Well, that and ensuring you were there to absorb their energy with the expressed purpose of lengthening your own life and thus extending your power base." She scrunched her face playfully. "I think he was trying to imply you were positioning yourself to become Yahweh when the time came, but he stopped short of being explicit. For a change. Barely."

"As far as blackmailing goes, I don't think you're supposed to give away all the details of your evil plot."

Uziel's short hair winged out at the ends, and those big hooks wiggled as she nodded. "Apparently you did." She paused, shifting closer. "Listen, Rev. Everyone in the Order is aware the two of you don't like each other. Neither of you has made a secret of that, and it's not usually even a problem. But stuff like this is. He didn't get anyone to commit to taking drastic action, but Jericho can be persuasive, if not out of persistence alone. His mother isn't helping the situation. She's connected and smart enough to know how to use those relationships to further her son's agenda. With enough time, Jericho could keep pushing and convince enough of the voting members to take these rumors to task. None of us have time for that. I'm sure you don't either."

I shook my head. "This is the last thing any of us need. I need to focus on the behemoth. There's…" How did I say this without giving away information I didn't want out until I talked to Pher about Hellion? "Information has come to light that I need to validate before I bother the Order with it. But it's troubling."

"I won't ask you to betray your confidences, but is there anything I can help with?"

This wasn't a matter of trusting or not trusting Uziel. I wasn't ready for that decision. This was the first time I'd ever seen her show her cards. Not to sound paranoid or anything, but this could be part of a longer play. Jericho would become more desperate as time passed. The harder I was on him, especially in front of his peers like in the last meeting, and as his fear of me exposing his friendship with the Nephilim who poured the First Bowl grew, he'd become more unstable. I needed more, on Arakiel, on Jericho, and on the Lamb of God herself, before I started slinging accusations around and found myself on the wrong side of justice.

I wished I could give something back to Uziel, to trade a tidbit for this assist of hers, but I had nothing to offer. Not until I could be sure. "I wish there was, Uziel. Right now, I'm still swimming for the shore, not sure how deep the water is. For all I know, I can stand and walk to land. The problem is, if I try, I might get swept back out by the undertow."

"Nice metaphor," she said. "Well, I don't want to keep you. I wanted to have this chat off the record, you understand?"

"Of course."

"That way, I figured, you could do what you needed to address it as soon as you could, but also keep yourself safe. He was practically begging everyone to 'bring you to justice' as swiftly as possible. Not that he got any movement, but there were a few reactions that made me nervous."

"Oh? How?"

"Call them signs he wasn't being completely dismissed. Not that you have enemies in the Order." She held up her finger, taking the part of a school teacher admonishing a pupil. "Most of the conversation centered on the collective shock and surprise of the 'news'," she said, hooking both her pointer fingers in the air, "of your dirty deeds, and the rest of us exercising caution. Especially when he started talking about a trial."

"A trial? Is he nuts?"

"He's a Judas," she said. "His mother overreacted often if you remember. Honestly, I'm not surprised. The good news is that no one, and I mean no one, agreed with him about taking immediate action. We know the work you're doing and how important it is for not only the Upperworld but for mortals as well. We've got a mess on our hands that only you can clean up. So his silly chat was shut down by several voices trying to talk sense about not risking you, even if what he was saying is true." She paused, her broad nose wrinkling. "Those words were actually said, and I thought he was going to lose his shit."

I didn't feel like chuckling. "Good."

"But no one outwardly turned on him, either."

"Maybe whoever was there took the conversation the same way you did?"

"Maybe. But are you willing to risk that?"

"I don't enjoy taking risks. Well, unless absolutely necessary or when doing so will make me look cool."

That was received as intended. "Tread carefully. He won't let this go, and I'm not confident he hasn't got at least one member thinking. Seeds were planted. They might never sprout green shoots, but if you're not careful, you'll have a field of kudzu on your hands before you know it."

I wiggled my hands. "Mmm, not as good as my metaphor,

but I get your point. Thanks for this, Uziel. I really appreciate it."

"You're welcome. For what it's worth, I don't believe him. You wouldn't blackmail him. We've used you for unscrupulous needs for ages, but blackmail? That's below you." She grunted and got up, leading me to the door. I was grateful for her incorrect assumption and followed. "If you had any problem with Jericho that was that severe, you'd just kick his ass and let the rest of us watch."

"Not a bad alternative."

"Agreed." At the door, which she opened just enough to squeeze me through while remaining hidden from the outside world, she said, "Take care of yourself."

"I will. Thanks."

Troubles followed me down the steps and through the Rift to my Overworld apartment. Once there, I found my cell phone on my nightstand, this time without stubbing my toe in the dark. Trying to ignore the early morning time on the display and the sleep I would not get, I called my mentor's Overworld phone number.

Pher has the longest voicemail recording in their brief history. Part of me wonders if he does it to discourage anyone from leaving him a message. I almost fell asleep while waiting for the beep to tell me I had permission to talk. When he finished his recorded allocution, I said, "Hey boss. Sorry for the early call. Had a long night. When you get this, let's chat about blackmail and the carnivals of souls."

I set my phone back on the nightstand and stared at my ceiling, willing sleep to come. Even if it did, I had a feeling nightmares would fill whatever rest I got.

18

BOLOGNESE AND BULL CRAP

I'M ONE OF THOSE RIDICULOUS RENTERS WHO NEEDS TO BE A homeowner so I can do what I want with my place. In a way, I guess I already have. I mean, there were missing walls between the apartment I lived in, situated at the end of the hall on the top floor of the building, and the two neighboring apartments I also rented for more assassin-related purposes. I could replace walls. Kitchens, though? You couldn't just do what you wanted to them. Trust me, I've thought about it. Often.

If I had my way, one of the three apartments would be a dedicated kitchen space. I enjoy cooking that much. If I had more people in my Overworld life to entertain, I'd be in my happy space more than I already was. Of course, that would tempt me to see if I could get away with converting one of the other apartments into a full-blown cooking space of such exquisiteness it would make any executive chef jealous.

A problem for another time. Tonight, I had one guest, and I was still scrambling to get dinner done on time. I'd blame Uziel. Her middle-of-the-night request for a meeting didn't do my Circadian rhythm any favors. After leaving the voicemail for Pher, I finally fell asleep, still dressed, and stayed asleep until way past the time when normal people were on their way to work. The rest of the day was a scramble to catch up, which left me feeling a little edgy.

Thankfully, Billee was willing to come by so I could talk things out while I cooked for her and she helped with the administrative aspects of our behemoth hunt—namely, finding lodging for the operation. That was a grander task than I expected when she started shooting me options. I think I balked at every price.

"We might as well rent a closet," I said at one point.

"Stop pouting, and keep cooking," she answered, a hand pressed to her forehead, pushing her long curls back, and leaning toward the monitor as if doing so would help her find the steal of the century. She stopped to sniff at the air. "What is that?"

"Ingredients," I said—told you I was feeling edgy.

"Don't be an ass. I'm already stressed enough trying to find a place to rent. Especially with your criteria, if you can call it that."

"The meal is pork sausage spaghetti bolognese," I said, drizzling olive oil into the pan before moving on to the unenviable task of removing the sausage from their skins. "And I wish I could give you better criteria, but I don't know what I can pull off or what I need. Just find the biggest place you can, with the most bedrooms. The Order might give me a team. They might not. I don't know. If they don't, I've got one myself. But I need to have a space to house as many as possible. Big. Think big."

"You don't even know how long you'll need it for."

"The video gave me an idea of where the behemoth is. That's all. I don't know how long we'll be there. All I need is to pinpoint its nest or cave or..." I waved the edged stainless steel spatula in the air. "Or wherever the damned thing sleeps, eats, and shits. Once I've got that, everyone can run for the hills. But if I have to use mortals, I can't ask them to drive from Olympia to the mountains every day."

"Yet you want them to take time off work or away from their families to go monster hunting?"

"Better that than doing it on my own and missing the behemoth because someone led it out of the Olympics and into Bremerton or across the Puget Sound to Seattle."

She stopped clicking on whatever sites she was perusing. "You really think that could happen?"

"My gut tells me it's only a matter of time. Our big break came when the Order found out about the behemoth. That allowed us to get a jump on the situation and hopefully will give me time to catch it before it gets its land legs under it. The thing will only get stronger the longer it's here. The only reason it's still tucked away in the forest is because it's too young to come out. But those buggers grow up fast. Before long, it'll be tearing up cities around the world at a pace that will make Godzilla green with envy. So, I cook. You pull off a miracle and find us a place that can act as our monster-hunting headquarters. Be creative. I know you can do it."

"It's going to be expensive, even if I can find something with five or six bedrooms."

"Find something bigger. We'll worry about the expense later. The Order is paying."

"Okay," she said, letting the 'ay' hang in the air as if she thought I was crazy.

Maybe I was. Everything swirling around in my head had a way of pushing me in that direction.

"Sorry if I sound cranky. There's a lot on my mind. I stabbed the pork as it sizzled in the heated oil, even though the innocent meat didn't need stabbing. I'd already broken the packaged block into smaller chunks. This was about frustrated vengeance, nothing more.

"No worries," Billee mumbled. "I'm used to you being an asshole."

I chuckled. "Thanks."

"Just the behemoth?"

"Huh?"

"Is it only the behemoth that's bothering you, or is there something else going on? Something that, oh I don't know, your familiar should know about so she can help? After all, isn't that what we're supposed to do? Support the Reaper in all things?"

"Partially, but you're dealing with enough. I don't want to add to it. You're already helping by looking for lodging." The laptop lid popping closed drew my attention. "What?"

Billee laid her hands over the cover. "Don't worry. I've found five places. I'll narrow them down later."

"Already?"

"Yes, Rev, it's not that hard. Well, not for a woman. Anyway, how dare you tell me what I can and can't handle?"

"I didn't mean it like you couldn't handle more. Just that…"

She stretched her thin neck as she jutted her head toward me. "That what?"

I sighed. "I want you to focus on the stuff I need your help with." Waving the spatula at the closed laptop under her hands, I said, "Like finding lodging. Five? Already? Impressive." I aimed the spatula at her face. "That's why I hired you. Right there."

One eye narrowed as the corner of her face curled up. "You didn't hire me. Remember?" Lifting her arm, she let the bracelet dangle. "I know. I know. I'm not your property. Anyway, what's bothering you besides my inability to handle a few big girl things?"

"Billee, I swear, it's not like—"

"Oh my god, it's fun giving you shit. I'm kidding, Rev. Calm down."

"You're an ass."

"I learn from the best."

We shared a short laugh.

I said, "Thank you. I needed that."

"You're welcome."

"To be honest, I'm just pissed right now."

"About?"

"A couple things." As a car honked on the street three stories below—five, if you count the two-story parking garage below the first floor—I told her about my confrontation with Hellion and Jericho's fabrication of the blackmail. "His mother has hated me for a while. A long time for mortals. Well over a couple of centuries."

"Why?"

The bolognese was still simmering, so I was free to share a short story about Maize Judas's history with me. "She used to hold Jericho's position. But the Order secretly assigned me to take care of a troublesome crime boss. Turns out, while isolating him, I discovered Maize was working with him on real estate deals that benefited her family. He used his muscle to make sure her family acquired prime property that was being held hostage by a private landowner. Turns out, it was an elderly guy saving it for his own family. Maize wanted it for hers. It would appall a good angel to take advantage of someone like that. Maize did. As a member of the Order, it would be uncouth to pressure the old guy. She did that as well."

"So she had this crime boss act as her muscle?"

"Bingo. All she had to do in return was influence policy for the Third Level where this dirtbag operated."

"Gross."

"That's politics for you. The rich get richer and everyone breaks their backs for them. Gender, sex, skin tone? That shit doesn't matter. It's all about the Benjamins, isn't that how it goes?"

"Don't try to be cool or relevant, Rev. You're too old. Seriously, though, that's gross and disappointing. I'd expect more of Heaven."

"Yeah, you'd think we'd have our act together. That we wouldn't be about classism and greed. But that's not true. Oh sure, ultimately, Yahweh uses us to keep the Balance, to ensure demons don't sway mortals too far toward self-centered motivation. We're supposed to keep mortals balanced between being motivated to act for the self and acting for the greater good. The Balance works wonderfully. That's how your kind has risen to dominate this rock flying through space. But in the Upperworld? We don't need to maintain a Balance. That's what our governing bodies do. The problem is, with ten ranks of angels, not including the Nephilim, only certain voices ever get heard on important matters. Even the ones affecting all angels."

"Let me guess," Billee said, her voice turning sour. "The lower ranks get screwed while the privileged get all the goods. The right kind of access. Advantageous opportunities. All the breaks in life?"

"Gee, it's almost like you're one of us."

"Humans have prepared me to expect the worst."

"Angels should be better. Sadly, we're not."

"I'm sorry."

"Not your fault, Sparky. You didn't do any of this. The Upperworld was fucked up long before you were a sparkle in your great-great-great-great-grandfather's eye."

"Gross."

"Not as gross as the way your father flirted with your mother."

"Stop!" She plugged her ears, laughing. "I don't want to know."

I winked and returned to my bolognese now that I had properly tortured my partner. My friend. Just having Billee around pushed the shadow of the Upperworld's bull crap to the periphery of my life. At least for the time being. She was good for me like that. I wished I could be as good for her.

Suddenly serious, she said, "I wish I could help."

"It's an Upperworld problem. You can't."

"Can't someone up there? I mean, the higher ranks of angels are residents just like everyone else, even if they're treated with kid gloves. But someone could stop them if they wanted. Right?"

"Sure, but no one will because they benefit too. Self-sustaining cycle of the elite."

"And that's how angels like Jericho and his mother, and Hellion—what a stupid name, by the way—"

"Don't say that to her face. She won't take kindly to it."

Billee was on a roll, not stopped by my interruption. "That's how they're allowed to continue with these abuses. And no one can help? At all?"

I suppressed a sigh. "Those who can help already are."

"Hmmm."

Without looking, I could tell she was tapping a finger on my counter from the sound of the faint click, click, click.

She snapped her finger. "Oh! What about that angel? The one who tackled you when we were trying to escort that drug dealer to the Veil Gate? She definitely owes you a favor. Maybe she's got connections she could use?"

In my stunned epiphany, I was aware of Billee searching my face for a clear reaction. I wasn't giving her much, because she'd just given me something I could use. A tactic I hadn't thought about because my brain was on overload.

"Sorry. Dumb idea," she said, shaking her head. "Not like I know how Heaven works. I was—"

"Billee," I said in a raspy voice, "you're an absolute genius."

19

LIVING THE PUG LIFE

WHAT DO YOU BRING AS A GIFT WHEN YOU'RE TRYING TO CHARM a woman you don't know and your visit to her home is unsolicited? What if outward appearances broadcast a message that the woman already had everything her heart desired? What if you are already the worst gift-giver in recorded history?

Standing at the gate of Cascade Cho's yard, I paused, caught in this dilemma. My hands were empty, and I was here with a favor to ask.

Poor form, Rev. Poor form.

But I didn't know Cascade outside of work. She had served as the Guardian Minister for longer than I sat in the complimentary chair for the Reapers. We worked together on issues of importance, but rarely outside of that. We didn't need to. I knew my job, and Cascade always seemed to be in the good graces of the Order, so she had to be squared away as well.

As I grew more and more jaded by my job responsibilities, giving over administrative tasks to the Order as they piled monster hunting and assassination assignments on me, my interactions with Cascade became more sporadic with each passing century. Standing in front of her gate now, I wished I'd stayed in better contact with her.

With a sigh, I reached for the call button, stopping when I noticed the design of the call box. It was iron and shaped like the head of a pug. A call button had replaced the dog's stub nose. I pressed it, feeling guilty. Those adorable dogs already had enough struggles without being portrayed in this light.

A moment later, a female answered. Her voice sounded thin through the box's speaker. "Yes?"

"Cascade? This is Rev Carver. Can I get a minute of your time, please?"

"Rev?" the woman answered as if the name was foreign.

"Rev Carver. The Re—"

"Oh, of course. Let me buzz you in. I'll meet you at the front door."

The gate buzzed, then clicked as the internal mechanism released the lock. I pushed down the handle and stepped into Cascade Cho's realm.

The house was another four hundred yards from the gate, but even from this distance, I heard dogs barking. Multiple dogs. Little dogs, by the sounds of their racket. The best home protectors in the Upperworld.

Don't get me wrong, I don't dislike dogs. In fact, they're pretty cool. The best of domesticated animals. But if that concerto of raspy barks was a hint, Cascade had a canine army inside that large home and I had a sudden vision of being swarmed by stocky, pudgy hounds too small to sound that aggressive.

The barking ebbed away as I neared. Like a solitary car on a nighttime highway, the barks disappeared slowly. The lock clicked and Cascade Cho, Minister of the Guardians, opened her door.

"I'm sorry that took so long, Rev. I had to put my babies away or they wouldn't have given you any peace. They get excited by company and I fear they would have been too much for the both of us."

"No worries, Cascade. I'm the one who dropped in on you unannounced. Apologies are mine. I wouldn't have if I didn't desperately need to talk to you."

Cascade Cho is fortunate to be above five feet tall and is losing the battle with gravity every day. For as long as I've known her, she's worn her hair short, and the way she wore it made the tips wing backward, making one side always look fuller than the other. Strange, if you ask me. But what do I know? I'm at the last stage in my life where others were starting to refer to me as middle-aged and my hair is still as long as it was when I was in school. Some of us are just too cool to outgrow cool hair, I guess. I'm not sure Cascade's short, winged hair was ever cool, and I was doubly doubtful she'd ever cared.

At the mention of needing to talk, Cascade backed away from the door, encouraging me inside. "Of course. Of course. The Reaper Minister comes calling and you answer. How does that saying go?"

"Which one?"

"The one about Reapers and chasing mortals down."

"No one outruns the Reaper?"

"Yes! That one. Such a neat saying. Good branding too. The Guardians need something like that. Of course, it needs to be more in line with what we do for mortals. You understand?"

"I don't even know where it came from or I'd hook you up with whoever first coined it to see if they could do PR for the Guardians. I'll have to ask around."

She waved a hand in the air. "Oh, don't bother with me. Just a silly thought. That's all. So, you need to talk. Shall we sit in the dining room and I'll get us tea?"

I knew enough about Cascade to know that no one denied

her kindness. She took it as a personal affront. "That would be great. I hope I'm not intruding."

"Not at all. I was puttering around in the garden when my girls and boys started barking. I wouldn't have even heard you coming if it wasn't for them. Which, of course, is why I have the little darlings around. They don't let anyone sneak up on the property. Plus, they're my babies, of course. Let me get the tea going. Have a seat. I'll be back in a snap."

She disappeared through a doorway twice as tall as she was, which only made her look shorter, and into her kitchen. Her disappearance gave me a minute to soak in the dining room.

Five-shelved corner stands stood in the two corners of the opposite wall. Clutters of knickknacks of pugs ensured the space had little free space. From tiny ceramic miniatures to clocks in the shape of her cherished dog breed's face, to painted spoons bearing pugs at play. Everything pugs. Just like the call box at her gate. Something told me the army of little protectors tucked away somewhere in a back corner of the house comprised nothing but the breed. If the snorting and sniffing I was hearing down the hall was a sign, I was onto something.

"It's black tea," Cascade called from the kitchen. "I hope you don't mind?"

"That's fine," I called back. "I'm the one intruding on you, and if I'm being honest, I'm not much of a tea drinker, so please don't trouble yourself. But, fair warning, I have an open mind, so I may end up loving it and drinking your entire stock."

Cascade clucked from somewhere unseen. "No fretting. I drink so much, both from the Upperworld and Overworld. Half of my pantry is filled with various teas. The mortals do such a good job with theirs, I tell you." Spoons clanked against ceramic. Pots thumped on the stovetop. Water ran. I just was just about to tell her how bad I felt for putting her out when she continued. "One thing they do well. A reason I'm eager to put myself on assignments again, even though I'm far too old for that. The Order would have my hide if I did, let me tell you." She clucked again.

I heard her coming and moved to pull out a chair for her.

Cascade carried a two-foot-long tray. On it, she'd neatly arranged two cups on saucers, two teapots, and a bowl of sugar. Another bowl, this one smaller, held packets of nonnutritive sweeteners. A tiny plate held slices of a lemon cut into eighths. A small glass container of a golden liquid dominated a corner. I staunched the flow of reactions I had to the cups and pots, all of which displayed painted scenes of pugs playing in grassy paradises. Ghastly. Absolutely ghastly.

"Honey?" I asked, pointing at the glass container, as she set the tray on the table between our places.

"Oh yes. Everyone has such interesting tastes when it comes to tea. I can never tell what I should bring out when serving. Just when I think I've thought of everything, my company will ask to add something to the teas I've never thought about." With an open palm, she waved at the impressive spread on the tray. "I do the best I can and hope I have what they want in the kitchen if I haven't included it."

"This looks magnificent. Thank you."

Cascade walked me through how to pour tea, including the entire straining bit, and what the different offerings on the tray would do for me.

"This is far more complicated than I thought," I said.

She pressed down the lid of her pot. "Most certainly."

"Probably why I just drink coffee. I'm a simple man."

"Tea isn't for those in a hurry," she said, her narrow eyes gleaming with excitement as she set the pot down and watched me. "Let it sit for a few minutes while we chat. I'm interested to hear what you wanted to discuss. If this has to do with you and Sage, I will feel bad that you put yourself through the trouble of coming to see me. There's nothing for us to discuss. She was in the wrong and is being counseled. I've even pulled her off any assignments until she finishes re-training. I'm sorry she interfered with your escort." Cascade's round face hardened. "A Guardian should never develop romantic feelings for their mortals. She knew that. I cannot express how disappointed I am."

I shook my head. "Actually, that's not why I'm here. But now that you mention it, I feel bad. I didn't want her to get in trouble. If I had my druthers, no one would have found out. Call me a sucker, but I don't mind giving good angels second chances."

"That's very kind of you, Rev, but she should have never acted that way and she needs to learn. I'm glad this came out. I fear what would have happened had it been another Reaper. A less experienced one." Cascade put a hand to her chest. "Can you imagine the nightmare the two of us would have had on our hands? My word. No. No. Though she's young, that does not excuse her. Multiple poor decisions are concern-ing. Had they not assigned you to her mortal, and she carried on in that way, who knows what the future would have brought? But if she isn't why you're here, what do you need from me? Don't misunderstand. I enjoy the company, but I worry the Reaper Minister isn't here for me to expand his beverage fancies."

"As sad as the situation with Sage is, I'm sadder to tell you there are bigger issues. Issues that interest the Guardians."

Her thin bottom lip jutted. She pulled her head back, which made the skin on her chin wrinkle.

I asked for her confidence, which she gave, and then shared my behemoth assignment.

"My. My." Her hand was back at her chest again. "That is disturbing. I've been through a couple of these types of mani-festations, and can honestly say there's always been good communication from the Council. From my experience, they've been clear about why He manifested His greatness in such a way. But for the life of me, I don't remember hearing anything about this."

"Because nothing was said."

"Thus why you're asking for my confidence?"

I nodded.

Cascade looked perplexed before tipping her hand toward my cup. "Go ahead and try that. You'll want a sip, but something big enough to determine whether or not it's to your taste. The honey, sugar, or sweeteners will help, if not. Not all in combination, of course." She clucked again, humored by herself before returning to the work focus of my visit. "This is unfortunate news, but I'm not sure how the Guardians can help."

"One of the greatest benefits of a good working relationship between the Guardians and Reapers is that we can call on one another in times of need. I hope you agree?"

"Most certainly."

"I'm in a time of need, Cascade. The Guardians have greater numbers than the Reapers, and I need to lean on your ranks now."

She turned her head partially. "How so?"

"You've got billions of Guardians."

"Don't remind me," she said before taking a sip of her tea, pursing her lips like she planned on holding the drink in her mouth until the end of this conversation.

"That kind of force is a power unto itself, and I need their eyes and ears. Right now, the behemoth is resting in a forest in the Pacific Northwest, in America. But it won't for much longer. Soon, it will be mature enough to head into the towns and cities around the forest. And beyond that. Until it's stopped. I can't wait. I need to know where it is, and I need that information before anyone gets hurt."

"I guess I'm confused. The Guardians aren't monster hunters. They won't know how to find or track this beast."

"No, but they're attached to their mortals. They'll hear

what their mortals hear. See what their mortals see. I need to cast a wider net."

"And you see the Guardians as the net?"

"Part of it. Yes."

"I don't know," she said, sitting straighter.

As if picking up on her unease, snorts and sniffs came from the far part of the house behind a closed door that ostensibly protected me from her pug army.

"I can't do it alone."

"What about the Reapers? Can they not assist their own Minister?"

"We don't have the resources," I said honestly. "We're already stretched so thin the Order instituted a draft to bulk up our numbers."

"I heard." From the back room, a pug barked, leading to a chorus of responses from the others. Yahweh and Cascade were the only two who knew how many dogs she had back there. "Quiet, Reggie. I'm sorry. They get restless when they're cooped up. There's too many of them and not enough space."

"I'm okay if you need to let them out. They don't sound that big. I think I can handle myself."

"You haven't met them," she said with another clucking laugh. "But we have to focus, and they won't allow that. They enjoy attention and keeping themselves closer to my heart than any visitor. Though I'd feel terrible if I left them there for too long."

"Sure thing." I couldn't tell if she was edging the conversation away from my request or not. After all, she'd made tea for us and commented on how it was a leisurely drink. "If I could rely purely on Reapers, I would. There's just not enough. Plus, being Reapers, they'd need their familiars to escort them, and I can't ask a bunch of mortals to traipse around a mountainous forest."

"But you'd ask the Guardians?"

"Guardians aren't mortal. I'd rather put them out to deal

with this behemoth than have innocent mortals put in harm's way." I spread my hands, giving up on the tea for now. "Plus, I'm not asking your Guardians to go out into the forest. Just to keep their eyes and ears open if their mortal heads in that direction." I snapped my fingers in a moment of clarity. "Just the Guardians in Washington. No need to drag others into this, unless you're willing to task those whose mortals travel into Washington to tour the national forest. I'd gladly accept that help as well."

"Rev," Cascade said in a careful tone, "I didn't even say I'd give this a stamp of approval with the Guardians in Washington. Something like this isn't our job."

"I understand. But I don't have a lot of options, and this is the most workable, the most effective, use of the Upperworld's resources."

Cascade pressed her lips together so forcefully that the top one almost went pale enough to disappear. "I'm loath to say this, because no matter how I do, it'll come out sounding pretentious and insulting, and it's not meant to be. But the Guardians' job is not to do assassins' work. What you're asking is problematic. Sure, we can keep our eyes and ears out. I concede. But I'm not one for asking for more than that. If they hear something and they remember to pass it along. Fine. If they forget, there isn't much bother. There are lines I don't like to cross. Doing so sets dangerous precedents."

"This is important work, not a line we need to worry about crossing."

"You say that, but we can't foresee all the results of such actions. Besides burdening my administrative staff to isolate the Guardians in that region would also change the relationship we enjoy by redefining our duties. Today, it may only be watching and listening for signs of the behemoth. A hundred years from now, though? A thousand? Mission creep begins with a single step."

"Something is wrong in the Upperworld, maybe with

Yahweh Himself, Cascade." I hated having to point out the obvious, but she had kicked into full-on manager mode, and the two of us needed to make a smart decision here. "You said yourself that you can't remember the last time a manifestation happened and you didn't get word beforehand. Think about it. Why would Yahweh manifest a behemoth and the Council didn't tell the angel responsible for all the Guardian Angels? Makes little sense, doesn't it?"

"I don't deny that it is concerning. Still, it's my responsibility to manage how operate and how our responsibilities, duties, and resources are separated. I know what's best for the Guardians, and I'm not sure this is it."

"And I know what's best regarding hunting demons and monsters, and it isn't sitting back and waiting for the killing to begin."

"Rev, that's hardly—"

"What's it going to be like for the Guardians when that thing walks out of the seclusion of the national forest and smack-dab into the middle of a town?" I said, now on a roll. "What about when it reaches one of the Overworld cities? Mortals will respond and I've seen this thing, Cascade. The fight will be ugly. Lots of destruction and death. You think the Guardians are busy now? They haven't seen busy. This isn't like the last behemoth manifestation. There were, what, hundreds of thousands of homo sapiens on the planet then? Now? Seven billion. Last time, the last behemoth could have roamed for years and only tripped across a few villages. Now? The damn mortals have covered almost every inch of the planet. This is going to be bad, and it's up to me to stop it before it starts. That's why I'm here."

"You have my empathy, but I'm not sure you have my help," she answered, and I could see it was troubling her. Cascade wasn't an enemy. She wasn't even an asshole. She was protecting her angels. I got it. I didn't have to like it, but I understood where she was coming from.

"If we don't work something out, I'm going to have to find a solution."

That one looked like it stung. "What does that mean?"

I pinched my lips. "I might have to go to the Order and ask them to decide on my request to involve Guardians. I respect you too much to do that. Which is why I'm here first. Let's figure this out together because I promise, this will get worse if I can't figure out what in the world I'm dealing with."

"How much worse?" she asked as her hand crept back toward her chest.

"It's very possible there are influential angels involved."

"In what way?"

Did I dare name the Lamb of God? Could I trust Cascade with that? "The higher ranks, possibly," I said instead. "Nephilim. Seraphim. Others possibly. I've got leads, but no solid information. I'm stretched thin. But someone is handling the behemoth, and I aim to find out who. Imagine the headaches you'll have on your hands when your Guardians report that back to you."

"I'd rather not," she said, and sounded like that was the absolute truth.

"If I'm right, this is a speeding train none of us are ready for," I said, feeling like I had her thinking. "Destruction of life on this level means one thing."

Her face hardened as she stared off in thought.

Not the time to relent. "If the behemoth gets loose in a city, there are a whole lot of mortals who won't have the chance to have their names entered in the Book of Planes. You know what that means."

"Hundreds, thousands of ghosts. In one incident." She might as well have groaned, such was the strain on her voice.

"And an Overworld thrown into deeper and deeper chaos. What will happen to so many Guardians who've lost their mortals without them being entered into the Book of Planes?"

It was almost cruel to ask, but I needed her to see the ramifications of denying me.

Cascade swallowed. Her Adam's Apple slid up and down. "Rev, I'm not resourced to handle that. The toll on their mental health... would be... I'd lose a lot of them."

"I know."

"The pain. The suffering. Depression." She pinched her eyes shut with each word. She kept them closed when she said. "Some of them might... I can't. I cannot think about that right now. Please, give me time."

"I don't have much."

Her response came out like gas leaking from a line. "I know. I'll give you my answer as soon as I have clarity. Please."

"I'm sorry to trouble you with this."

"It's okay," she said, and I think we both knew that it wasn't.

I took my leave, tea unfinished, so she could release her pug corps. They barked at me all the way to the gate and long after I was outside it, clarifying their stance on the troubles I'd just brought their master.

20

BULGOGI AND BLACKMAIL

THREE DAYS. THREE FRUITLESS SEARCHES OF REMOTE REGIONS OF the Olympic National Forest. Exactly zero behemoths. Just to rub salt in the wounds, no Nephilim or Lambs of Gods made appearances either.

One thing that had come out of the investment of three days of my life I'd never get back was an answer from the Guardian Minister. I guess a few restless nights were enough for Cascade to find the motivation to agree to see things from my perspective, if not completely, at least a good chunk of it. Details were still being ironed out, but I could count on the Guardians' help. Exactly what that help would look like. I still didn't know. The terms were still unclear. One definite? Under no circumstances would they unmask. The one super-power Guardian Angels had, the ability to remain unde-tectable while in the Overworld, by mortals and immortals, was off the table.

"Eyes and ears only," Cascade had said, stressing each word. "They will not show themselves. I don't care what it is, unmasking will not happen. I've moved closer to meet you where you are. Now I need you to meet me."

I agreed. Once again, not liking Cascade's point of view,

but understanding it. The problem was all mine now. What to do if someone helping me, directly or indirectly, had their life, limb, and safety put in jeopardy? Better come up with something, and soon, because the Guardian Angels were going to stay behind their secret curtain and do what they could do to help their mortal—emphasis on 'their.' Immortal or another Guardian's mortal, it didn't matter. Each Guardian was to stay out of getting physically involved.

Still, this was a win, small as it may be. And I had my mentor to thank for it. From what I understood, Pher was the olive oil to Cascade's pan, the butter to her toast, the PB & J to her jelly.

Which was why I was cooking for my mentor. Cooking and complaining, until he made me accept I wasn't getting another inch from Cascade, so best not push it and have her retract her agreement. The true reason he was here. Well, that and he missed Juniper, who had gone home to her parents again while gramps returned to the Eighth Level for a new session for the Order.

"You know, it never ends," Pher said, standing by the balcony door and looking at the night-time setting over Olympia. The capitol buildings were illuminated in a rainbow color for an event. I wasn't sure what was happening in my adopted home, but that's because I didn't have time to buy milk, never mind ensuring my social calendar was up to snuff.

"What never ends?"

"These sessions," he said, unclasping his hands he'd had behind his back, and gesturing at the night. "Every time I turn around, there's another one on the schedule."

"Maybe the Order should focus a little more on events besides the latest offerings at the snack and coffee tables. Bet business would go a lot faster, and you'd get a lot more done if you actually met during a meeting instead of filling bellies."

"I'll have you know everyone puts great care into those

218 | PAUL SATING

baked goods and coffee," Pher said, still facing the night. "No sense in letting them go to waste. And we focus while in session. We have to. There's too much business waiting on votes to be wasteful or get distracted by tasks. Of which, many are yours."

"Such as?"

"Cascade," Pher said. That was important enough to mention and make sure was registered by the intended target. "And this business about the carnival of souls? What in the Upperworld made you say something like that?"

Pher had turned back to the night before mentioning the term I'd heard from Hellion. Was that because it disturbed him or he was just that fascinated with creeping fog and yellow streets creating an ambiance any serial killer would be happy to call home?

"What does it mean?" I asked as I casually trimmed the scallions for the bulgogi bowl, their sharp scent tickling my nose. By Yahweh, I love bulgogi night. Since I'd re-focused on preparing Pher's next free meal, I didn't see his reaction. I heard him coming—you have to pay attention to things like that when you're an assassin-slash-monster hunter-slash-demon hunter. He was at the edge of my kitchen island, almost directly behind me.

"Are you sure that's what Hellion said?"

I'm as white as you can get in the Pacific Northwest while still having an iota of ethnicity to me. Pher's black. We ain't related, any more than that wonderful little granddaughter of his would allow me to claim dibs on him. Even without blood ties, the way Pher asked made two things instantly obvious. First, he knew he'd get my attention and make me answer. Second, he got my attention and made me answer.

I sighed. "One billion percent. Whatever it is, boss, I can't shake the feeling that it's bad."

Pher made a sound like ach. I'm not sure if it was a sneeze he cut off, a cough that just couldn't be bothered, or that thing the fly-infested cartoon cat always used to say. Regardless, I don't think he expected me to name the Lamb of God.

"Too late now, but you shouldn't have gone to see her," he said in back-to-back record-breaking sluggish speech.

"I know." I stopped trimming the scallions before I ended up including the ends of my fingers in the mix. I set the knife down and turned. "But I've got a job to do. I don't have time to play around. Not with the behemoth growing stronger and someone handling it. We know that wasn't a demon in that video. No way Yahweh would manifest a behemoth to become the Underworld's plaything. That was an angel. The only reason I haven't already dragged that angel before the Order is by the saving grace of distance and limitations of modern mortal cameras."

"This is going to cause problems. Ones that will last long after you've rid the Overworld of the behemoth. I wish you'd asked. We could have attempted to help. You took that away."

"No one else needs to be at risk, boss. If I upset Hellion, and I'm sure I did, that's one thing. If I'd involved the Order, the Reapers, and the Guardians, who's to say any of you wouldn't have tripped in Hellion's path? At least this way, I'm the only one she tears limb from limb."

"You're crazy, lad."

"Like bat shit."

He shook his head and moved to my wine rack to select tonight's pairing with the bulgogi bowls. After a smattering of grunts as he squatted, he said, "You're not getting a morning star if she kills you."

"What?"

"You heard me."

"But what if she does?"

"Guess she better not," he said, holding the rack and swaying. For a second, I thought he'd pull the damn thing down on himself, but Pher steadied himself and the swaying ceased.

"Gee, thanks," I said in response, once my heart stopped skipping.

"Ah," he exclaimed with a smack of his hand on the bottle of Chilean Shiraz, "here we go. This should work. Right?"

"Impressive, boss. You take care of the wine, let me get to this," I said as I shot a thumb at the last of the carrots needing a little TLC by way of trimming and peeling. "Pour me a tall one."

"Good. I need that too."

We both got to work. Once the food preparation was done, the pork was seared and dumped into the pan with the carrots to start their bake, we were ready for a chat.

"So, what is it?"

Behind his glasses, his eyes were flat.

I shrugged. He knew better than to think I'd move on until I understood Hellion's threat. "The carnival of souls?"

Pher rocked his head. "Stupid saying from a long time back. In the Eighth everyone used to walk around using the term 'a great harvest of souls' whenever a Yahweh was resetting something in the Overworld. I don't know how well you remember those times. You were so young. Yahweh and Lucifer got on much better than they do now. Back then, they could do those things and cull the crop, if you will."

"Yikes, Pher. Sort of a casual way to talk about celestial genocide."

"I know. I just don't know a better way to put it. Anyway, that's what it used to be called. I guess that made it land more softly for a lot of angels. I don't remember when, a long time, that's for sure, it changed. Mostly from those who think Yahweh was overstaying his welcome. The types who were ready for a new regime. They took a soft saying like that and twisted it. The more questionable decisions Yahweh made, the more often He made them, the firmer the saying stuck as 'carnival of souls,' because a lot of angels saw what was happening and didn't like it."

"So what?"

"The pettiness grew between Yahweh and Lucifer. Lots of angels saw how the humans were being treated, and I'm sure demons did, too. At least those with access to these kinds of discussions. Some of the more humanitarian types, who saw a different path to the same goals, got real loud in proclaiming mortals were being used as pawns. Everything worsened, especially when many of the pre-historical civilizations were wiped clean in wars, floods, famines, and such. If I remember correctly, that's when it stuck."

"Hmmm," I said in equal eloquence.

Pher laughed richly. "What's that mean?"

"If that's the reference, then why in the world would Hellion say it to me? I mean, I get why she'd know it. She's ancient, like you."

"Careful, you only have a few more years of good knees yourself."

I ignored that all-too-real fact. "But I wouldn't know it. Not unless it was still a common saying. Which it isn't. I know because I've been all around the Upperworld, and hung with you big-wigs, and I've never heard anyone use it. Her saying it to me doesn't make sense."

"Unless its meaning has changed."

"To what?"

"That's the problem," Pher said. "I'll bet only she and those who run in her circles know. But one thing I've always found true about Hellion is to never let her get too far out of sight, or out of mind. The moment you do, it's not pretty."

"Duly noted," I said with a sigh and a long drink, emptying my glass and sliding it toward Pher for a refresh. It was also a chance to keep the guilty-admission ball rolling. "Since we're talking about dirty business and baring our souls, I have something else to tell you. About Jericho."

Pher's head flopped forward. "Do we really want to talk about him?"

"Nope, but that doesn't mean we can ignore him or the problems he causes."

"What is it this time?" my mentor asked as we clinked now-filled wine glasses.

"Me," I said, not bringing my cup to my lips and stopping Pher.

"What about you?" he asked over his wine glass.

"I blackmailed Jericho."

"You—" Pher's lips clamped together. He set his wine glass down. "You what? You couldn't. No. Not possible. It's just not. I thought the word in the halls were just ridiculous rumors."

"Sorry, but it's true. Just not in the way Jericho says."

"Well, that's not surprising." His hand went to his beard. He gripped it, pulling it down like he was ringing water from a washcloth. "What is this blackmail you're talking about? What in the world did you do?"

I explained everything about uncovering Jericho's past friendship with Arakiel Hale, the Nephilim who possessed and released the First Bowl. With a shrug, I said, "So he figured he'd focus blame on me to distract everyone even more. Finally, when he was desperate enough, he weaved his own tale about blackmail."

"Except that's the only detail he got right."

"Yep."

Pher was still stroking his beard. "This might be a problem. I'll have to work with the Order. You know that, right? We can't have the Reaper Minister running around black-mailing officials. That makes honest officials nervous and crooked ones paranoid."

"I know, boss."

"Plus, Jericho's mother doesn't need any other reasons to hate you. Hell, boy. They're Seraphims. Who messes with an entire family from the highest order of angels?"

"Someone looking for a fight. Or someone who doesn't

care what they think. Or someone who is crazy. I don't know. Pick one?"

"Someone who doesn't think he has enough problems is more like it," Pher said, lifting his wine glass. "Here's to the craziest bastard in all the Upperworld."

"Here, here."

The wine didn't last as long as my feelings of trepidation about the trouble I might have caused myself.

21

OUTBACK AND SNACKS

"Why couldn't God have released the behemoth in June? It's nice around here in the summer." Billee groaned as she pulled herself atop the boulder.

Bear chuckled, a deep rumbling sound. He stood a few feet in front of us, looking down into the next valley for any signs of the monstrosity.

"There's a lot of reasons to question Yahweh," I said, "but timing isn't one of them. We don't have a sense of the seasons in the Upperworld like on the earth. What's summer for you is just another day for us."

"Sounds boring," Billee said as she sniffled.

"It gets old," I admitted.

"What's the Upperworld?" Bear asked, still surveying the rises and troughs of the valley.

"We call it Heaven," Billee answered for me as she moved closer to the big man. "See anything?"

"Fuck all."

Thank Yahweh Bear's vocabulary didn't bother Billee. I'd numbed her to caustic words, I guess. A monstrous man in his own right, I found he had quite a tempered personality. I wouldn't call him soft. Men his size and with his military background were too dangerous to slap that attribute on, but this was a guy who would spend more time hugging people than fighting them. The Green Berets had made him that way, but that only formed part of who he was. A civilian for five years, remnants of that harshness remained, but a kinder, dare I say more human part of the man dominated his personality. His language was simply a leftover of his past life that stubbornly refused to fade with the rest of his previous identity. Though I doubted special forces people like Bear ever truly let go of who they used to be.

Billee had never been in the military, but she was tough, too. Words couldn't hurt her.

"We keep going that way," he said, pointing off to the north. "One advantage we have is the flora. If we were in the open prairies or in some incredibly inhospitable environment that stopped vegetation from growing or stripped all the trees from the land, we'd be fucked. But here? Anything that size can't get around without making a mess."

"And we follow the mess," I said. "Lead the way."

We started out on the trail of the behemoth.

My big break had come when there was a sighting just west of Brinnon, an unincorporated clump of houses and buildings that existed in name only, if I'm being flippant. As a Census Designated Place, Brinnon didn't exist in the sense of how we think of towns and cities. Yeah, it's that sort of place, nondescript and forgettable. But hey, someone in Brinnon saw the behemoth—well, they saw something they didn't understand, and it scared the bejesus out of them enough to take to the internet and tell any troll peeking their heads out from under their bridges. Thanks to the fervor it kicked off, where most users responded with critical comments about the poster's mental health, it came across my radar. Not that I spend time on social media. Trust me, I don't. I'd rather hike across Death Valley on my hands and knees, armed only with a canteen of salt water. But one of Bolt's boys, like most teens, apparently spends all his free time on different platforms. He was the one to see the online arguments and told Bolt, who reported it to me.

See? My net strategy was working. Vindication!

As soon as the sun rose, Bear was on his way to my place. Billee beat him because I'd given her a heads-up and she was practiced at responding with expediency. It didn't hurt that she lives ten miles closer to my place. When Bear arrived, we made sure we had everything we'd need to spend the day hiking in the forest in late January. Good times.

Bolt's boy had gleaned enough from the online fight to give us a good starting point. It didn't hurt that Brinnon was such a small not-town, and we could find someone willing to start us off based on what they'd heard in the local rumor mill.

The Dosewallips River feeds Hood Canal from the north-west. Rocky Brook Falls was the nearest landmark the local could point us to, so we started there and found our first clue within minutes of getting out of Bear's truck.

Don't give me a lot of credit, the signs were hard to miss.

The falls were a local attraction, modest, but picturesque. I understood why they attracted people with very little else going on in their local community that didn't involve church. The Pacific Northwest is littered with waterfalls. These falls were one of the tamer offerings, so small a visitor could walk to within a body's length of the base. In fact, during the summer, plenty of mortals frolicked and played in the pool the falls fed.

Well, they used to.

This summer, no kids—or adults looking to embrace their youthful side—would play in the fall's pool. The behemoth had made sure of that.

It had gone through its "terrible twos" a little early and tore the place up. Out of frustration or boredom, I couldn't tell, and the mysterious witness hadn't provided that level of detail in their online reporting. But what might have been a quaint recreational area before the behemoth's arrival was now a scene of devastation. Uprooted trees had been tossed around. Shards of trunks told me the beast had thrown a handful of the trees at the falls as if the sound of rushing water had upset the beast. Trees that had stood forty, fifty, sixty feet, and higher were now thick, jagged splinters of their former selves, all clogging the pool they now buried.

Boulders, bigger than Bear, and weighing tons, had been tossed about too. Pushed downhill. Kicked uphill. Apparently thrown against the falls and broken apart. The rock mixed with the splintered trees in a way that made them look like nature's attempt at spaghetti and meatballs.

As disturbing as the destruction was, the behemoth had left behind a part of itself that might lead to its downfall. Footprints. Everywhere.

In this region, especially at this time of year, it's easy to give yourself away because of the soft soil. That only gets easier when you weigh ten tons and sink four feet into the land with each step. Bear stood in one and I took a picture so he could show his ex-army buddies. The ridge of the print came up to his broad chest. It was a funny picture, even considering the serious situation.

Four hours later, we were deep into the forest and still following the trail of prints.

"This goes on forever," Billee said.

The day was pleasant enough for the time of year, but it was going to be a short one. They all are in January in Washington state. Between the relative cold and the looming sunset, I think she was getting nervous about being caught this deep in the forest. The scene at the falls, the remnant of the behemoth's might, probably helped to unsettle her. I couldn't blame her. I felt wholly unprepared now. Even though I'd seen the behemoth on a cell phone video, what had been captured in digital format hardly did justice to a creature that could tear apart a waterfall. The behemoth was a force, one we couldn't meet in dying sunlight.

"We'll get to that next rise and reassess," I said. "Then we'll need to head back if we don't get at least a nibble, if not the whole damn bite."

Neither of the mortals argued.

Another half-mile later, toward the bottom of the slope and almost at the valley floor, we pulled up. No one said a word. Bear winced. Billee gagged. I put a gloved hand to my nose and mouth.

"Good God, what is that?" Billee said.

"Something dead," Bear answered, still wincing but swiveling to find the source of the stench. He pointed left of the trail. "Coming from over there."

"You can tell that?" I asked, amazed.

"Been in too many dangerous places to not have learned how to pinpoint the smell of death," the big man said, looking pained.

I had no response.

We followed Bear as he crept forward. The fern-covered terrain rose in short swells before dipping away. Trees grew close together here. Combined with the flora, that made the going slow. We needed to be careful. No one, especially Bear, needed a broken ankle this far out into the nothingness. We didn't have the time or capacity to lug each other back to civilization, and spending the night in the forest fell far short of my vacation destination list. Being the good adult I am, I reminded the pair of that fact.

"It's a mess in here," Bear said, bending underneath the dropping branches of a bigleaf maple before pulling up. The way he stood erect, I knew I couldn't wait to see what we'd stumbled into.

The ferns and trees had blocked my view whenever the rise or Bear hadn't. Moving beside him, I now saw what stopped him.

Trees uprooted. Smashed. Broken. Snapped. This extension of the heavily populated rainforest was now a wreckage of a clearing. The forest flotsam didn't hide the discarded meal the behemoth left behind.

Deer and elk, what remained of them anyway, lay scattered around the clearing.

"Oh my God," Billee said, pulling up and staring wide-eyed at the poor animals.

"Twenty-six by my count," Bear said, his eyes bouncing along their carcasses as he recounted. "Yep. Twenty-six."

Billee groaned. "What in the world could eat that many animals? Especially this size? Rev, how big is this thing?"

"You saw the footprints. Let's just hope this isn't a single day's meal," I said, finding it hard to stop the calculations in my head. The prints were enough to reinforce my estimation of its size. This carnage reinforced the fear I had that the beast wasn't long for the isolation of this forest. Maybe it was hungry, maybe starving, and that's why it threw a tantrum at the falls. This was bad. Very bad. "Let's see if we can pick up the trail again. Then we'll head back. We've got about five minutes to find this thing or we're going to be racing darkness." I scanned the broken and devastated wildlife. "We're not prepared for anything more."

I gave the team an extra five minutes to pick up the trail. Though the space was trampled and compacted by the behemoth's time here, that didn't mean the terrain wasn't difficult to navigate. The indentions it left behind in the moist soil only added to the hazards of traipsing around. We had split again, but stayed close enough to hear each other's voices should we need to come to one another's rescue or shout a warning to high-tail it away from the scene.

Just before I was ready to call everyone back, Bear whistled. "Rev?"

His voice carried across the clearing from the far side.

"Coming. Where are you?"

"Here! I see you."

I pinpointed his voice. Behind trees that had survived the behemoth's feast, he waved. "Billee? Let's round up."

"Gladly," she said, her small hooded head barely visible beyond the moss-covered mounds of dead vegetation. Together, we joined Bear.

He stood on the rocky banks of a river. Pebbles and rocks of all sizes lined the water. Bear pointed off to the side. "There's one last footprint, then... nothing. Figure it went into the river, though I don't see anything on the far side."

I scanned the opposite bank. "It could have gone either way."

"Or walked up the river. You know? To cover its tracks. You said someone was working with it, right? Maybe they are trying to keep its presence hidden as much as possible."

"Good point," I said. "That water can't be more than ten or fifteen feet deep."

"Moving swiftly though," Bear said, cocking his head.

"Yeah, but this thing is a freaking tank. It'd plow right through that like it was a mud puddle."

Billee wrapped her arms around herself, her gaze flicking toward the gray sky. "So what do we do?"

I sighed. "We head back and figure out how to raise an army. Now that we have an idea where it is, we can be faster next time. But we still need more eyes."

"Is that smart?" she asked.

"Yep," I said, gesturing behind us at the field of dead wildlife. "Because the behemoth is growing and getting stronger. Probably running out of things in the forest to eat, and I don't think it's interested in becoming a vegetarian. We have to find it soon, or 'almost soon' might be too late."

"I've got some old Army buddies I could call," Bear said, spreading his hands.

"You do?"

"Yeah. Bunch of them are local. Wouldn't be hard to round

them up. They're itching to get back into the outdoors. Do it all the time, from spring to fall. We're getting old, so we don't get out much in the winter, except to hunt. This is something they'd definitely be down for."

"The Green Berets too?"

"Not all. But I know a few Special Forces guys. They might have contacts too. They should."

I nodded. "Great. Let's work on that as soon as we get home. I've got people I'm going to call on, too."

Billee groaned. "Tell me it's not the kids."

"It is. But I also have another type of crew ready to help." I didn't tell her about the Guardian Angels joining the fight, at least in their own way, as I watched her face harden. "Either they help me find this thing so I can stop it, or this monster gets out into the populated areas and does a bunch of nasty shit to a bunch of innocent people. I swear this is on the up and up. No coercion, I promise. This isn't Hollywood. It's not pretty, and it's not clean." I turned to include Bear, so he understood where I was coming from as well. "There are no Rules of Engagement with the behemoth. And if my gut is right about who is directing it, ethical rules would hand the bad guys the advantage. They won't fight fair."

The ex-military man looked grim but nodded.

"We don't let anyone walk into this blind," I said, more to him than Billee. She already knew how this played out. "Tell them what they might see. Just leave out comments about angels and immortals. That freaks people out, and I don't need to take time away from this to break you out of a mental ward."

He chuckled. "You got it. Lips sealed. Wouldn't be the first time I couldn't share the nature of the job I'm on."

I moved to him and extended my arm. He took my hand, and we shook. I didn't let go. "Thank you for this, Bear. I know you didn't sign up for this. I appreciate it."

He shook his head, looking embarrassed at my gratitude.

"Not a problem, man. Wasn't kidding when I told you I'll never forgive myself for what we did to that pastor guy. I mean, he's doing better, but, still. His life will never be the same, even after he heals. For the rest of my life, I'll be making reparations."

"I'm not asking for that."

"I know," he said, his jaw clenching. "I am. It's the right thing to do. Don't worry about my boys. They'll be good. They know what they're doing, and more importantly, they know how to keep their mouths shut."

"I like the sound of that," I said, and we finally let go of each other's hand. "Let's get out of here before we end up having an unplanned overnight camping excursion in the Olympics."

Two hours later, we were on the last rise, a thousand feet above the valley. We were looking down on a human-made trail that would help us pick up our pace and get back to the warm truck. I looked behind at the vast stretch of green. Even with Bolt's group and Bear's ex-military friends, tracking the behemoth was going to be a tall task. I needed more. The Guardian Angels would be an immense help. Though I appreciated Cascade making accommodations, they weren't enough. I'd even be willing to buy her an atrocious knick-knack to fill any empty spot in her home if she'd give a little more. This much territory required bodies to canvas it before the behemoth started its body count.

We were on the back side of the last hill when a deep boom rolled through the forest. Life stilled as the thick sound reverberated in all directions at once.

Bear had his hand to his heart, looking pale enough that his freckles nearly faded into his cheeks.

My pulse raced. "You okay?"

He blinked. "Sorry. Little PTSD there. Sounded like an ordinance. Took me back to places I don't want to be anymore."

"Understand. You good now?"

The rumble was fading, rippling miles away.

"Yeah."

I turned to find Billee staring off, back up the hill we'd just traversed.

"Billee?"

"What was that?" she asked. Her brown skin had drained as well.

"If I had my guesses, I'd say our mysterious pet is getting restless." I looked up at the sky, suddenly feeling uncomfortable with how low the sun was behind the gray clouds. "We can't do anything today, and dusk is coming. We need to get out of here while the getting is good."

"Can it find us?" she asked.

"I doubt it," I said, listening for another sonic boom. When the quiet revealed no secrets, I said, "That was miles away. There's no way it's aware of us."

"Miles? But I felt that. Felt it, Rev. The air moved."

"That happens," Bear said. "When I was in the war, the shock waves from explosives would hit you like a wave in the ocean. They're no joke. Even miles away, they'd make tents sway and knock shit over."

Billee's arms wrapped tighter around her waist.

"Let's go before my toes freeze," I said and started toward the path, knowing after what we'd found today, frozen toes were the least of my worries.

22

TATTLETALES

"You what?" Puriel asked and actually broke her typical stoic posture to lean forward and cock her ear like she hadn't heard me.

Around the table of the Order of Thirteen, heads swiveled in my direction, eyebrows raised, and even Sid looked about to say something—and getting him to say anything is a monumental task.

"I've got a bunch of kids and ex-military people rounded up in a mountain retreat. Got a great deal on it, though I had to book it for two weeks to get the owner to come around to having that many people in it. So I'm going to need the funds deposited into my Overworld account."

"Not that bit, Mr. Carver," the President of the Order said, laying her hands on the table and rolling her fingers together until they interlocked. "The part about you involving children. Mortal children."

"I warned you about him going rogue," Jericho mumbled from his chair halfway between me and Puriel.

Her hand shot in the air, a single finger extended. "Not now, Jericho."

Pher snickered. So did Turiel. Jericho, even after being

publicly chastised, showed absolutely no emotional reaction. If anyone could corner the deadpan comedy stand-up market, it was him. Well, if he had the personality for it. Thankfully, the Upperworld was safe from being exposed to his sense of humor.

"You," Puriel said, her finger dipping at me. "This is unconventional."

"The boy has a way with convention," Pher said. "I'd swear he's allergic to it. But we'd do well to remember that, above all else, he's effective."

"Yes, but putting mortals in harm's way?" Dumas said, his white eyebrows furrowing. "This is unacceptable. Surely we all see that? We would never tolerate this from another Reaper or Guardian."

"Yet he gets away with it," Jericho said, jumping in unsurprisingly. He would take advantage of anything that shed me in poor light. I expected nothing more from the spoiled brat.

"He's not getting away with anything," Uziel said in my defense. "Are we serious?"

"This is serious." Puriel's mouth puckered, and not affectionately. "Convention or not, I don't care about that. What I care about is that you've made these decisions without even broaching the subject with us."

I spread my hands in an ever-widening lateral plume. "Because of this, right here." That got interesting facial gestures and throat clearing, let me tell you. "Listen, I don't have a lot of time. If you don't like the way I conduct my business, the business this body assigned, then fire me and let someone else chase down the behemoth."

"Don't be like that, lad," Pher admonished.

Jericho scoffed but said nothing.

"Why Rev? You're perfect for the job," Turiel said, sounding genuinely concerned.

I looked her way to nod, seeing her smile. A smile that was dominated by her two broad front teeth. "Thank you."

"Unconventional, yes," Samael, the Vice President, said, tapping the table with a thick finger, "but what's more concerning is the ethics of the matter." I started to reply, but he held up a hand, palm aimed at me. "Allow me time to make my point, Rev. The major issue many of the Order members have is that you didn't approach us first before taking unilateral action. That's the sticking point. But I also agree that we can address this another time. After you've taken care of the behemoth."

Convenient. Punish me once I did their dirty work. If I lived to be punished. "The behemoth is growing, literally and figuratively. I give it another week or so, and it'll be tromping around the Overworld. What then? You think you're frustrated now? Wait until the Council is breathing down your necks because they delegated this to you, and you wasted precious time complaining about my methods." I motioned at the angel to my side, also placed at the foot of the table to communicate her standing with the angels of the Order. "Cascade is on board with the Guardians. It's not like I'm dashing into a fight and pulling everyone along with me. But I can't do this handcuffed. This will be nearly impossible as it is."

"But children?" Dumas said, emphasizing the last word.

"He's just setting up his excuses for something else he's pulling, probably behind our backs," Jericho said to Puriel.

I think even Pher growled.

"You're welcome to come to the Overworld with me, Jericho. Like I've said a thousand times, I need the extra hands. Pitch in and do something meaningful for once."

That received a round of snickers from Turiel, Raphina, Zephon, and even Sid. But Dumas and Harut's scowls encouraged their peers to keep proper decorum. The others, the more senior of the Order, didn't react at all, keeping their faces neutral.

"Did you check the Book of Planes for their names?" I asked Camael, the Order's Secretary.

He nodded. "I did. None of them are named."

I spread my hands at the minor victory. "There. See? They're not slotted to die, so they're as safe as they can be."

"That could change," Dumas said with a scowl only hidden by his thick white mustache. "Taking them into the forest to hunt the behemoth. Anything could happen. They could fall off a cliff or a bear could catch them unaware. They'd be lost. Senselessly. All because of your decision to involve them."

"Beelzebub could run them down while crossing the street when he's had too much to drink," I argued, growing exhausted by the need to argue.

"Not all at once," Jericho said, having the nerve to look at Cascade. "The Guardian Angels could protect them from that if their time hasn't come." He looked away, bypassing me in an instant. "But the behemoth stomping on fifty teenage mortals would be a political disaster."

"Rev," Jerah, the Chief of Internal Relations, said, looking as if he was already preparing an apology, "I hate to say it, but I agree with Jericho on this. As the conduit between the Reapers and the Guardians, I speak with both interests in mind. Yes, none of us enjoy putting mortals at risk. There can be no doubt of that. Yes, I understand you have a job to do and I appreciate the fact you're likely the only one who can do this without getting a reaction from the demons. But this might be a step too far."

I appreciated Jerah and never had a problem with the man. I didn't now, either. But he was wrong.

I rubbed my face in frustration, wanting to scream at this listless body of angels.

Cascade, who had been quiet throughout, cleared her throat. "If I may?"

"Of course," Puriel said.

Cascade stood to address the Order. I'd never thought of doing that. If this worked in her favor, maybe I'd have to give it a go the next time I needed them to hear me about relieving me of my Reaper duties. "Ladies and gentlemen, I understand everyone's reservations about Rev's decision. Please note, we've had lengthy discussions and I'm in favor of him utilizing the Guardians how he will, in accordance with our agreement. None of the Guardians will unmask. They'll help how they can, but I won't have them exposing themselves to mortals. The ramifications of such actions would be a bigger problem than the behemoth, given time. We can't have that. I want my support of his plan to be clear. Doing otherwise, I feel, creates bigger problems for all of us."

Her message shared, Cascade slowly retook her seat. Never dropping her head, she instead met our superiors' eyes. She had their respect in full, based on what I saw around the table.

"Your Guardians are all on board?" Puriel asked.

"Not all," the Guardian Minister said. She wore a white business suit today, which only embellished the aura of power emanating from her. "But they'll come around because I expect that of them. They know where I stand on the issue." She delayed just long enough to send a clear message to anyone who'd been paying attention. "Some are more thick-headed and stubborn than others, but I have full confidence. You have nothing to worry about from the Guardians. We'll do what we can to help Rev and the crew he's assembling. I hope the Order will as well."

Wow. Calling out her superiors to support me? Cascade was definitely getting an ugly knickknack if I survived this mess.

"Thank you," I whispered.

She stared forward, her chin clenched as if she was daring anyone to question her stance.

Puriel held her own head in a similar stance. She titled it a bit, hardly noticeable. "We will think on this."

I rocked back in my chair, almost tipping it. "We don't

have time to think. The Safe? The First Bowl? Worldwide pandemic? A behemoth handler? Unless you've got an answer to why Yahweh manifested the behemoth, we can't wait."

My implied question hung in the air for only a fraction of a second before my mentor contributed to my point. "We haven't. The Council is still silent. If they know something, they're not sharing it."

I flung my arm out. "There you go, then. Whatever reason Yahweh has for the behemoth, the Council doesn't know, but they agree it needs to be stopped. All the while, someone is preparing the beast to march on the world. For all we know, it could be one of the Four Horsemen."

Turiel gasped. Sid coughed up his coffee. Uziel stared at me.

"You can't know that," Dumas stammered. "You sh— shouldn't say things like that without having very solid information at your fingertips."

"You're right, I can't," I said. "But no one at this table can dispute the signs that we're becoming vulnerable. Can you?" I let the silence linger, but only for a moment. I was done with the politics. We needed action, not words. If they didn't like it, they could fire me. Then we'd all win. Well, except for the future of humanity, and maybe even the Upperworld, if Hellion was indeed wrapped up in this subversive mess. For a bunch of thinkers, the Order was short of ideological feedback. "That's what I thought. Here's the deal. Not everyone is a willing participant in life. Some of us get screwed over once or twice, and we remember those times forever. Life fucks others every single day. No one wants mortals to get hurt, least of all me. I'm the one putting them at risk, and I'll do everything in my power to ensure their safety. Everything. But I'm going to do it because the behemoth needs to be stopped. Now. Not next week. Next month. Not whenever the Order is bothered to decide for me what's appropriate and what's not." I met Puriel's stiff gaze with one of my own. "You tasked me to take care of the behemoth. Now I'm telling the Order to get out of my way and let me do the job you're forcing me to do."

If the meeting room doors weren't so thick, I'd bet I would have heard Brock cracking up outside. The air crackled with anxiousness as everyone, myself included, waited for Puriel's response.

"Rev, we trust you to complete the task," she said, her thin lips barely moving. "We trust you to protect as many of the mortals as you can. Thank you for your candor."

"You're welcome," I said cautiously, expecting much more. From the glances and head swiveling at the table, I think most of the Order did as well. She didn't give them a chance to voice any uncertainty, though.

"We'll adjourn the meeting," she said and stood.

As chairs rolled back under the table and the Order broke off into small clumps of whispering angels, I thanked Cascade once more.

She rested her hand on my arm. "You are in an unenviable position. Good luck."

She drifted away, pausing only to smile and say short farewells to Turiel and Uziel. Then, she was out the door, leaving me with the thirteen angels who could extend my misery with a short vote.

Dumas drifted by without a word, heading toward the doors. Jericho walked alongside him, leaning in to whisper something.

They were almost at the door when I heard Pher call out. "Dumas. Hold for a moment, please. There's something I'd like to talk to you about. You too, lad."

At my inclusion, Jericho, who had halted beside Dumas, straightened his back and spun, leaving the room as rapidly as my good mood shriveled any time he was around.

The other Order members slowly departed. I remained

next to my chair. Dumas stayed by the door. Soon, it was just the three of us at one end of the table, Puriel and Samael at the other, pretending not to be hanging back.

"What do you need, Pher? I'm busy," Dumas said once the three of us were together.

"Let's get right down to it," Pher said, his demeanor so un-Pher-like. "What do you know about the carnival of souls?" He waved his hand back and forth. "I'm not talking about the old days. I mean, a recent phase. Have you heard anything?"

"I hear rumors, and rumors bore me," Dumas said, scrunching her furry eyebrows.

Funny, I thought, for him to make a point of saying that when he was essentially Jericho's confidant in the Order. Dumas was very likely included in the smaller council Jericho had called to spread the lie about my blackmail efforts. Jericho was a walking rumor, yet Dumas didn't seem bored enough by him to not associate with the idiot.

"Don't play," Pher said, taking the same tone with the elder angel as he did with me when I acted like a punk. "What do you know? Ignorance doesn't suit you. I can read it on your face. You've heard things. Give it up. What's going on with the carnival of souls?"

Dumas's gaze swiveled between me and my mentor. The old man was unsure, questioning. Calculating.

But I didn't have to worry. Pher was on him like sparkles on a unicorn's ass. "Now, Dumas. You've heard it. Start dropping names and specifics, or Puriel and I are going to have a conversation about your relationship with Jericho. If some of the things I've been hearing are true, they might make her and the rest of the Order concerned."

Ah, look at my mentor, getting into the blackmail game himself. I couldn't have been more proud.

Dumas pulled his notebook tight against his chest. "Ju— just things, Pher. Like I said. Nothing but rumors."

"Enlighten me." Pher took a small but measured step forward.

From the far end of the room, Puriel and Samael conversed quietly, but I caught them looking our way. They tried to act as if the folder on the table was the center of their discussion, but they couldn't fool a fool. I'd busted them.

"Just th—that the Nephilim are engaging in something," Dumas said. His bony hands holding the notebook quivered.

"Engaging? Like what? With who?" my boss pressed.

"I'm not sure," Dumas said. "You asked what I've heard and I'm telling you. Supposedly, they're targeting angels and archangels. For what purposes? I don't know. But that's what I've heard."

"Targeting them how?" I asked.

Dumas kept her gaze on Pher. "Jericho is the Chief of Security, and this is most definitely a security issue. Go ask him. I don't know. Leave me out of this."

He turned, swayed a little at the swift movement, and bolted from the room as fast as an angel his age could reasonably be considered to be bolting.

In sync, Pher and I groaned.

23

TO TRACK A BEAST

MOVING AN ARMY THROUGH AN EXPANSIVE WOODED AREA IS slower than crossing a country on your own. Especially unfamiliar land. Even if it's mountainous land. Even if you have one or two mortals with you, and one of those mortals is your familiar who never seems to be warm enough. But an army? They slow things down, especially when the vast majority are a bunch of kids and young adults from a small city, unaccustomed to harsh hikes in the dead of winter.

"They're doing well," Billee said at my side.

I scanned the line in both directions. Forty of Bolt's crew actually broke away from their parents. It helped that it was the weekend, providing the teens with a ready-made reason to get out of the house. As someone who's never had kids, I know enough parents who'd be more than happy for their teens to disappear for a day or two every month. Looks like I was doing everyone a favor. I wasn't complaining. Forty was great. A super-shot of their focus, and then I could return each one of them to their parents.

I would return every last one of them.

"Bear's crew is helping," I said, noting them, spread along the two lines of civilian kids.

"I can't believe he could get eight guys to help on such short notice," she said. "Though I could do with a few women in this crew. Being the only one in a group of fifty? Too much testosterone for me."

"Bear is a good guy. If he knew a female Green Beret, I'm sure she'd be out here. I'm not sure they have them, though."

"Not until 2020," Billee said. "Though one graduated in the eighties, they denied her graduation. Right up until she filed a complaint."

"No females until 2020?" I said, shocked enough to pull my attention away from my careful assessment of our wild surroundings.

"The military hasn't exactly been an organization that leans forward on issues if they don't involve shooting or bombing things," Billee said, eyeing Bear. "But he seems like a good guy. He has, ever since the first time."

"Yeah, I'm grateful to him almost as much as I'm grateful for you."

"Me?" she said, pulling back her hood with a gloved hand. The wind blew a strand of long curls back into her face and she tried to swat at that, but it wouldn't be denied. Each time she moved her hand away, the wind blew the strand right back. She finally gave up. "Why me? He's the one adding expertise." She leaned closer, lowering her voice. "And they're all armed. Did you notice?"

I laughed. "Yes. I did. And I'm glad. I don't know if I'll need their help, but I'm glad to have it just in case."

"What do you think we'll find? I mean, really?"

"Unless the behemoth is on the move, I expect to find it or its nest."

Her eyes widened.

"Now or never, Billee. I don't want to fight this thing in Shelton's downtown."

"I understand. I just… I don't know. Out here, with so many people, I feel a lot better. At least until it dawns on me that we're really doing this. We're really getting close, and that makes it real. And the more real it feels, the more frightening it is."

"I totally agree."

"You're scared?"

"Shitless."

Billee's shoulders dropped. "Classy. As always."

"Over here!" a youthful voice called from the right end of the line.

"Stop!" I didn't want the formation to break.

"Halt!" Bear's bellow, on the heel of my command, stopped everyone. I wasn't jealous. The authority in his voice made me want to comply with whatever he said, too.

"Come on," I said to Billee.

She stepped out of line with me. I whistled for Bear and tipped my head. He jogged up behind us, small clouds of white breath puffing in front of his face.

This half of the line, civilian teenagers who were learning about search operations on the fly, interspersed with experienced Special Forces ex-military, held steady. Keeping their place, they craned their heads to get a glimpse of what was called out.

The day was bright but as cold as an annoyed grandmother's disposition.

"Try to stay warm," I shouted as we jogged up the slope. Each member was spaced out by twenty feet. We weren't looking for needles in haystacks here. The creature we sought was three-quarters as tall as the western hemlock trees filling this part of the forest. Spread out to cover as much ground as we could so we overlooked nothing, I had to repeat the order every fifteen feet. But word spread up and down the line and soon everyone shuffled their feet, blew into gloved hands, or tucked their faces as deeply into the collars of their jackets as they could to stave off the chill while they waited.

Reaching the teenager at the crest of a rise. He was thin

and handsome. Probably had no problem drawing the interest of anyone he wanted and probably never would until his "dad bod" took firm hold two decades from now. The kid pointed downhill.

Thirty yards away, we would have missed the pile of shit if we hadn't stretched the line so far.

When I say shit, I mean, literally, a pile of shit. A big, ole, stinking pile of shit four feet high.

"No animal makes something like that over a lifetime," Bear said with a nervous grunt.

"Takes a big one to crap that much."

"How big is this thing?" the kid asked.

I looked up at the hemlocks.

He followed my gaze and then said, "Seriously?"

"Almost. Yep. I'm serious."

"Well, that explains that." He tipped his jaw toward the pile of behemoth dung.

I moved closer.

"What are you doing?" Billee asked.

Without turning, I said, "Seeing if it's warm."

Before I reached the pile, I knew we were safe in the immediate term. Without the aroma of fresh dung and with no white tendrils of steam rising from it, I didn't expect the pile to be hot or even lukewarm. It wasn't. Not that I touched it, of course. That was unnecessary. But I got as close as necessary. An assassin's work is sometimes dirty.

"We're good," I said, waving everyone back into a ready stance. "Let's keep moving."

A few miles later, we found more deer carcasses than I ever cared to see again. I apologized to the crew, knowing the ex-Green Berets probably had seen worse in their time, but the kids hadn't, and I didn't want them feeling like I was picking on any perceived fragility. Teens, especially boys, can be like that. The smell was thick, and I nearly gagged when the wind shifted and I swallowed a particularly over-whelming batch of dead animal.

One of the ex-Green Berets spoke up as everyone processed what they were seeing. "When we were shopping in town, I heard a local talking about shit going down at farms in the area. Lots of cattle turning up slaughtered a couple of mornings in a row. Said the farmers were talking about everything being fine when they headed in for the night, but then waking to a massacre. Anything left outside at night was dead in the morning. By the way the guy described it, sounded a lot like this."

Great.

"If the behemoth is attacking farm animals, Rev?" Billee said, her voice full of tension. I didn't need her to finish her comment to agree with her.

"The good news, if it can be called that," Bear said, nudging me with his elbow and jerking his head up along the clearing, "is that we have a nice clue about which path to follow."

"Let's hope that leads to the prize," I said.

Two or three of the kids grumbled. They were getting cold and unnerved. I had to keep in mind that they were necessary sacrifices. I would protect them the best I could, but they were going to see some shit, literally and figuratively, today that they would never forget. Still, I didn't need to overload them unless the situation demanded it. I also didn't need to break their minds and send them back to their parents as half of who they were when I took them away.

"Let's hurry and follow it. No more need for the search line. That'll just slow us." I took one more look at the group, seeing a mix of fear, trepidation, and something that looked like hunger in their faces. The trail might lead to another dead end if it crossed a river and obscured the behemoth's tracks. It might split off, forcing us to resume the search line. As much as I wanted to send these kids back to the rented house to eat all the junk food we brought and spend the rest of the day surfing porn on our renter's internet, I needed them here and as focused as they could be under the circumstances.

I found Bolt among the throng. He was standing at the front of the collapsed column formation. As if understanding my dilemma, he bit his lip but nodded, once, stiffly.

"Let's do this," I said and led everyone up the trail.

The sun was trying to poke through the clouds, intermittently successful, at least until the cloud cover swept through again. The constant ebb and flow of sunlight made the shadows dance in the deeper parts of the forest on either side of this channel cut through it. In the back of my brain, I knew those shadows were nothing to worry about. It was too big, and from what I'd seen on the cell phone video, too much of a lumbering beast to stalk us in the small spaces provided by the forest. But in the video, the beast had been grazing and bathing at dusk. Each time we'd been in the Olympics, we hadn't seen the scale or nail of it. The booming sound we heard during our last trip had come as dusk was setting. Now, if farmers in the area were noticing consistencies in the timing of when something attacked their livestock. That pointed at nighttime events, meaning the behemoth came out under the cloak of darkness. If that was the case, we wouldn't have to worry about the spawn of Yahweh stalking us as long as we had daylight.

But Hellion or one of her Horsemen could.

At that thought, I hurried everyone along at a slow jog. Just because we had more bodies to help with carrying any potentially broken ones didn't mean I wanted to take unnecessary risks and put my theory to the test.

We came out of the channel. The forest on both sides peeled away. For six hundred feet, the slope dropped. Deep gouges cut apart the hill in alternating grooves that could accommodate modest boats had Mother Nature filled them with rainwater.

"Jesus, that thing climbed down this hill?" Bear asked, astounded.

"Apparently so," I said, following its trail with my eyes down and along another path carved through the forest floor. A broad swath of trees had been toppled and trampled. From up here, they looked flattened.

"A food trail," Ricardo, one of the ex-Green Berets, said from the edge of the cliff.

"What?"

He pointed at the trail of flattened trees. "A food trail. It takes that route to find food. Probably daily."

Bear grunted. "Bet he's right, Rev. Look at the way the path looks almost smooth. The trees were knocked down recently, but look how flat they look. A high-use trail if I've ever seen one."

"Like something is constantly coming and going," I said, seeing what they were getting at.

"You see trails like that when you're really close to an animal's nest," Ricardo said.

"Are you telling us we're close to where the behemoth lives?" Billee asked.

Someone in the group whistled excitedly. Had to be one of the ex-Green Berets. A kid groaned. Another one whimpered in a way that made me feel for him because I knew he'd now take a ribbing for that for a long time from anyone too stupid to be equally as scared.

Ricardo closed one eye, extending his arm and raising it along the path of the behemoth's trail far below us.

"What's he doing?" I asked Bear.

"Trying to see if he can find you this bastard's nest," Bear answered.

"There!" Ricardo said suddenly. "Look at the range across the valley. One. Two." His hand looped in the air. After a second, I realized he was counting the mountain peaks three or four miles away. "Five. Six. Six peaks from the center of the food trail. To the left. Get to the sixth one and look down. About a fourth of the way above the tree line." He paused, giving us a chance to follow his directions. "See it?"

"Is that what I think it is? A cave?" I asked.

"Looks like it," Ricardo said.

"That's big enough to drive an airplane into," Bear said in a voice etched with equal parts shock and excitement. "Think that's it? Is that the behemoth's nest?"

I looked up. Not toward Heaven, but at the sun, obscured by clouds. Too low in the sky. The cave was a few miles away. We'd never make it today.

Smacking a hand against my leg, I turned to lead the group back to civilization. "Let's get a move on. I've got a big day tomorrow."

24

RIGHT TO FIGHT

"The hell you are," Bear grumbled. "We're here. That's a couple miles. We can make it."

I shook my head. "Not safe. It'll be dusk by the time we get there. At best. We'd never make it back tonight, even if I take care of business in a few seconds. I can't have a bunch of innocent people around. The kids definitely can't be out here."

"Yes, we can," Bolt said, stepping forward.

"No, you can't."

"We haven't gone through all of this to not get the payday," he said with the level of bravado only a teen could pull off.

I turned on the group. "Listen. This isn't a joke. Not a video game." I shot my arm out blindly behind me, hoping it was in the region of the behemoth's cave. "If that's where that thing is, you're not going to see a zoo animal. What's inside that cave will kill you. It will kill all of us. Me included, most likely. Sorry, but this is where the fun ends. We head back."

"I can take you in," Bear said, looking down at me, which is weird because I don't come across many people taller than my six feet.

"We'd never make it out of the forest before nightfall. Tomorrow."

"And you'll be in the same boat then, except more tired because you're going to haul ass through the forest to get here in time. Why not do it now? I've got protein bars. We rest, and then head over. You kick its ass. I help if I can. Then we camp." He reached underneath his armpit, patting his backpack and grinning like a goofball. "I've got a ton of arctic gear. All the guys do. Someone will lend you their pack and we'll be okay for the night. I promise."

I delayed too long, empowering his goofy grin to split his orange mustache and beard even further.

"Dammit. Did you bring the other stuff I asked you to pack?"

"Got 'em."

"All of them?"

He nodded. "Not one shy."

"I'm going with you," Billee said forcefully.

"Absolutely not. You'll be close enough back at the rental for me to bullshit my way out of any problems the other side has with my work here. Stay there."

She pulled her head so far back that her chin touched her chest. Flicking a hand at Bear, she said, "Oh, a man can join you, but not me?"

The ex-Green Berets laughed. One of them crossed his arms like he was about to witness the most epic showdown ever. I knew better. I'd fight the behemoth ten times before I took on Billee once.

"Rev, you know you're not allowed to act here without me. Don't try to tell me that trying won't get you in trouble. I know it will," she said, driving her victory home. Even though she and I were the only two who knew exactly what she meant, the other guys thought they understood, so she won just the same. As an angel, I couldn't act on my own. Already agreeing to allow Bear to accompany me because I needed him if I was going to survive the frosty night meant I'd possibly impact the Balance. Demons would have a conniption if they discovered that, so having my familiar along for the ride might not be mandatory in this situation, but it was pretty damn close. If I was lucky enough to defeat the behemoth, and didn't have Billee by my side, I'd return to the Upperworld embroiled in controversy I didn't need or want. My familiar had to come along and she knew it.

"She'll need one of the arctic packs too," I said in defeat.

Billee got a high-five from Manny, who handed over his pack.

Ricardo tipped his chin at Bear.

I didn't even get a chance to ask what that meant when Bear said, "Of course, man. Come along. We are going to need you."

I waved my hands from side to side. "No more people."

"He's good at tracking. If that thing isn't in the cave, he'll be able to find it way before I can," Bear argued.

"Rev, you already said someone else might be involved," Billee said, jumping into the fray. "While you're engaged with the thing, I'd feel much better having Bear and Ricardo around. Assuming you're both carrying?" She looked between them. They responded by patting their jackets.

"I've got some surprises in the backpack if we need 'em," Bear said.

"Surprises? Like what?" I asked.

He pushed out his bottom lip. "Let's get the guys on their way back to the rental, and we'll talk about it as we head to the cave."

"The only way we do this now is if the rest of your guys head back, too. I don't want forty high schoolers walking through the damn forest on their own. Agree or no deal."

Bear grinned. "I was just about to tell them that exact thing. Just me and Ricardo. Billee and you. Four against one. We'll kick its ass."

I wagged my finger at him. "None of you are fighting it."

He winked. "We'll talk about that on the way."

"So? Are we good?" Billee pointed to the gray day that was slowly darkening. "Daylight is burning."

"Are we going to go through this again if I decide to wait until tomorrow?" I asked.

My familiar, my partner, my friend, smiled. "You bet your ass."

"Fine," I said, deploying my best pouting routine. "Let's get this over."

25

FIRST OF HIS WAYS

I ALMOST WISHED FOR CRICKETS. BULLFROGS WOULD WORK TOO. Maybe even those annoying cicadas that seem to cover every inch of Mexico. Even they would have been welcome now. The night was that still.

"I thought you said we'd see it at dusk?" Bear said, watching the cave's entrance.

"I did, but cut me some slack. I've never seen the thing in person, and all I had to go on was a cell phone video and whatever your man heard in town. This is OJT for all of us."

He slapped Ricardo, and the pair shared a laugh. "The military taught us all about OJT, didn't they?"

"You better believe it," Ricardo said, slapping him back.

"Let's just hope you're right about this, Rev. I hope you're not pulling guesses out of your ass." Billee held up her torch, giving it a shake. "Because these are outdated tactics here. I'm not even military and I still know that."

"Yeah, man, if you needed to blind the damn thing, I could have snagged a thousand tactical flashlights. Especially now with these LEDs. They're crazy bright." Bear looked genuinely disappointed now that it seemed to dawn on him he could have used flashlights instead of torches.

"I know they're..." I playfully scrunched my face at Billee "... apparently old school, but torches are all I had at my disposal. Well, actually had a contact sell me his. Works for a traveling show in Portland. Anyway, I need firelight, not flashlights." I stopped, catching myself on how much I wanted to share with three mortals. "The nature of this beast is such that I think I'll have something more effective against it. We'll see."

"We'll see? We'll see?" Billee said, her words rising in pitch.

"I can't know for sure. Not until we test it for real."

She shut her eyes and looked like she was about to shake her head, but it only shot to one side and she held it there.

"What?"

Billee gave her head a tiny shake. "I just can't with you sometimes."

"Can't what?"

She flung up an arm, pointing off in an indiscriminate direction. "You're protecting everyone in the world before you understand the nature of this thing."

"I have to."

"You can when you understand it. When you have more resources. Not taking chances like this."

With the softest voice I could manage without sounding patronizing, I said, "Billee, someone has to, and that's fallen to me. You save people every day in your job. I do too. My office just exists in the open air and not in a stuffy office." I said that bit with a wink. Billee had never invited me to her office, even after hours, to protect my privacy. "And I know what I'm doing. Trust me. I wouldn't have been assigned the job if I didn't. Sorry Sparky, but you're going to have to go with me on this."

She cocked her head but said nothing.

"So." Ricardo drug out the word. "We wait for your signal. You wake it up or whatever you're going to do, to get it out here. At the signal, you'll light our torches, and we run around the clearing, lighting the rest we just spent ten very tense minutes setting out. Is that it?"

"In a nutshell."

"And you have to be the one to light the torches, why?" Bear asked.

"It needs to be Angelfire," I said.

"Angel what?" Bear leaned closer like he hadn't heard me.

"Sounds like the name of one of those loud bands you white boys listen to, Bear," Ricardo said with a shove to the redhead's shoulder.

"It's not, but it might be the only thing that saves us," Billee said, pressing her lips together and looking my way from the corner of her eye.

She'd have to get over caring about my welfare enough to get through tonight. After that, I might not be alive to find out how disgusted she was. If I walked away from this, I'd deal with her reaction then.

I looked back at the dark mouth of the cave. "It's something special I can do. That's all. Just follow the plan and we might get out of this."

Billee snorted. "All of us better."

"We will," Bear said, looking between us, then holding Billee in his attention. "Are you sure you want to take the last torches? That's a long run."

"Absolutely," she answered. "I'm fast."

"She is," I said before they could reignite the discussion about who was going to take the torches to the furthest point of the flat, rocky clearing. "Let her do it."

"Okay."

"Everyone ready?" As I waited for their individual responses, I planned on giving each of them a hard, uncomfortably long analysis.

Billee was the first to break that opportunity, followed by the two ex-Green Berets in chorus.

So much for hard analysis to determine the genuine level

of commitment coming from the three. They better be as tough as they believed they were, because this was happening.

I looked at Billee. "As soon as that thing steps out of the cave, get your torches in the air and, for the love of all that is epic and good, keep them there until they're lit."

"Yes sir," the two military guys said, making me question whether they were going into an engrained auto-response mode.

"Of course," Billee said as if she was trying to be patient with a child. I was about to turn when she stopped me with a word that cut through the tension in my brain. "Wait."

I faltered.

Billee's gloved hand wrapped around the wrist of my heavy jacket. "Please don't do anything crazy. I know I've been a nightmare to deal with since the case... the death with dignity, and I'm sorry."

"Billee, don't worry. It's all part of the job. I understand. You're not the first."

It really sucked trying to have this moment to bury the hatchet and move on from Billee's struggle to accept that some people, mortal and immortal, simply didn't want to have to face another day of pain. But I wouldn't step away for a quiet moment and risk the behemoth waking and flossing its teeth with Bear and Ricardo.

"And I'm sorry about giving you grief about the job," she said, shaking her head. Mad at herself, if the way her mouth bunched up under her nose was any indication. "Who am I to whine when you're forced to do something you don't want to do and had to do it far longer than I could even imagine? That was wrong of me, to put that pressure on you."

"None of this is worth apologizing for." I squeezed her shoulders for good measure. "One is a personal value, and that's nothing unique. The other is because you're still adjusting to the demands forced on you. Trust me, it takes some people much, much longer. You're totally fine and, I swear, we're good."

"Thank you," she said, looking on the verge of the kind of tears that came with absolute relief, but showing a timid smile.

I stood from behind the knoll, my presence now obvious to anyone in the cave. I used my last check-in with the squatting mortals to see if I could spy any of their Guardian Angels hiding behind rows of moss-covered tree trunks and thousands of lush ferns. None of the three Guardians were present or accounted for. Just the way Cascade and I agreed. Just the way I hated it. The three mortals should be safe, but if anyone threw an unanticipated wildcard into the fight between me and the behemoth, all bets were off. Let's just hope that if the time came for the Guardians to unmask, they would.

Not worth the drain on my focus, though. I couldn't control them and their actions. I could only control myself.

"Okay then," I said to the three mortals. "Follow the plan. Light those torches and keep your eyes open for anyone sneaking up on me. I don't care if they're two hundred yards away. If you see someone, you shout. And last but not least—"

"We know. Stay the fuck out of the fight," all three said at once. They should have it memorized. I'd only said it about three hundred times over the trek to the cave.

I wagged my finger like they were misbehaving children. "Don't make me say it again. Now, let me go pick a fight with an oversized domesticated pet."

Before I could emerge into the clearing, Billee snagged my wrist for the second time. "Please, be smart."

"I will."

"Kick its ass."

"I'll try."

She yanked her hand, tugging my arm down. "Win. The world needs you."

Instead of replying, I patted her hand. She released me and I stepped out onto the compacted shelf of hard-packed moss, soil, and most definitely, stone. The mouth of the cave yawned. Darkness was past the fulcrum, tipping the night sky toward sheer blackness, accelerating by the minute.

I waited, standing in front of the cave. Feet spread. Hand near Maggie.

"Psst." Someone hissed from the covering rain forest shrubbery. "What are you doing?"

"Waiting," I whispered harshly, not exactly in the mood to give away my tactics in case someone was inside the cave, waiting and far more ready than me.

I didn't doubt they would be. The one advantage I had against the behemoth and its handler was my awareness that there was a handler. They didn't know that I knew about them unless all of this was a setup for the biggest screw job in the history of screw-jobs outside professional wrestling. I was going to hold this advantage as long as I could.

The behemoth might be stupid, but its handler wouldn't be. The silence was tactical. They wanted me inside the cave.

There was no way in hell I was going in there.

I needed to make sure whoever might be inside wasn't someone I wanted inside, and there was only one way to do that. So I opened my big mouth and shouted, "Hey, if you're not a big, fat, ugly, scaled monster of biblical proportions, you've got thirty seconds to get your ass out of that cave." I waited while my voice carried into and echoed around the cave. Once it faded, I finished, "If you think I'm joking, or if you actually are a big, fat, ugly, scaled monster of biblical proportions, stay where you are. Where you are is where you'll stay for eternity." Once again, waiting for the echo to fade, I started counting. "One. Two. Three."

You know how that goes.

I counted one number after the previous. I took my time, adding an extra half-second between each. When I reached thirty and no one stepped outside the cave, I didn't wait. I was done playing.

I reached into my jacket, sliding Maggie from the holster, and pushed my Ability into the revolver's chamber. The night lit as the beam of pure white angelic magic roared forth in a thick beam. It resounded as it struck the cliff thirty feet above the cave entrance, shearing rock from thicker slabs. Piece by piece, the cliff splintered and cracked. I forced more Angelfire into the .327. The grip vibrated in my hand. Stainless steel, magically enhanced, heated under the pressure, but it would hold. With weapons, assassins had to know their stuff. The tinkering I'd done with this revolver over the past few years gave me the confidence I needed.

In chunks, rocks, pebbles, and even boulders, the cliff collapsed in front of the cave, choking it off.

I cut off my Angelfire. Wisps of white smoke uncoiled from the end of the barrel. I aimed Maggie at the ground and waited.

"Rev, wha—what happ—"

Before Billee could finish, the muffled roar of one pissed-off lizard reverberated from behind the new wall of rock I'd just created.

"That's the signal!" I waved them into action.

Three torches rose into the air. I lifted Maggie and sent three bursts on-target, lighting each of their torches with Angelfire.

"Go! Go! Light the rest." I reminded the shocked humans, who dashed from cover even before the behemoth shattered the wall of stone choking off its habitat. Billee and the two ex-Green Berets were on their own now, hopefully following the plan. Plans were great right up to the moment someone threw the first punch. Then they went to shit, and you had to trust that everyone would do their jobs and adjust on the fly.

I punched by collapsing the cliff side. Let's hope a behemoth counterpunch wasn't in the plans.

Rock and boulders sprayed away from the cave from an unseen force. I dove out of the way, hearing the rock thunder down around and beyond me, crashing against the world, snapping hundred-year-old trees. I spared a split second of worry about Billee and the ex-Green Berets being hit by the wreckage. The human body wouldn't stand a chance against a fist-sized rock flying at the speed of this explosion of stone. No time for those types of thoughts. All part of the job they'd signed up for. Well, except Billee. That poor, beautiful soul never had a say in the matter of how the Upperworld used her. I'd make the behemoth hurt extra slow if it hurt her.

As the last of the rock rumbled away, down the pitched slope leading away from the cave and to the valley below, the world underneath me shook as the behemoth stalked forward.

Let me tell you, it looked a lot smaller in the video. A. Lot. Smaller.

Another benefit of the video? I didn't have to smell the overgrown crocodile. Now, sharing this wide arc of compacted earth, with it stomping toward me, its thick aroma hit me long before my brain processed its enormity. The beast smelled of something between funk and decay.

"You're one nasty fucker," I said, slowly getting to my feet and looking up, up, up.

The behemoth stood thirty feet tall, from paw to the crown of its two horns. Covered in dark green scales, each the size of a serving dish, it could have easily spent its entire life in the forests of the Pacific Northwest going undetected. Against the cliffside, it stood out, in color and sheer immensity. Legs as thick as red cedar trees stretched from its flank to the ground, supported by four-clawed paws. Claws, razor sharp. Claws that were easily two feet long. At least if it raked me, I wouldn't feel a lot of pain for long.

Smaller, tan scales covered the beast's underbelly. Every inch of Yahweh's creation was armored. Defensive beyond comprehension. No vulnerabilities except for its eyes. And those were a long, long way away and constantly moving as the beast roared and thrashed its head.

Offensive too, my experienced mind shouted.

Claws that could shred a skyscraper. Horns that could pierce the side of a battleship. The behemoth's gut glowed. I couldn't get a good look at it, but pale light pulsed from the area just in front of its hind legs, where you'd expect a belly button. I'm not the brightest assassin in the world, but I know enough to be wary of glowing parts of bodies. If Yahweh had also armed this killing machine with a laser beam upgrade, I was going to be pissed.

This thing wasn't supposed to exist. According to everyone supposedly in the know, there was no reason for this most recent manifestation. The time for a reset wasn't now. Something was wrong; everyone in the Upperworld's inner circles attested to that. So if something was wrong, it was very wrong. Yahweh could have armed this thing to be indestructible and like nothing He'd ever created before. Who was I to say? I'd never met the ruler of the Upperworld, the yin to Lucifer's yang.

But I wasn't taking chances and making costly assumptions. You didn't survive as an assassin for long if you did.

The behemoth pounded its tree trunk-thick leg. The ground rumbled, forcing me to spread my legs to steady myself.

The area around us brightened as the three mortals spread the torches burning with Angelfire. The behemoth didn't notice, and that reaction played perfectly into what I needed.

I spun, lifting and firing Maggie. Angelfire burst forth, striking the first torch on the edge of the clearing. I swung in an arc, pushing the source of my Ability into each flaming torch. Towering Angelfire roared on each head as I connected one to another. All around the clearing, I swept the beam until every torch was lit.

A line of white flashed from the first torch, horizontally and seven feet above the ground. The second torch flared even higher, now reaching twelve feet in the air. The white horizontal beam continued, from one torch to the next, until blazing white Angelfire ringed the clearing. Once the beam connected each torch, the flames reached higher until they were at chest level with the monstrosity before me. The horizontal beams rose with the torch fire, now fifteen feet above the forest floor, allowing the mortals and me to pass under them. With the cliff wall to its back and the ring of Angelfire all around the clearing, there was no escape for the behemoth. It wouldn't be able to get through the ring of Angelfire without slicing its legs out from underneath it. The beast was too stupid to understand what I'd just done. It was a prisoner as long as I was alive to hold the Angelfire. Now, my only challenge was staying alive to hold the spell.

The blazing Angelfire lit the clearing like stadium lights. Quite a spectacle for any wayward winter hiker, I imagined.

"Keep your eyes open for anyone else!" I hollered to the mortals in hiding.

The behemoth growled and lowered its head, looking every bit like a bull ready to change. The smartass in me wanted nothing more in that moment than to walk up to it and boop it in the nose for all the headaches its presence had created in the past two weeks. But one look at its rippling lips, pulled back and exposing teeth half as long as I was tall, told me I had better ways to get the beast's attention.

I whipped my Ruger up, taking aim.

The thing about being an experienced assassin is that exposure to stressful situations is a wonderfully creative mechanism. They talk about soldiers, business people, and doctors being cool under pressure, and there's a reason for that. It's because somewhere in their early career, they got their asses kicked. A lot. Those ass-kickings taught them valuable lessons and made them better at their jobs because they learned how to be better prepared. A self-feeding loop. Assassins go through it too. We get a bad rap, but that's because of the high-profile scumbags who assassinate. Not assassins. There's a difference. Hell, people in my profession have felled dictators or stopped them from rising in the first place, saving millions of people from utter misery and lives of hardship. We're the heroes no one knows about. If all my ass-kickings throughout my career prepared me properly, I was about to add a kill to the impalpable list of great accomplishments by assassins because I was cool under pressure.

"Fuck you," I said slowly as the behemoth growled.

Its maw still opened, the behemoth roared again as I pulled the trigger.

Maggie flared with Angelfire. The beam of white flashed between me and the monster, splitting the air as I propelled it at Yahweh's pet lizard.

This spell wasn't about containment, like the barrier I'd set around the clearing. This was about destruction. I wanted to barbeque the bastard where it stood and then go looking for whoever was handling the beast in Yahweh's stead.

My spell hit the behemoth right in the nose. A nose that was as wide as a bus. A nose that should have contorted in pain before turning to gooey green ooze.

Instead, when my Angelfire hit, bolts of white shot in every direction. Fizzling into the ground or ricocheting into the sky and fading out, my Angelfire did no harm.

The behemoth curled back on its hind legs and roared, dropping its long snout open and exposing three rows of teeth. Drool plopped to the ground from both corners of its mouth, deep enough to clean my boots in if I wanted to.

I stood, stunned. Never had that spell not evaporated whatever it hit. Not only had it not done so this time, but it didn't even hurt the giant lizard.

The behemoth lunged. My brain fog lifted just in time to recognize the threat.

Its large front legs pulled up and slammed into the ground in unison. Somewhere, I think I heard rock cracking. I couldn't be sure because I was too busy flying backward.

The ground rushed up to meet my back. Bolts of pain exploded from my shoulders to my hips.

I rolled, scrambling to my feet and drawing Maggie. I didn't have time to fire, though.

The behemoth was on me with surprising speed, lowering its horned head. Horns that, I'd only noticed now, curved to fine points, meant to not only pierce but to barb and secure. This bastard was designed to torture its prey.

"Get up, Rev!" Billee pleaded from somewhere in hiding.

Cursing her to stay quiet and hidden, I couldn't tell her that's exactly what I was trying to do.

The behemoth hit me as soon as I stood.

Fortune smiled. I try to stay in the best shape I can, but when you're middle-aged, that's not as easy as when you're going through puberty and the few centuries—years, for mortals—that followed. Once that phase of life ends, so do the good times of eating like shit and still looking like you're in a gym eight hours a day. But I'm in decent shape for someone my age. That meant I was thin enough to fit between the behemoth's horns and take the brunt of his forehead square on.

Let me tell you, I thought hitting the rocking clearing after the beast's first attack hurt, but that had nothing on this. The top of the behemoth's head was flat but scaled. When it struck, I felt like I'd just jumped from a skyscraper and met a concrete sidewalk face-first.

I flew out of the clearing, barely missing my ring of Angelfire spell, and tumbled down the slope. Feet over head. Head over feet. Ass over both, it seemed. I fell and fell. Losing sense of all sight and sound in the fall, I focused on compacting my body so I didn't accidentally snap an appendage.

The slope was clear of anything that could have broken me in two. The behemoth had actually done me a favor with all of its previous hunting. By using what Ricardo had called its food trail, the monstrosity had compacted the earth so much that it left no trees standing to snap me in half, no jagged rocks or boulders to rip me from navel to neck. It hurt, sure. Being propelled at this speed down a hill would. But I didn't die, and that's what mattered.

Once the falling stopped, I took a moment to catch my breath. But only after I made sure my spell hadn't slipped.

"Whew," I said aloud to the silent night, seeing the intact ring above. The behemoth was still a prisoner, and my mortal team was safe.

I grunted as I pulled myself up. The rock shells below me slid, and I almost fell on my face again, catching myself just before I did. "Dammit, I'm too old for this shit."

My jacket was torn to shreds. Thank Yahweh it was too cold to wear my duster. Had I been, I would climb the slope and drag out the behemoth's death if it was the last thing I did. My insulated snow pants didn't fare any better than my winter coat. If I wasn't in the middle of a fight, I'd probably feel the chill. As it was, with Angelfire coursing through me and my adrenaline pumping, I didn't notice how cold the night was.

Stalking my way up the slope seemed to take an eternity. The clouds above were calm, withholding their precipitation. The night was silent for miles all around us as if the animals of the Olympics waited to see who would come out on top of this struggle. A wind cut across the slope, a gentle nudge. In all, it would have been a serene evening if not for the grunting beast waiting to tear me apart for caging it in.

Outside the ring of Angelfire, I leveled my gun at the behemoth's head and fired. Just like the last time, my beams deflected off scales, shooting in all directions. Fifteen shots pumped into the damn thing and the only difference was I'd irritated it more.

I couldn't keep firing at the behemoth from outside the circle. For one, at some point, I was going to get tired and my magic would weaken enough that the magical fence would slip and free the beast. Second, it had layers of scales that deflected my attacks. Doing the same thing and expecting different results was the very definition of insanity, wasn't it?

I needed to get closer. I needed to find another weakness. Another way to kill it without becoming the newest version of Jonah of the whale.

Slinking forward, I dodged the behemoth when it charged.

Its bulk made stopping difficult, and the beast careened into the ring of Angelfire.

The zapping and sizzle were intense. The collision shot sparks fifty feet in the air and a small shock wave that flung me toward the beast's cave.

The behemoth screeched in an octave too high for something that large.

I rolled as it turned away from the ring of Angelfire. Across its broad front shoulders, a wide line of black showed the result of my barrier. It hadn't cut through the beast, but the thick scales were singed and crumbling as it turned toward me.

As they fell away, I noticed small spots of leathery-looking flesh. A small target, but if I could buy time, then I could target the injury. One accurate shot and I might just bring the beast down.

The behemoth roared and charged.

"Shit," I cried out, caught between the cliff walls and tons of pissed-off gecko.

I waited until the safest last moment and dodged to the right. The behemoth couldn't stop and ran face-first into the cliff. Behind it, I leveled Maggie, waiting for it to turn so I could take aim at its wound.

What my dumb ass didn't think about was the fact that the behemoth was also equipped with a twenty-foot tail.

I thought about how I'd left that part out of the equation because I was so distracted by its rows of teeth, large horns, and absolutely frightening claws. I thought about how I'd left that part out because I was distracted by its fresh wound, exposing a vulnerability. Its underbelly was protected by smaller, thinner scales that might be susceptible to injury. I even thought about it when I realized the glowing pale light from its belly button might be a secret weapon I needed to be wary of. But all of those thoughts came too late for me to do anything about twenty feet of solid tail swinging in my direction.

By nothing but luck, I'd stopped far enough away that I was toward the edge of the tail's radius. Had I stood closer to the back of the behemoth, the speed of the swinging tail would have been slower, but the thicker part would have struck me. As it was, I was far enough away that this part of its tail was 'only' three feet wide.

But it was moving fast. Physics, am I right?

Something inside me snapped on impact.

One minute I was standing, taking aim at the behemoth. The next, I was bent at the waist and flying again.

When I landed, it was atop a large fern that slightly cushioned my fall.

I couldn't draw a deep breath. In fact, drawing even a slight whiff was difficult, and quickly approaching impossible proportions.

"Rev! Get up!" Billee screamed from somewhere in the cloud of my mind.

My vision blurred. The blazing light of my Angelfire ring was blurry and… was it fading?

No!

I snapped my eyes open, inhaling deeply through my nose. I wasn't going down. I couldn't. Those three mortals would die if I did. Their Guardians were keeping them safely hidden, but even three of them teaming up wouldn't do much against the behemoth once I was gone. They'd be prime pickings without a snowball's chance. If I died, the behemoth would be free of my ring trap. Whoever its handler was would speed up the preparations to release the beast on the world after it finished chomping on my partner.

Still, it was hard to stand when you couldn't breathe.

My pulse galloped as I pushed myself to my feet and hobbled toward the clearing.

"Rev! Please!"

Panic filled Billee's cries. They drew me nearer, like a magnet. She was good people, that familiar, that friend of mine.

I didn't see her, but I almost feel her presence. Somewhere close, hidden by her own smarts and supernatural angelic help. I'd buy her Guardian a beer if I lived through this.

Back on level ground, holding my side and trying to find a way to stand that wouldn't send shoots of pain through every inch of my body, I took aim at the rock above the behemoth.

Funny thing about severe injuries, they cloud your thinking. I carried the mana stone and could heal myself, but doing that hadn't crossed my mind until now. I hadn't been hurt enough to worry about it. I was used to pain. Another benefit of having tons of experience doing a shit job. And, honestly, I was tired. Of these fights. These missions. These never-ending tasks.

I kept going because of Billee and the two innocent men who depended on me to follow through on my part of the deal. I did it because the behemoth would kill tens of thousands of mortals once it started stomping around the Overworld. I didn't do it for myself. I hadn't before, and never would.

The mana stone, secured in a zipped pocket, sat unused.

Which was why I was in as much pain as I could tolerate without curling into a small ball and waiting for the beast to flatten me with a stomp. Which was why my thinking was clouded and my reactions slowed.

And which is exactly why I didn't see the boulder, a remnant of my attack on the behemoth's cave, sitting within the radius of its tail. I didn't see the threat the small boulder, about the size of a Great Dane, was until the behemoth swatted it. Hitting the boulder like a batter hits a baseball, the boulder grew in size as it approached.

I didn't even have time to curse when it struck me and my vision shut down.

26

IN HIS LIGHT

VOICES.

My hearing was recovering before my vision.

The world was still foggy, but I could hear. That was something. Voices. Three, to be precise.

"Fuck." I groaned, trying to roll over and discover, much to my tempered anxiety, that I wasn't able to.

Alive, goddammit, I was alive. How? The physics of the behemoth's strike should have—

I groaned again, this time with more ferocity, fed by dreams of payback and relief about still drawing breath.

Strength pulsed through me, returning in volumes as the mana stone activated.

The magic of the All, the essence of everything, channeled through the stone and into me, filling me with life and vigor. The damn mana stone. Wouldn't even let me be put out of my misery by Yahweh's overgrown terrarium escapee.

Mana stones are like that, ensuring the viability of the named individual. Thrown around, knocked down, beaten, clacked, scraped, and sanded, the stone might tolerate a lot, but one thing it wouldn't put up with its holder dying.

Blasted, cursed stone. At least now, I could save Billee and her two ex-military cohorts.

The world zipped back in a flash. Suddenly, I was aware of how cold the night was. Definitely January. Despite the time of year and the chill in the air, my shirt clung to my back and armpits. I hoped it was sweat despite the cold air, and not blood. Puffs of clouds were faint against the backdrop of the night sky. Three mortals were screaming in panic somewhere very close. The ground shook with each step the behemoth took.

Yet, I couldn't help anyone because the boulder that should have killed me during the beast's attack pinned me to the earth. My legs were trapped underneath it, but at least my upper body was free. Bones would have shattered had it not been for the mana stone. Plastic action figures on a stovetop would be more unmalleable than my legs if it weren't for the essence of the All repairing the damage the behemoth had done. I was still a sitting target, though.

But thanks to that damn stone, I was aware. Aware that the beast still raged and that my mortal partners were in trouble. Big trouble. The mana stone might have saved my life, but it'd done nothing to preserve the Angelfire gate I'd set to corral the behemoth and protect my mortal teammates.

"Fuck," I said, drawing out the word, partially because I was tired, and partially because I couldn't see clearly enough yet to pick out small humans fleeing from a colossal terror.

My pistol in hand, I took aim on the boulder pinning me. With a single burst, the large rock shattered into gray dust. I wiggled my toes inside my boots, happy to see the mana stone had done its duty.

Rolling over, I popped to my feet, feeling like I was ten thousand years old again. Damn. Nothing hurt. Nothing even ached. Energy pulsated in each fiber. I swear, I could have squeezed in an epic workout if the behemoth's hideaway had a gym and three mortals didn't need me to save their hides. The way I felt, I could have bench-pressed the damned beast.

But then I saw it slam a thick leg down just feet away from my partner.

"Billee. No," I rasped, taking aim at the behemoth.

It towered over her. My familiar, partner, my friend, may have stumbled in fear or had tripped, but either way, she was on her backside, trying to scoot into the tall bush. Even if she did, it wouldn't matter. The behemoth could now follow.

Unless I kept it trapped.

Firing Angelfire into the barrel of my Ruger, I found a torch, still in its strategic place, and lit it, swinging the spell around the ring, striking each of the torches. It's not as impressive as it sounds. Pulsing with the dying remnants of the mana stone's power, I was re-energized as if this was the first time I'd cast in this fight. The beam was wide and not only caught the torches but the trees behind them.

The night burned with Angelfire.

The behemoth stalked Billee, towering over her and drooling globs of saliva that were bigger than she was. Its tiny, relatively speaking, black eyes greedily zeroed in on her. It hadn't seen the rebirth of me or my magic. As it moved to take another step, the ring of Angelfire reconnected, and the stupid beast walked right into it.

A flash of fire burst across its lowered head.

"Ha!" I yelled as it bellowed in pain and jerked away. "Run, Billee!"

The behemoth pulled back and, for a second, I feared it would sacrifice its life to stomp hers out. Thankfully, the agony must have been too much. It pulled away from the shocking impact of the newly reborn ring of Angelfire before falling back on its front paws.

Billee had been getting back to her feet, but when the behemoth hammered the rocky floor again, the ground jolted. She stumbled, still far too close.

"Goddammit, get away." I aimed my gun at the raging behemoth, firing into its back, knowing doing so would do nothing but piss the beast off.

The broad scales deflected my magic, of course. The scales on its back were probably the thickest on the beast. But I wasn't trying to kill it—though that would be nice. I was trying to pull its attention away from my friend.

Billee stood up, her face drawn in overwhelming fear. The creature thrashed and bellowed. To the side of the clearing, not more than a hundred feet away, both Bear and Ricardo hid behind a boulder the size of a shed, waving Billee toward them.

She took a last look at the behemoth, then turned, like she was searching me out.

"Run, Sparky. Goddammit," I said, keeping a portion of my attention on her as I fired uselessly into the behemoth's scaled-covered back.

She cupped her hands, shouting something in my direction I couldn't hear over the roaring beast. I think she realized it was futile because she dropped her hands and did the last thing I expected. She sprinted toward me.

"No," I gasped.

Billee is fast, but not fast enough to outrace a beast with the radius of a hurricane over the open ocean.

She was twenty feet away from it, thirty if my judgment was crap, when it swung. I don't even know if she was its target. Maybe it was just pissed about the fresh injury I'd delivered and was lashing out at the world.

I screamed, pouring—no, not pouring; I was pushing—power into my spell, even though I knew it would do nothing to the behemoth. Almost in slow motion, underneath my constant stream of Angelfire, Billee closed, still shouting. From my periphery, I saw the behemoth's wide tail arc in her direction.

I stopped firing. Angelfire wouldn't save her. Only I could.

I raced toward Billee.

She was within ten feet. "The navel, Rev. Shoot its navel! It—"

Billee, the mortal assigned to be my familiar so I could operate in the Overworld without getting the demons' panties in a twist, tasked without her consent and obligated to a life of servitude, didn't get to finish. Billee Brand, my three-hundred-and-fifteenth familiar, was putting her life at risk and showing more courage than any supernatural associate of mine, mouthed her last words.

The tail closed. I roared, pulling my power away from the ring and channeling all of my strength into this beam, firing at the behemoth's appendage. Billee's steps fell as if in slow motion. Beyond her shoulder, in the clearing's periphery, a Rift opened, and a Reaper stepped through. Anapheil. She held a scroll in her hand.

We made eye contact. Ever prompt, the consummate professional. Before she executed the order to escort Billee to the Veil Gate, I shouted, "Wait!"

Anapheil stopped just outside the Rift as the behemoth's tail collided with Billee, bending her so viciously that her head almost touched her feet. I nearly vomited.

As she sailed through the air and crashed into the over-grown vegetation, I raced forward, shouting at my Reaper peer. "Stay right fucking there, Anapheil!"

The distance to the behemoth shortened. I fired at the beast's head, needing to draw its attention. The plan worked. I was halfway to it when it turned on me, snarling and drool-ing, unhinging its jaw to show an impressive array of sharp fangs, rows deep.

I blasted its face. I blasted its arms. Its paws. Its legs. I knocked a few claws loose, and the behemoth bellowed. I shot out an eye and it filled the night with a piercing cry of pain. And then it roared back, its tree-sized legs ready to come down and crush me.

I drew on the glowing belly of the beast, filling my mind with the pale light that radiated from its gut. This was for Billee. This was for the two guys hiding somewhere in the bushes. For all the mortals of the Overworld, this beast would terrorize if I didn't take it down now. This was for me because I was tired of being used. I pushed all I had left into the shot of Angelfire.

The beam was as thick as a cedar tree and it struck the behemoth's glowing gut.

There was a sucking sound, a loud whoop that sounded like it was coming from behind the mountain and racing in our direction, growing as it neared. Its pitch increased until it stabbed my ears. I winced and bent forward, blocking my ears and hoping the noise wouldn't split my skull open.

The glowing orb of light in the behemoth's gut expanded as the noise heightened its pitch. It pulsed, dimming and brightening in an ever-increasing rhythm until I thought it would send me into a shock. Then the vacuum of sound evaporated as if it was sucking back in on itself. A blissful moment of utter silence stopped the madness, and I feared Billee had been wrong. She'd sacrificed herself for absolutely no reason. Whatever she thought might happen if I shot the stupid lizard in the gut hadn't come to fruition. Whereas I lived for nothing, Bille had died for nothing.

In that moment, I would have yanked Yahweh's eyes out if He was standing before me.

Then the light in the behemoth's gut exploded outward.

The wave of light and sound was so intense it forced me to turn away. Even then, the skin of my eyelids turned pink, moving to primrose, and then flashing to pure white, like I was staring straight into the sun itself.

The light swelled. But I felt it. Oh Yahweh, did I feel it as the immortal energy of the behemoth flooded into me. Power. Rage. Animalistic hunger.

I'd absorbed energy from immortals for thousands of

years, but never so much at once. My body shook as it fed on the remnants of what had been the behemoth. I chugged to drink it all in. Every muscle, every fiber shook. My hair tingled. My heart galloped. My lungs expanded until I feared they'd burst. My biceps, hamstrings, and quadriceps fired like pistons. Ten-cylinder Lamborghinis had nothing on me.

I'd never felt so alive.

The urge to rend, to tear the mountain apart, coursed through me. I was indestructible. All-powerful. I could tear the Underworld apart. I could feed Lucifer his ass and still have time for a snack before I stomped into the Upperworld and demanded Yahweh set me free of the eternal slavery I'd been tricked into lest He prefer the same fate.

In an even quicker flash, the transfer of immortal energy evaporated. Darkness fell over the mountain.

I panted. Hearing the sound muffled in my ears.

"Billee," I croaked when my mind cleared. "God, no. Billee?"

I scrambled to the overgrowth where I'd seen the behemoth fling her. With a twitch of the trigger, I set the closest torches to an intense blaze to give me enough light to search.

I found her crumpled in a heap. Pellets of snowy dirt covered her cheeks and forehead. I saw no blood. The way she'd landed looked so natural. So peaceful. She could have been sleeping for all anyone knew.

I heard the crackle of torch fire. The dirt beneath my feet and all around Billee glowed as Anapheil brought the torch closer. "Rev?" she said quietly, drifting close.

"Don't you dare," I announced to my Interim Minister, watching Billee's chest rise and fall slower with each breath.

"I have to," she said, holding up the scroll. "This was delivered a few minutes ago. I haven't received assignments since taking the interim job and Pher signed this one, so I knew it was important." She squatted at Billee's still head, looking down at her. "Your familiar?"

"Yes," I said, trying to calm the shaking in my voice.

Anapheil reached over, laying her hand on my knee. "I'm sorry. And I hate to rush you. I can give you a few moments if you'd like?"

"No," I said, shaking my head stubbornly. "I don't need it because you're not taking her."

Anapheil gave me a look that told me she didn't understand. "I can't reassign this, Rev. You know that."

I snapped at her. "Don't do it, Anapheil. Not... not yet."

She patted my knee and stood. "Okay. I'll let you say goodbye."

But goodbyes wouldn't be said. Assassins can be stubborn like that.

Unzipping my pocket, I pulled out the mana stone. The power of the All in one hand, the stone's quill materialized in my other. Holding the point to the stone, I recalled what I knew about how these devices worked. Feeling the quill's tip raked across microscopic pores, I scratched out my name. "You've got too much to do to leave me now, Billee Brand." With the supernatural feather of the quill, I dusted off the residue of my work, watching with distracted amazement as the stone's surface smoothed. Flipping the quill and pinching the point, I wrote Billee's first name, pausing at her last. "Just don't hate me for doing this to you."

Then I scratched her last name on the stone and slipped it into her pants pocket.

I watched her face, ignoring Anapheil's short shuffling behind me. Those closed eyes had wept with untold numbers of mortals who'd poured their hearts out to her, hoping she could rescue them from life as I was now trying to rescue her. I watched for a sign of a twitch from the thick-lipped mouth that had imparted sage advice to those in need, that had delivered so many snappy reposts to my jaded snarkiness. I listened for a drawing of breath from the chest that was filled with so much love, for family, friends, and strangers. For humanity. Her hands, the ones she'd used to grip me and plead for me to act smarter than I was, the hands she used to tend to the injured with, remained still. Behind her tight black and tan curls was a mind like none other. A mind that dealt with the incomprehensible like a champ, that formulated a fairer worldview than I could ever manage with a hundred of my lifetimes, that was astute enough to eschew her biases for the greater good. Inside her chest sat a dormant heart that knew the denial of love, a transcendent experience she might never experience on a truly intimate level now because of her unsolicited duty to the Upperworld's whims and needs.

What way was this to end a beautiful life?

Had I used the last of the mana stone's power? Was it limited to saving one owner's life per day?

"Come on, Sparky," I whispered my plea, lowering my head to her hand. I nearly pulled back at feeling its lack of warmth.

"Rev?" Anapheil asked tentatively.

"Stay. There," I grumbled miserably into my partner's stomach.

If the mana stone failed Billee, I was marching straight into the Order's meeting room and dropping my retirement papers. I was so beyond done, I might just—

Billee gasped and rocketed to a sitting position, knocking me off balance. "Rev?" Her gaze bounced around, from the ferns she'd crushed, back to the empty clearing.

I sat up and back. The confusion on her face was clear, and she didn't need me freaking her out by making her wonder why I was laying my head on her. I put my hand on her shoulder. "It's okay, Billee. It's gone."

"Wha—what happened? I remember running. To—" She stopped, putting her hand to her forehead and staring at the ground as if she was trying to focus on a singular thought. "I wanted to tell you to shoot the circle of light in its gut, and... well, that's all I remember."

"Rev, what did you do?" Anapheil said from a few feet away, her arms at her side and the scroll dangling in her grip.

Sparks of white light formed in the air around the scroll. At first, no more than a handful of bright, floating sparks. Then a dozen. Two dozen. They swirled in the air and began rotating around the scroll, wrapping tighter with each rotation. The scroll illuminated, surrounded in the white glow, and then flashed. By the time I could open my eyes again, Anapheil's hand was empty.

I smiled with a healthy dose of snark—not aimed at her, specifically, but at the decision-makers who put Billee in this predicament. "I just freed up your evening."

"The Order will... Once they find out," she said.

"Let me handle them," I said, flicking my hand at her empty one. "Looks like it's time for you to head home."

Anapheil looked down at her now-freed hand. "I guess so. See you around, Rev."

"See you."

The Interim Minister stepped through her Rift, shaking her head. Once she was through, it collapsed and the world reignited with life.

"Rev? Where the fuck are you?" Bear was shouting as he burst from the foliage near the center's edge of the clearing. "Rev?"

"Over here!" My gaze never left Billee.

"Rev? That you? Where are you?"

I raised my arm, hoping he could pick it out in the night because I wasn't leaving my partner until she proved to me that the mana stone had done its job. "Here."

Within seconds, the two ex-military men were barreling through the greenery.

"What the fuck happened?" Bear asked, putting a hand to his beanie-covered head, his gaze swiveling between Billee and the empty clearing. "Where is that goddamned thing?"

"You okay?" I asked my partner tenderly.

282 | PAUL SATING

She reached out her hand, clasping mine. "I'm good. Great, actually. Here, help me up."

I stood, pulling her to her feet.

Bear shook his head. "Jesus, Rev. You can take an ass kicking. The Green Berets would love to have someone like you."

I brushed off my pants. "I'm sure they would. But—"

I stopped when I stood straight again. As an assassin, I live by a code of situational awareness. It's like having a tiny radar station in your head, always scanning, always watching. Good thing, too, because when I caught sight of the ridge atop the cliff, my breath caught.

Astride a pale horse, holding a torch in its hand, a rider looked down at us. Donning a black robe, it would have blended in with the night if it weren't for the torchlight. The Horseman of Death. A lemming of the Lamb of God. The behemoth's handler. Hellion was so busted.

Before any of the mortals caught sight of the Horseman, a Rift appeared a few strides in front of his pale steed. He kicked at its flanks and disappeared into the black of the supernatural realm.

"Uh, Rev? Are you okay?" Billee asked behind me.

When I broke away from staring at the blank ridge, I saw she was glancing between me and where I'd been looking.

I covered my scowl at catching one of the Four Horsemen of the Apocalypse and the troubled future now implied by his presence. "Yeah. I think I'm just a little paranoid now." I pointed at the cave mouth. "Anyone up for a fire and a campout in Mother Nature?"

Bear patted his bounteous backpack. "I brought the dehydrated snacks!"

I chuckled. "Mmmm, sounds yummy. I can't wait."

27

ENDINGS AND BEGINNINGS

"It's crazy to think they won't remember a thing about the entire trip," Billee said, her hand still resting on the handle of my passenger side door. "You know they'll ask you what happened."

"I'm more concerned with their parents wondering why their sons went to an overnight party with ex-soldiers," I said. "Let's hope no one says anything. Not sure that command stuck. I was exhausted by that point. Slept like shit in that cave."

"I wish you didn't have to do it at all."

"Me too," I said, watching her. "You okay?"

"Yes," she said, looking down and nodding tightly. "I am."

"What is it, Billee?"

She exhaled, her lips fluttering. "Promise me you'll talk to me about this thing." She patted her pocket that held the mana stone.

"I will. Just not right now. I've got to wrap up some business. Plus, we'll have plenty of time since you hold the stone and I absorbed the energy of the behemoth."

"What does that mean for you?"

I looked out the car's window at the dreary Olympia day and snorted. "That I'm never going to fucking die."

"Gee, that's a cheery thought."

"Hard to be cheery when you're the Grim Reaper."

Billee didn't respond. Not at first, and not verbally. Instead, she reached over and grabbed my hand. "Don't worry. I'm here and I promise to eat as many of your free dinners as I can for as long as possible. Just think, an eternity of free food!"

I looked at her and laughed. "Deal. We'll get together in a couple of nights. I'll cook and we can talk about what holding that mana stone means."

"Sounds perfect. I'll bring the wine."

"Thank you," I said with a forceful wave toward the wind-shield. "Do you think you could teach Pher how to stop mooching off me, too?"

"Nah. More fun this way." She popped the door open and put a foot outside.

"Hey," I said, stopping her. "How did you know to shoot the behemoth in the gut?"

Billee's face scrunched as if she thought I was joking. "Uh, the Bible. Job 40:16. Duh. Maybe you're still getting over having your butt handed to you. Honestly, I thought you knew that?"

"Yeah, well, I put little credence in that book, but it's nice to see my familiar has been studying."

"Familiar again, huh? I thought we were friends."

I held her gaze until her smile slipped. I wanted her to know I was serious. "We are, Billee. Dear friends."

"Good," she said, standing and backing away from the car, her hand on the door, ready to close it. "Shoot me a message when you want to do dinner. I'm already ready. See you, Rev."

"See you," I said and waited at the curb until she disappeared inside. "You poor, poor sucker."

With a sigh, I pulled out and headed home, ready to finish this business.

Before heading to the meeting with the Order, I swung by Cascade's place, setting my gift by the gate. I rang the call box.

"Yes?" Cascade said a moment later, barely audible over the din of barking pugs.

"Special delivery," I said, and stepped into the waiting Gateway before she could peek out her window and catch me.

Someone might have to help her carry' the box of ceramic plates to the house, but it wouldn't be me. A surprise gift can't be a surprise gift if she knew who it was from. Plus, a dish set of plates with painted scenes of pugs at play, pugs relaxing, and pugs swimming in a lake was probably the tackiest thing I'd ever bought for anyone. If she hated it, I didn't want to be held responsible. I also didn't want my name associated with such a thoughtfully atrocious gift, even though I truly hoped it brightened Cascade's day.

"I thought the Council would be here. Hell, even just one of them. You know, to show they gave a shit?" I said to the room of angels I reported to.

"Language," Dumas said with a shake of his head, the end of his overgrown mustache fluttering.

"They're 'busy' handling other things," Uziel said. I think I caught a note of exasperation in her voice.

"I'm sure they are," I said just as skeptically. "Maybe finding out why Beelzebub was in the Overworld."

"Nope," Pher said.

"Maybe the identity of who broke into the Safe to steal the First Bowl?"

"Not that either," Sid answered, raising his eyebrows.

"Well, let's hope they're putting Hellion to the question about why one of her Horsemen was handling the behemoth. Because if I was in their position, I'd be curious why they weren't informed about a Horseman acting as an agent in the Overworld."

A tense silence followed.

Politicians, am I right?

Puriel moved the discussion forward. "We're very pleased by your performance, Mr. Carver. That was not an easy mission to complete."

"You're telling me."

She held her lips pinched for a moment, then said, "But you don't look at all satisfied."

"Or content," Uziel added.

"Not much has changed," I said, spreading my hands. "Not for me. Tomorrow will be just another day. Everyone will have moved on. I have to as well."

"You should be happy," Turiel said, chipper as always. I didn't fault her for having absolutely no clue how discouraging the entire mission had been. She couldn't be at fault for not comprehending how the job was exacerbated by the ton of nasty shit swirling around the Upperworld and the fact no one seemed too bothered to put their neck on the line to uncover why. I mean, she was a politician. What can you expect?

"If I could be, I would be."

Turiel slouched as if my response was a punch to her gut.

Her reaction wouldn't stop me from making a point. "Not until I get back what I've lost."

Puriel, maturity providing her a social awareness Turiel lacked, was more somber, yet still made her gratitude evident. "We're in your debt, again, Rev. If the Order can thank you, please let us know. If it's within our power, we will do it."

As much as I appreciated her gesture, it was an empty one, and we all knew it. "When the Order is ready to release me from all Reaper obligations or give me my Morning Star, then I'm all ears. Until then, I'm afraid your 'thanks' will have to do."

Heads dropped around the table. Pher pinched his lips, rolling them like he was going to say something, and then pinched them closed again. A sure sign he was going to give me a talking-to after this.

"If Anapheil were ready, maybe," Puriel said, "but she's not."

"Not even close," Jerah said, concentrating on his hands.

"Plus, we enjoy having you around," Turiel said cheerily, flashing a smile filled by her two broad front teeth. "You're not only good for the Reapers. You're good for us." A quick round of murmured agreement followed her statement. Neither Jericho nor Dumas joined in.

I snorted. "Glad I could help. Maybe I can get a day off to recover, if that wouldn't be too much to ask."

Pher nodded vigorously, and he never does anything with vigor that doesn't involve his granddaughter. "Absolutely. I agree."

"Consider it done," Puriel said without looking around the table for a vote.

"Thanks."

"Let's adjourn then, so you can enjoy it," she said and stood, signaling the end of the meeting.

I was only too happy to be away.

"Nice work, Rev," Brock said from his guard station when I stepped out of the meeting room. "Heard it was a big one this time."

"You can say that again. Big, dumb, and ugly. Just like you."

He winked.

"Hate to be rude, but I'm going to get out of here and relax for a bit. Need to decompress from that shit."

"Totally understand. See you soon."

"Too soon, I'm sure." I waved over my shoulder, more than ready to sprint away from the Order because Brock had just said the truest thing I'd heard today.

I was halfway down the stairs to the lower floor when Pher called my name. I stopped and turned to see him halted at the edge of the first step.

"You headed out?" he asked, wearing a quizzical look.

I couldn't lie to Pher. I respected him too much, and he knew my tendencies too well to fool him. A thousand times out of a thousand, when leaving the Order's meeting room, I opened Rifts in the hall to take me back to the Overworld. This time, I hadn't. That wouldn't get by him.

"I'm going to take a walk," I said, motioning at the ceiling, though there was nothing above me of interest. Right now, not even the higher floors where the Upper-world's most powerful angels were doing whatever powerful angels did, mattered. Not even the penthouse of the tower, the personal residence of Yahweh Himself interested me. I was just motioning to motion, to burn off the emotional crap in my gut. "I need to clear my head."

"I understand," he said, and I believed him. Whatever was going on around the headquarters, Pher would fill me in when he could and when talking about the Upperworld's machinations was safe. "I've pinned Jericho down about the carnival of souls."

"Oh? What did he have to say?" I asked, trying to hide my utter lack of desire to talk about work.

"He'll look into it."

"Of course, he will," I said, stepping down another stair and sending a clear signal to my mentor that I needed some 'me' time. "Let me know how that turns out. Just not today, okay?"

"Of course, lad," Pher said, pinching his lips. "I'm sorry. I should have recognized you might need a little peace. An incredible thing you did. For everyone."

"Thanks."

He clasped his hands. "Listen, Rev. I know you're not much into reading."

"Yeah?" I said, sensing there was a 'but' coming.

"But—"

Bingo!

"You might be interested in something I've been thinking about," Pher continued. "Job 40:19. Remember it?"

"Nope."

"He is the foremost of God's works; only his Maker can draw the sword against him." He paused, his eyes never flicking away. "Do you know what that's referring to?"

I rubbed my face, not caring what Job or any of the dudes who appropriated old stories and claimed them as their own thought. The last thing I cared about, especially right now, were politicians, especially those from the time before electricity, running water, or indoor plumbing. "No, Pher. I don't."

"It's referring to the behemoth." His dark cheeks flashed with excitement.

"So? The behemoth is dead. Unless Yahweh is going for back-to-back manifestations? If he is, task someone else. I'm all behemoth'd-out."

"The last manifestations took teams of angels to kill. You did it on your own. The only angel ever to accomplish that."

I shifted my weight. "What's that got to do with some irrelevant Bible story?"

Pher leaned an arm on the railing. "One interpretation of the passage is that only Yahweh's sword can kill the behemoth. You don't find that interesting?"

"You're looking at me as if I should."

"Then maybe you should."

I blinked, hard and snappy, in a moment of pensive thought. "Wait. Are you saying that I'm in contention to be the next Yahweh because I killed an overgrown iguana?"

"See? That's what a lot of angels think. I bounced it off Dumas and he said that's not what it means at all. He's of the opinion, and so am I, that it is a metaphor. Yahweh still drew the sword. After all, if He didn't, you wouldn't have been able to do what you did. No, boy. You are Yahweh's sword."

"Oh great. As if I needed another job title. What? Is Reaper Minister, assassin, monster and demon hunter, and bread crust cutter not enough? Do we have to add a new one to the mix? Please tell me it comes with a pay raise and actual vacation time."

Pher laughed. And laughed. And laughed.

I waved, turning down the stairs and taking them two at a time, without stopping. "I'm leaving. I'll see you later, boss."

"Enjoy your day," he called out.

I was three floors below him before his laughter finally faded away.

Yahweh's sword. Ridiculous. Right?

Maybe I'd wait to see if I got called to meet with the Upperworld's head honcho before I accepted the gig. As if I'd have a choice.

Right now, I didn't care. Reaper. Divorcee. Assassin. Undesired bachelor. God's Sword. For the rest of today, and as long into tomorrow as I was allowed peace and quiet, I was just going to be Rev Carver. Maybe then I'd figure out who in the hell I was.

THE END

WANT THE DEMON'S PERSPECTIVE?

Enjoying Rev Carver and want to read more from this story world? *The Zodiac Series* shares the same story universe as the *Rev Carver Series*. Newsletter subscribers get *The Fall of Aries*, book 0 in *The Zodiac* for free. You can also pick it up on Amazon. Book 1 in *The Zodiac Series* is titled *Bitter Aries*. Pick them up and start the demons' side of the story.

ALSO BY PAUL SATING

FICTION

Urban Fantasy

Rev Carver Series (Same Story World As Zodiac)

Angel Assassin

Angel's Creed

The Zodiac Series (Same Story World As Rev Carver)

The Fall of Aries (Free for newsletter subscribers)

Bitter Aries

The Horn of Taurus

The Gemini Paradox

Cancer's Curse

The Pride of Leo

Virgo's Vigilantes

Libra's Liberation

Epic Fantasy

Hexed Heroes Saga

Thornbane Trilogy

Thornbane the Lost (Coming 2023)

Thornbane the Demon Witch (Coming 2023)

Thornbane the Free (Coming 2023)

Battleborn Books

Bloodborn (Free for newsletter subscribers)

Battleborn Trilogy

Fireborn

Rageborn

Battleborn

Bonebreaker Trilogy

King of Bones

War of Bones

Breaker of Bones

Crown of Thieves

Birth of a Thief (Free for newsletter subscribers)

Horror

12 Deaths of Christmas

The Plant (Free for newsletter subscribers)

Suspense

RIP

Chasing the Demon

Nonfiction

Novel Idea to Podcast: How to Sell More Books Through Podcasting

Podcasts

Audio Fiction Podcast

Horrible Writing Podcast

(Free for Patreon supporters!)

GET EXCLUSIVE CONTENT

More stories! Get exclusive Paul Sating fiction, including free audio books, in podcast form!

Get more stories each month by becoming a Patron! New exclusive fiction each month!

Become a Patron & enjoy more content!

NEVER MISS OUT!

Get the latest news, special deals, exclusive stories, first looks at book covers, and more by signing up for Paul Sating's newsletter!

Sign up for Paul's newsletter to follow all the news and special deals for upcoming novels, and to catch up on the latest regarding his podcast at http://www.paulsating.com.

ACKNOWLEDGMENTS

Most of this book was written over the span of three days. Sure, that sounds great, right until you hear that I was at the keyboard, literally, from before sunrise to well after sunset. My body didn't feel right for over a week afterward. Now, before you feel bad for me, I was on a writing retreat, a few miles from Mt. Rainier, in the middle of winter. In a tiny home. No one around. No cars. No people. No TV. No dogs. No nothing. It was absolutely glorious. So glorious, in fact, that I'm looking to schedule another for this year—even though I don't know what I'm working on... yet.

I wouldn't have spent the money on it if it weren't for the first person to I was thank at the end of these things. Maddie, the light of my world. My wife made me (because she already paid for it and told me it was non-refundable, so I had to go) take advantage of the trip. Wow, what a genius she is. You think I'd listen to her more often. URME!

Nikki and Alex. Keep working hard for your dreams now so you don't have to do it when you're my age. Love you, girls!

Patrons. You are crutches to my wobble, the splint to my achy wrists, the ibuprofen to my headaches.

Finally, *Paul's Epic Peeps*, the team of readers who get to see these books first and help me prepare them for the world. You're loud and proud and I adore you!

ABOUT THE AUTHOR

Paul Sating is an author, podcaster, and self-professed coolest dad on the planet, hailing from the Pacific Northwest of the United States. At the end of his military career, he decided to reconnect with his first love (that wouldn't get him in trouble with his wife) and once again picked up the pen. Years on, he has published tons o' novels and is living the dream... though he still has occasional nightmares that he's back in the military and deploying to some obscure location around the world.

When he's not working on stories, you can find him talking to himself in his backyard working on failed landscaping projects or hiking around the gorgeous Olympic Peninsula. He is married to the patient and wonderful, Madeline, and has two daughters—thus the reason for his follicle challenges.

Find out more about his other books and free podcasts from his website: paulsating.com.

CONTACT PAUL

How to Contact Paul Sating

Published by Paul Sating Productions
    P.O. Box 15166
    Tumwater, WA 98511
    paul@paulsating.com

Follow Paul:

- Facebook: www.facebook.com/authorpaulsating
- Bookbub: bookbub.com/paul-sating
- Goodreads: goodreads.com/author/show/16982359.Paul_Sating
- Instagram: @paulsating
- Pinterest: pinterest.com/paulsating
- Twitter: @paulsating